HAVEN REQUIRED

HAVEN REQUIRED

A LOCHLAN ELLYLL NOVEL

BY

HS PAISLEY

ISBN: 978-1-9995236-7-1 (ebook)
ISBN: 978-1-9995236-6-4 (paperback)

To you, the reader.
Thank you.

CHAPTER ONE
Lochlan

The squeak of small wheels echoed off the dank walls as my thumb frantically rubbed the metal cuff at my wrist. The sound of sliding metal on metal had me closing my eyes. I knew what that sound meant. I knew the pattern.

Light streamed through the narrow window in the heavy door. It illuminated the concrete walls, the bloodstains, the bile.

"Hello, Lochlan," said a bland voice.

Panic shook my body and the Proxy made a soft sound of approval. The door was wrenched open. The Proxy pushed a cart through a shallow puddle of muddy water and into my cell.

A man in dark coveralls followed him in and placed two objects on the ground. I didn't need to look to know what they were, or who he was. I knew the pattern. The second man's blue eyes flared with excitement before he flicked the lights on. I was momentarily blinded as my eyes adjusted.

"How are we feeling today, Lochlan?" the Proxy asked. He wore coveralls too.

I rubbed the cuff at my wrist again, trying to stay calm. I shook the long blood-matted hair off my face, squinted against the light, and looked up at him.

"Do you feel strong today?" The Proxy grabbed the short chain linking the cuffs on my wrists, pulling them over my head to a hook on the wall. My body weight pulled on my dislocated shoulder. I swallowed a cry of pain.

"Not so strong then, hmm?" he said. His clammy hands felt through the holes in my torn shirt. I flinched and turned away.

He laughed.

I tried not to shake. Not to scream. I tried not to cry out for the brothers I missed so much, for the mother I'd never known, for Zemila, for death. But my efforts were in vain.

I always screamed.

He always liked it.

"Right there," he said, and I gasped. "There's that xiphoid process."

His cold, bony fingers found my sternum, pressing hard under my rib cage. "You know I like to pull on it a bit. Makes it easier to find that spot."

He'd never told me what "spot" he was talking about. I thought about asking, but the long thin metal rod he'd pull off the cart stole my focus every single time.

"Lochlan," he breathed, excitement clear in his voice. "You're shaking. Are you scared?"

"Do it already." I met his dead brown eyes with my green ones. He smiled, and it was a knowing smile. I cursed the waver in my voice. "Do it."

The Proxy held my gaze as he slowly pressed the long thin rod up and underneath my ribs. I couldn't draw breath; the pain was excruciating and I knew it would only get worse. There was a spot it would touch inside my chest where the pain had me screaming for death.

"Eyes here, Lochlan." The Proxy grabbed a fistful of the unkempt hair on my chin. "You know I like to see when it happens."

Blue Eyes flipped a switch on the machine. It was slow at first. The metal rod in my chest seemed to heat, intensify, then pain exploded through me. The Proxy push deeper into my chest and I was burned alive.

Strength left me and my head lulled to one side. The Proxy kept his hand on my chin, pulling my face back to his. He smiled as he dug that rod into my chest. I screamed, and screamed, and screamed. Then everything was quiet.

Zemila was there.

I thanked the Gods for this small mercy, even though I knew it wouldn't last, I knew it wasn't real. She would leave me. She always did.

I knew the pattern.

CHAPTER TWO
Zemila

Twin jets of flame flew over clean white snow, racing toward Zemila. The snow melted as the fire roared and Zemila tried to breathe.

Trapped, trapped, trapped!

"Breathe," Zemila told herself aloud. The pink and purple sunset of the Rocky Mountains did nothing to soothe her. "Feel the earth. Feel my hand in it. My mind in it."

Zemila's thoughts became real. The earth beneath the flames heaved, rolled, smothering the fire. The melange of frozen emerald grass, dark mud, and half-melted snow made an ugly pattern criss-crossing the wide lawn.

"Again!" Ember said from the front porch of the red brick house. Llowellyn looked up at her from a patch of nearly untouched snow and opened his mouth to protest, but too late.

Ember threw fire at Zemila, without pause. Zemila tried to think, tried to move, tried to breathe.

"Mine, mine, mine," Greg Simmons screamed from deep within Zemila's memories.

Zemila couldn't breathe, she couldn't do anything, she was trapped, she couldn't—

No, said a smooth voice. A voice, foreign yet familiar.

No, Zemila realized. No.

She wasn't tied to a chair with duct tape over her eyes and mouth. She didn't have a knife to her throat. She wasn't helpless like she'd been when the Famorian Simmons had taken her eight months ago. Here and now, she had fire before her and earth below.

She had control.

Zemila lifted her hands, creating a pedestal with the ground under her feet. Keeping herself aloft, she crafted a wave of earth and covered the flames. As the fire died, Zemila let the pillar of earth return her to the ground.

The moment her feet touched down, she sagged, exhausted.

"Ag mo dúil fás." Llowellyn knelt, sinking the fingers of his right hand into the now-tilled dirt. Long dark hair fell from his loose braid into his eyes. Bright green grass sprouted and froze in the cold mountain air.

"I don't think that was all together necessary," he muttered. He stood, readjusting his heather gray toque.

"I wasn't ready." Zemila brushed snow and ash off her coat, feeling deflated, and annoyed.

"Maybe I'm wrong, but . . ." Ember put her hands on her curvy hips. The porch light cast a long shadow in the gold evening light. "Is Balor going to ask if you're ready? Is the cartel?"

Zemila froze mid-swipe of her thick-lined pants.

"What did you say?" Zemila whispered.

"I think you heard me." Ember stepped off the porch, ice in her voice. She wore boots, jeans, and a T-shirt. Snow melted around her as she walked. "But if you need me to repeat myself, I will."

Zemila's heartbeat pounded in her ears.

"Ember," Llowellyn cautioned.

"Is a Demon King, who has already killed you once, going to ask if you're ready?" Ember paused a few feet away from her, feet planted, eyes hard.

"Stop it." Zemila fought the quaver in her voice.

"Ember, that's enough," Llowellyn said.

"Is the cartel who kidnapped your boyfriend going to ask you if you—" Ember moved forward. "are—"

"Stop it!"

"—ready?" She shoved Zemila.

"Ember," Llowellyn chided as Zemila stumbled back.

"No!" Ember yelled when Llowellyn stepped forward. A jet of fire burst from Ember's hand, creating a wall of flame. Llowellyn was on one side, Zemila and Ember were on the other.

"No one will ask if you're ready, Zemila!" Ember said, keeping the wall of fire alive with one hand, pointing a finger at Zemila with the other. "No one will make sure you're prepared before they come for you."

"You're right," Zemila squinted against the bright inferno, raising her hands in surrender.

"What was that?" Ember said, tucking her dark red-gold curls behind her ear.

"I said, you're right," Zemila repeated. Ember shoved her again. Zemila stumbled and slipped on a bit of ice. "Hey!"

Llowellyn tried to get closer, but the flames kept him back.

"Don't you think I know I'm right?" Ember shouted, moving to shove Zemila again.

"Stop!" Zemila screamed, lifting Ember into the air with her gift. The wall of fire was extinguished as Ember was thrown through it. She hit Llowellyn hard and the pair crashed into the fresh, frozen grass.

"Oh God," Zemila rushed forward. "I'm sor—"

"Don't you dare give me sorry!" Ember was tiny compared to Llowellyn. She pushed herself off his chest. "You're too goddamned sorry. Do your 'sorrys' do anything for Lochlan? For yourself? For him?" She nodded to Llowellyn, still on the ground.

"No. You're wallowing in self-pity about making the right call in the moment. That's why you can only tap into your true abilities when you're pissed. You put up some kind of barrier in your mind! You've convinced yourself you're not strong, that you're an Earth Driver. But I feel you pull on my fire, my element, when we train. You're something else, something more."

Zemila grit her teeth.

"You have got to get over it, girl," Ember said. "You need to get past whatever's holding you back and accept what's happening to you. He needs you."

Ember flicked her eyes to Llowellyn again, still on the ground. "I need you." Her voice softened and she stepped forward. "Lochlan needs you."

Zemila looked away. Her eyes stung.

Ember sighed. Reaching up, she placed a warm hand on Zemila's cool cheek. The heat of Ember's palm thawed something cold in Zemila.

"I believe you can do this," Ember said. "But that's not enough. You need to believe it too." She let her hand fall, then turned to Llowellyn. Zemila watched Ember kneel and speak to him before brushing a bit of dirt from his beard and planting a kiss on his cheek.

"I'll start dinner," she said, walking up the stairs to the front door. "Come in when you're ready."

Zemila looked to the tree line. Her eyes found the well-worn path in the woods she'd walked down every day for the past two weeks. That walk calmed her. It helped her forget how much was waiting for her when she returned to the city.

Right now, she didn't want to walk down the small dark path. Right now, she wanted to run, and scream, and curse the Gods. She'd wanted that from the moment she'd woken up this morning, only to realize Lochlan's soft touches and gentle kisses were a dream.

Zemila wanted to yell and cry and spit all her venom up to the unrelenting skies. She wanted to pour all the hurt and guilt and shame and hopelessness out of herself, to never think of it again. She wanted to scream until her voice was raw and there were no words left.

But she stared into the woods, trying to breathe. Trying to figure out how she could do better, do more, be enough.

"Enough or not enough isn't the way to look at it," Llowellyn said.

Relief flowed over her body and loosened her neck at the same time as she felt a hand on her shoulder. She turned.

"You're not doing that on purpose, are you?" Zemila asked, meeting Llowellyn's green eyes.

"Danu," the demigod cursed. "No. I'm sorry."

Llowellyn was working on controlling his gift, like she was.

"It's okay," she said. "Sometimes it's the only relief I get in my day."

Llowellyn was an Empath, and although he couldn't read minds, he could read feelings. When the feelings were strong, it was almost the same thing.

"You've come very far," he said. "And there is still road ahead of you."

"How is that any different from not being enough?" she asked.

"It's reframed as a positive." His smile went all the way to his bright green eyes, so similar to Lochlan's. "That makes all the difference."

She could read his expression in the dim light. She squinted at him, then scoffed. She recognized that look. "Spit it out, Llowellyn."

"Were your parents Gifters? An Elemental, maybe?"

"An Elemental?" Zemila rolled her eyes, knowing what this was about. "My parents were Human, not Luman."

"You are so much more than you think you are," he said.

She knew Llowellyn didn't believe she was an Earth Driver.

"If you say s—" she started, but Llowellyn raised a hand, his body going rigid.

"Ga éist," Llowellyn muttered, tilting his head. "I thought we were up here alone." He took her hand, moving quickly across the starlit lawn to the porch. ". . . that no one knew about this place."

"That's what Dyson said." Zemila could barely see the driveway now the sun had fully set. She heard an approaching vehicle and a moment later, a dark green Jeep Cherokee with tinted windows screeched to a halt, spraying snow and gravel.

The driver's side door opened and a figure stepped out.

"State your business here," Llowellyn said, pulling Zemila behind him.

The new arrival was backlit by the Jeep's headlights. Zemila couldn't make out the person's face. She only saw an outline—and the glint of fangs.

"State my business?" said an accented voice she recognized. "This is my home."

"We have permission to—Mila, wait!" Llowellyn tried to catch Zemila as she pushed past him.

Ignoring the newcomer's defensive posture, she launched herself at him, burying her face in his neck.

"Zemila?" Sahrias's voice was shocked. "Child, what are you doing here?"

"We . . . I . . . .we—" She wanted to tell him they'd checked with Dyson, with Tarin. She took a breath and tried to speak, but it was no use.

"You're all right," Sahrias said, his arms tightening around her. "It's going to be all right."

They held each other for a moment longer before Zemila stepped back. She wiped her face and surveyed her old teacher, her mentor, her friend.

"Si, it's so good to see you," she sniffed. "It's past when you said you'd call. I was worried."

He sniffed. "I'm only a few months late."

"Six months," she corrected. "Six months late."

"Happy New Year to you too." His tone was light, but his dark eyebrows pulled together as he looked at her. "I feel I've missed much in your life."

"You have no idea," she said.

φ

Sahrias looked as regal as ever, leaning against the kitchen's marble island. His smooth dark skin, tailored black button-up, slacks, and a casually held glass of red wine—Sahrias had a classic look that never went out of style.

"Your grandfather, Balor," Sahrias pointed at Llowellyn. "One of, if not the most powerful Demon Kings of the last fifty lifetimes, is not actually dead."

"Correct," Llowellyn nodded. He stood opposite the large island, near the stove, next to Ember.

"You and Lochlan must fulfill a prophecy of killing him three times, once for each of you. The first time being your late brother, Lugh, with the necklace I gave Dyson," Sahrias pointed at the thin chain hanging around Llowellyn's neck.

"You gave Dyson a piece of it," Llowellyn said, tucking the small stone entwined in gold wires under his shirt.

"Pa, my grandfather, cast some kind of protection spell when she gave it to Lochlan." Ember put the lid on the chili and turned, her tone icy.

"Hmm . . ." Sahrias considered the Fire Gifter before continuing. "Lochlan has been taken by a drug cartel and, at that point, you had no idea who was working with . . ."

"The Proxy," Zemila answered, pulling her brown cardigan closed and crossing her arms. "We don't know much about him."

Re-hashing everything that had happened over the last year was hard. She craved a cigarette but was trying to quit . . . again. "Nemo and Jenner found some financial records that basically confirmed the Ruiz cartel is working with, or for, the Proxy."

"And the only way you know how to kill Balor is with the weapons of your brother." Sahrias turned his dark eyes to Llowellyn. "The Tools of Lugh."

Llowellyn nodded.

"The Spear is in Austria," Ember said, still glaring at Sahrias. "We've been trying to figure out how to get it." Her tone was cold, rude.

"Okay, what is your deal?" Zemila spat at Ember, confused at her hostility.

"Excuse me?" Ember turned fire-bright eyes on Zemila.

"Why are you being—"

"How are you so buddy-buddy with this guy?" Ember jabbed a finger in Sahrias's direction. "After what he did to Dyson."

Sahrias sighed heavily as if he'd known this was coming.

"Because I was there," Zemila shot back. "I was one of the people Dyson and Lochlan left behind without so much as a 'see you later.' Cut the shit, Ember. You know half the story."

Ember inhaled a long breath. It looked like she was biting back a retort. Her shoulders relaxed and she started to take another deep breath. Then she froze.

"Stop it," Ember said to Llowellyn. "I can feel what you're doing and I want you to stop."

"It's unconscious," Llowellyn said. "I'm sorry, I'm still working on control."

Zemila uncrossed her arms, her jaw relaxing. She felt it too.

"You're the Empath," Sahrias said, examining the bowl of fruit on the counter. "And the craftsman, then."

"Yes." Llowellyn turned narrowed eyes to Sahrias. "How do you know?"

"Have you tried crafting to help re-engage your Magic? To work on your control?"

"I– No." Llowellyn blinked at him. "I hadn't thought of it like that."

"Let's say you crafted a replica spear—I assume you made the original." Sahrias chose a bright red apple and looked up.

"Most likely," Llowellyn answered. "There is a stone at the center of it Lugh acquired somewhere . . . I think. But a replica wouldn't be able to—"

"—kill your grandfather," Sahrias nodded. "It would be able to replace the original, would it not?"

"Which is in Austria," Zemila reminded him.

"Would it not be easier to have the Spear brought to Washington?" Sahrias polished the crimson fruit on his shirt.

Ember scoffed. "Of course, but how?"

"I can help with the location of the item," Sahrias raised a dark eyebrow at Ember before looking to Llowellyn.

"I repeat, how?" Ember said.

"Once it is in DC," Sahrias continued, ignoring Ember's question. "Remember, a good heist is always simpler than you think. You need only three things."

"Gods Below," Llowellyn said, sitting up a little straighter. "You're that vampire. I thought your name was William."

"It was, for a time," Sahrias said, too casually.

"What vampire?" Zemila looked between Sahrias and Llowellyn.

"What three things?" Ember asked.

Sahrias took a bite of the apple.

"Si, What vampire?" Zemila repeated.

He swallowed and Sahrias said, "It's hardly worth getting excited about. Reality is always more mundane than the stories. Did Dyson ever tell you about Rayyan?"

"She was an ex of yours," Ember recounted. "And what are the three things?"

" 'An ex' is putting it mildly," Sahrias grimaced.

Llowellyn let out a small laugh. Ember glared at him.

"There was a rumour." Llowellyn looked from Ember to Sahrias, hope filling his bright eyes. "A story. The origin of a legend was a woman who worked with a vampire."

Sahrias shook his head. "She earned that name long before I met her. She earned that name before I was born. She brought me along when I would be useful. But there were many who used the name, who built the legend."

"What does this have to do with the Spear?" Ember growled. "And what the hell are the three things?"

Zemila raised a hand. "I'd actually like to know that too."

"For a good heist, a clean heist, you need the right mark, the right distraction, and the right exit. That's all."

"Okay." Ember leaned back on the counter behind her, unimpressed.

"The right mark is not one in Austria," Sahrias explained. "If for no other reason than international travel makes your exit considerably more difficult."

"Hmm," Llowellyn nodded in agreement.

"Unless you have connections there." Sahrias raised a brow at Llowellyn who shook his head.

"The right distraction will depend on when you plan to take, or switch, the Spear. I will leave that to you." Sahrias took another bite of the apple. To Ember's great annoyance and Zemila's amusement, he took his time before speaking. "I will get the artifact to DC."

"Hoooooow?" Ember dragged out the word, her impatience clear.

"I have my ways," he smirked. "And deep connections in the art world."

"I'll bet you do." Llowellyn smiled. "How often do you do this?"

"Not much anymore, not, ahh, not without the Robin." Sahrias looked mournfully into his glass of wine. "It never felt right without her."

"No," Zemila whispered, looking back and forth between Sahrias and Llowellyn. "No way. Does Dyson know?"

Sahrias shook his head.

"Yikes," Zemila smiled. "Si, if she wasn't mad at you before . . ."

"The Robin?" Ember asked.

"Rayyan," Zemila answered. "Rayyan Hode, sometimes The Robin, and sometimes—"

Ember's eyes went wide. "No way . . ."

"I thought you'd know by now," Sahrias smiled at Ember. "All the stories are real."

CHAPTER THREE
Lochlan

"Oh God, oh God, oh God."

I couldn't see Zemila. I never could. But I felt her warm body beside me. I felt her hands in my hair and her lips on my skin.

These dreams. These dreams are the reason he hasn't broken me.

"There is no god but God. There is no god but God. There is no god but God."

No. No, go away.

"There is no god but God. There is no god but God."

No. She was slipping away. No, not yet, don't go. Don't leave me.

"There is no god but God. There is no god but God."

What is that chanting? Why is it taking my pain away? As Zemila slipped from my fingers, I felt my other hand tangle in the chant, in the prayer. It was a lifeline. It was power. It felt good.

"There is no god but God. There is no god but God—

أشهد أن لا إله إلاَّ الله و أشهد أن محمد رسول الله

—Oh God, oh God, oh God."

I was back in the dank, dark, concrete room. By the thin light slipping in under the heavy metal door, I could see a kneeling figure.

"There is no god but God. There is no god but God—

أشهد أن لا إله إلاَّ الله و أشهد أن محمد رسول الله

—Oh God, oh God, oh God."

Someone was in here with me, and he was praying. He was pouring his Spark into the words. Powering the prayer with his life force. And I was healing myself with it, I was stealing it. I didn't mean to, not at first. But the relief was too sweet. Too intoxicating. Too powerful.

And I was so very weak.

I wove my mental Magical bonds deeper into the rhythmic chanting.

If I kept pulling, I could heal myself. If I kept pulling, I could get free.

But, no, my body was too broken for that. I would never be able to heal myself with the Spark put into prayer.

But if you ate his Spark, a dark voice in the back of my mind said. If you ate it, you would be strong enough to heal. To escape. To return to Zemila. To keep her safe.

Yes. I gripped tighter still to the invisible bonds in the darkness. The bonds that tied the words to the Spark, the Spark to the soul, the soul to the life.

Eat it, the voice said. And you will be with her.

Yes. I found the man's Spark with my Magic. It was bright. It pulsed with the connection all life had to the Anima, to the World Soul, to Magic.

Eat it, the dark voice repeated. And you will have your Magic. She is waiting for you.

Yes, I thought again. And pulled.

The chanting faltered. There was a choking gasp. I pulled harder. I tasted it. My body surged with power.

Just a little more, said the dark voice. A little harder. She is waiting for you. She needs you.

I pulled again, forcing my Magic deep. Then, familiarity hit my senses.

"Gods," I croaked, releasing my hold.

I was so close. So close to eating his Spark, to being free, to being back with Zemila. So close to straying down the path of Dark Magic and not caring. So close to losing myself in the rush of power, the sense of rightness, the knowledge that I would be unstoppable.

But that familiarity, that hint of my own Magic, of Llowellyn's Magic.

I knew who knelt quietly on the other side of this cell. I'd healed the man now trying to catch his breath. I'd vowed to protect him.

"Why are you here, Qillian?"

"Lochlan?" he asked.

"What are you doing here?" I repeated, squinting in the dim light.

"Oh, thank God, it's you."

I heard the muffled sounds of movement, the slosh of a shallow puddle. I turned my right wrist back and forth, feeling the power I'd pulled from Qillian. The metal cuff warmed as it slid against my skin.

"Don't thank your God. I almost killed you because of Him," I said. I could feel his Spark mix with my own Magic, healing my deeper wounds.

Qillian crawled toward me. I tried not to think of what he crawled through.

"Why are you here?" I said again. I could scarcely make out his silhouette when he moved passed the sliver of light at the bottom of the heavy door. His broad shoulders looked thinner than before. His normally neat dreadlocks looked frizzy and unkempt.

"I . . . I don't know. I've been here for months. We're in a compound," he said. "Have you seen anyone else here?"

"A compound . . ." I echoed. In the faint light, I saw him nod.

"From what I gather," he said. "They'd move me sometimes. I saw enough to make me think underground and ex-military. They took me from Heaven. I was with Avery, my friend, and they knocked me out cold. I haven't seen her since I've been here. They won't tell me why I'm here or where she is." He paused. "Are you . . . okay?"

"Okay?" I said, trying not to laugh. It would hurt too much. What came out was a half wheeze, half cough.

"All right," he said. "Stupid question. Are you restrained?"

"Chained to the wall."

There was another shuffling sound, and Qillian was in front of me running his handcuffed hands over my body. I hissed in pain when he hit the break in my leg, the fracture in my ribs, the constant ache in my shoulders. My broken wrist was healed and I rotated my right hand again.

"It's a hook," Qillian said. "But it's about three inches up to get the chain off it."

"Danu," I cursed. I'd fallen asleep with my arms restrained overhead several times, but in a room where I couldn't see the sun, that meant nothing. Nothing but the ache that turned into blinding pain when I moved.

In the dim light, I heard more than saw him stand. "Ready?"

"Do it," I said.

Qillian lifted the chain, pulling my arms up with it. I sucked in a breath, I knew nothing but the roar of agony in my shoulders, and then . . ."Lochlan? Lochlan, can you hear me?"

A palm on my cheek. My face held between two hands.

"Lochlan," the voice said. "Lochlan, stay with me . . . يا الله ساعدني . . . help him be all right."

A rush of Spark surged into my body and I flinched away from the contact.

"Thank God," Qillian said, not noticing I had stolen more of his Spark.

"Lochlan, don't do that again," he said. "You went limp. I thought you were . . . I thought . . . We need to get out of here."

"That has never occurred to me," I said.

"Ha ha," Qillian said dryly. "Do you need help sitting up?"

I could feel the new infusion of Spark. I moved my foot and was surprised at the lack of pain. That leg had been broken. I took a deep breath. My punctured lung was healed too. I was slumped low on the ground, and when I tried to move, my body barely responded. Qillian's Spark had done much, but my body was still weak, broken.

"Yes," I said, keeping my Magic in check as he touched me.

"Sorry, sorry, sorry, sorry, sorry," Qillian whispered as hoisted me up the wall. "God, you are skin and bone."

"I haven't eaten since I got here," I said.

Qillian's mouth fell open. "Lochlan, it's been nearly six months. How have you survived?"

"Magic." I started to shrug, but stopped at the white-hot pain shooting through my shoulder.

"That's how they've kept me trapped." I explained. "My Magic keeps me alive. These?"

I shook my hands and the chains jingled lightly against each other. "Child's play if I had a fraction of my usual power. But they keep me starved and bleeding. All my Magic goes to keeping me alive."

"They thought you would kill me," Qillian said. "When they put me in here with you, they said they would be back for the body."

He paused. I thought he was looking at me, but I couldn't see in the darkness.

"If you can't even sit up on your own, how did they think you were going to kill me?"

"I almost did," I said, and silence met my words. "When you pray," I explained. "When you think well of someone, when you give someone a hug, there can be transference of power, of energy."

"Okay," Qillian said.

"There is an energy, a power, that runs through and connects every living thing, Magic and non-Magic alike. The Anima Mundi flows through all of us. As you prayed. Did you not feel it? Did you not feel something being pulled?"

The soft rustle of Qillian shifting was my only response.

"They thought I was going to kill you to save myself," I told him. "And if you'd been a stranger to me, I would have. I would have pulled that power right out of you."

"Queen Anne," he said. "She collected something from the people playing in Heaven."

"That's right," I confirmed. "She did."

Queen Anne, Inanna, Queen of Heaven when the ancient Sumerian deities had reigned supreme, had opened a casino in DC and called it Heaven. Her sense of humor.

"When you were praying," I said, shame and bitter longing coating my words. "I was so desperate, so broken . . ." I looked toward him. At the outline lit by the space under the door. "I took it."

"You took it," he repeated.

"I started to," I sighed. "It was power I longed for. I felt your prayer, and I pulled. I lusted for it. It was a lifeline. But then . . ."

"Then what?"

"Then I felt you," I swallowed. "And I could have continued. I could have pulled until I was strong enough, until I had all the power your Spark could produce, until I was freed. I would have been."

But at what cost. I could not have yet another soul on my conscience. I could not start down that path again. No matter what. I took in an unsteady breath.

"My freedom is not worth your life," I finished.

"So, instead, we'll both die in here?" Qillian's tone was angry.

"What?" I squinted in the darkness.

"Instead of you getting out and being okay," he said. "We will both die in here because you won't do what's needed?"

"Qillian, I would have killed you."

"Lochlan, I understand, but Queen Anne said—"

"I don't care what Inanna said."

Gods Below, I'd curse her if I could. Spouting off about a prophecy to this kid who'd already almost died trying to protect me.

"Lochlan," Qillian placed a hand on my shoulder. I flinched away. "She said you are needed. That you will be needed in this lifetime and in lifetimes to come. That you will deliver a message and change the course of—" He reached forward and I flinched away again.

He paused. Looked at me.

I felt his intention.

Danu, he's smart. Too smart for his own good.

He grabbed my shoulders and pulled me toward him. Bowing his head, I felt a rush of power push at my senses. His head fell to my shoulder as he muttered under his breath. I couldn't make out the words, only the feeling, the power, the rush of energy as he forced his Spark into my body as he prayed.

CHAPTER FOUR
Zemila

Adrienne Jace's eyes narrowed as Zemila slid a latté and a seven-layer square across the wide Intelliglass desk. Sunlight poured through the wall-to-wall windows which offered an unobstructed view of the city.

"Why are you trying to bribe me?" She raised a perfectly shaped black eyebrow.

"You let me work from home over the holidays." Zemila smiled and sat down in a black straight-back chair, across from the CEO of JACE Co. Media. "Can't a girl show a little appreciation to her boss?"

"You've been back for over two weeks." Ms. Jace's sable eyes seemed to look through Zemila. "What do you want?"

"Ms. Jace, you called this meeting," Zemila reminded her. Adrienne's stern features softened.

"I want you back in Lowtown." She took a sip of her frothy drink. "You were better with that demo, and Rabski is moving over to the Clemens story."

"Hmm." Zemila flicked a piece of lint off her white button-up shirt.

"Don't give me that look." Adrienne pointed a manicured finger at Zemila.

"I have no idea what you mean, Ms. Jace," she smiled sweetly. She was sure Richard "Dick" Rabski had begged for the Hale Clemens scandal. "It seems totally in-character for Rabski to gravitate towards a story about a wealthy, soon-to-be-disgraced art collector, instead of low-income families having their homes burnt down. Who is on the Cartwrytte story?"

She'd go back to Lowtown, she'd write about the fires, but they were a symptom. She wanted to write about the cause, and though she didn't know why, she felt it connected to the murder of Maggie Cartwrytte.

"There's nothing new on the Cartwrytte story," Adrienne said and Zemila pressed her lips together. "People don't care anymore. That's the news cycle."

"And the FirstGen bill?" Zemila asked.

The Right Waters Party had been trying to push a bill mandating all immigrants register their generation of arrival. When Maggie Cartwrytte, wife of a Right Waters Party member, was found dead in her home by her husband, the bill gained traction. There was footage of two First Generation kids carrying out the murder, but the story was fizzling out.

"Those two kids might never clear their names," Zemila tried.

"That was seven months ago," Adrienne said. "As far as the people are concer—"

"It's going to slowly gain traction in the House and no one will—"

"Lowtown," Adrienne said, ending the argument. "Have you seen what Candle is doing to that neighborhood?"

"I have. That drug is very damaging, but Ms. Jace—" Zemila protested.

"Zemila, who is in charge here?" Adrienne snapped.

"You are, Ms. Jace." Zemila studied her black oxfords.

"Uh huh," Adrienne said, skepticism clear on her face. "Rabski's good with that artsy crowd, and all those—"

"Criminals?" Zemila supplied.

Three days ago, the Washington Post had published an article about Hale Clemens, the featured collector at the Day Dream Ball. Apparently, his acquisition habits were less than reputable. The Day Dream board had postponed the gala to find a replacement. Kennedy Virtue's name was at the top of the short list.

"Rabski has connections in that world," Adrienne said.

"I'm sure." She fought not to roll her eyes. Zemila might have been upset that Sahrias had given a story to the Post if she hadn't been so damn impressed.

"Rabski has connections within the art world and is better equipped to—" Adrienne's black eyebrows drew together. "Why am I justifying my decisions to you? I'm your boss."

"You are my boss," Zemila grinned.

"Must be a sugar high from your not-a-bribe." Adrienne took another sip of her latté.

"Must be," Zemila shrugged.

"Any news on my Irish Prince Charming?" Adrienne asked and Zemila's spine stiffened. "I want to see that boy on your arm in a tux in April."

Lochlan had gone to the Ball with Zemila last year. That's where he'd met Adrienne. Or where they became reacquainted.

"He's in the Rockies with his brother." Zemila tried to keep her tone casual. "They have a friend with a place up there."

"Uh-huh," Adrienne said.

Zemila saw the accusation in her eyes.

"Well," Adrienne went on, "the Ball isn't until June now, assuming they find a replacement for Clemens. Gives him plenty of time."

Zemila forced a smile. "I will relay the message when I speak to him next, Ms. Jace."

"All right," Adrienne said and Zemila stood. "Lowtown. Talk to Rabski. See where he left off. Go."

Rabski sat alone in a cluttered room he shared with three other journalists. The sound of his inconsistently long and short fingernails clacked and tapped on the projected keyboard.

"What do you want, Alkevic?" he barked without looking up from his projection. "I'm working here."

"Ms. Jace put me back on the Lowtown story," Zemila said, refusing to let him get a rise out of her. "I need any new leads or storylines you have."

"Nothing," he said. "Bye."

"Excuse me?" Zemila squinted at him.

He paused his furious typing to look up. His eyes were narrowed, and his thin lips twisted in a grimace.

"Nothing? Candle is flooding the streets, people are amped up, they say making people more—"

"Yeah, yeah, more encounters with police, more aggressive, stronger, starting fights, blah, blah, blah. You want me to do your job for you, beautiful?" He shoved the sagging sleeves of his blue collared shirt back up his forearms. "Don't you just bat your eyelashes at the cameras?"

"Okay," she said, losing the battle with herself to take the high road. "When you're done covering the easiest story of the year, send me your notes on Lowtown. Thanks."

She moved to leave, but his voice had her turning back.

"Easy?" Rabski scoffed. "Do you know how hard it is to get a hold of this guy? Do you know what I had to do to secure a meeting?"

"Oh." Zemila raised her eyebrows. "Did you have to work hard to get a meeting with a criminal?"

"He's not a criminal," Rabski snapped.

"He sought out stolen artwork, Dick." Zemila didn't know why she was picking a fight with him.

"Whatever, Alkevic," Rabski rolled his eyes, he waved a thick hand through the air. "You fuckin' FirstGen."

The last part was said so quietly she barely heard him.

"What's wrong with being an immigrant, Richard Natan Rabski?

On his business card, it was Nathan. In English, it was Nathan. But Zemila pronounced his middle name in Hebrew, like she'd pronounced her uncle's name, like her mother had pronounced her grandfather's name.

"Both our families immigrated here," she said. She saw the tops of his ears turn pink as she walked off. Or maybe that was wishful thinking.

φ

A blur of images projected onto the living room wall. Jenner scanned the pictures at lightning speed. Zemila rarely understood what Jenner was working on and today was no different.

"I'm not hungry." Jenner's eyes didn't leave the projection.

His black hair was longer than usual, his signature red hoodie looked like it hadn't been washed in weeks, and his normally warm caramel skin was chalky. Zemila had stopped asking when he'd last slept. Now she just tried to keep him fed.

"You have to eat—" A ringing interrupted her.

"Nemo." Jenner picked up the call by tapping a small disc on his neck. Zemila could only hear Jenner's side of the conversation.

"Sí," he said. "The alarm system is disabled . . . yeah, well, hopefully you'll get something this time. No . . . no. Okay."

He tapped his neck again and started coding.

"Jenner," Zemila said, "Jenner." But she could tell it was no use.

The first few weeks after Lochlan had been taken were hard. But compared to the following months, that pain was nothing. Zemila knew now what true torture was.

It was helplessness. Uselessness.

Knowing you had tried everything you could and knowing it wasn't enough, then trying to live, to keep going, to move on.

Is that what this is? Zemila thought as she walked down a narrow hall to the kitchen. Is this moving on? No. This is surviving. This is not breaking when there's nothing to do but wait and hope and try to not hate yourself every second of every day.

"Did he take it?" Camile asked. Though Jenner was older than Cam, she had stepped into the role of older sibling, of caretaker.

Zemila shook her head and sat across from Llowellyn at the square table pushed against the kitchen wall. "He barely eats when Nemo is on a job."

Camile hung her suit jacket on the back of a chair and sat beside Llowellyn.

"Jenner barely eats anyway," Llowellyn said. "Any idea where Nemo is today?"

"Lowtown's Candle supply," Cam's brown eyes pinched in concern.

"Trying to get to the top of the Ruiz family. I try not to know too much, but I know it's getting worse."

Jenner and Nemo were recruited to help track Lochlan and a few other people Queen Anne had lost when the Ruiz cartel destroyed her casino. Heaven.

Zemila wasn't sure why Nemo had said yes. He'd been held hostage by Queen Anne, the bogeyman of Lowtown, for weeks after being caught cheating at her roulette tables. But Queen Anne had resources they didn't. Resources that could help find Lochlan. Or at least that's what Nemo said when he'd told Zemila what he was doing.

"I miss my dog." Zemila pushed back from the table, rubbing her eyes. "I might go by my place. Do you want to come?" She looked at Cam even though she knew the answer. Nemo was living at Zemila's bachelor apartment. Zemila was staying in Lochlan's room.

As a lawyer, Camile couldn't, or shouldn't, be in a relationship with one of the employees of the Lowtown crime boss. Zemila didn't know where their relationship was now.

Cam sighed and shook her head. "You should go, though. If you see Nemo . . . I don't know. Tell him I hope he's safe."

Zemila tried to smile. "I think I'll go tomorrow. I hope I'll see him at Heaven before—"

"Training?" Camile asked.

"Training," Zemila echoed.

"Inanna will be eager to see you, I'm sure," Llowellyn said. Although Zemila, and everyone she knew under one thousand years old called her

Queen Anne, Llowellyn had a different relationship with the Goddess. One Zemila tried not to think about.

"You're not coming?" she asked.

"I've my own work," he said, nodding in the direction of the back yard. Llowellyn had emptied out the unused shed and created a work station.

"The replica," Zemila said. He nodded.

"It's an interesting exercise. It's . . . working, I think. We'll see. Sahrias sent you this, by the way." Llowellyn flicked his fingers over his watch, tapped his wrist. Zemila felt her own watch buzz.

"You spoke to him?" Zemila tried to hide her jealousy. Though Si had promised to be in touch, it had been two weeks since they were in the mountains and she hadn't heard from him.

"Very briefly," Llowellyn said.

"Oh my God," Zemila's eyes went wide. "It's Kennedy Virtue's personal email and a list of board members."

"Board members?" Camile leaned forward to read.

"The people who will pick Clemens' replacement," Zemila explained.

"Who's on the board? Maybe one of them is a client or something," Cam said.

"I'm out of the loop," Llowellyn said. He'd been spending most of his time working on the replica spear and regaining his full connection to Magic. "Why does this help us?"

"The charity for the Day Dream Ball is APECA," Cam said, as if that explained it.

Llowellyn blinked slowly at her.

"The Association for the Preservation and Expansion of Creative Art," Zemila filled in. "On the surface, this year's 'charity' is rich people giving other rich people an opportunity to show off their private collections."

"Where is the charity part?" Llowellyn asked.

"Many donate to show their collection. Some donate a piece to auction," Zemila said.

"We have a couple partners at the firm attend the ball every year. I don't know if they are art fans or just—"

"Snobs?" Zemila supplied.

"Right," Cam smiled.

"Clemens is out and Virtue is on the short list of replacements," Llowellyn asked. "Is the Spear—"

"He's shown it in events like this before," Zemila nodded. "The board has to pick him, and he has to say yes."

"We can make that happen," Llowellyn said, more confidently than Zemila felt. "The Spear will come to DC."

CHAPTER FIVE
Lochlan

Qillian held my shoulders, muttering under his breath and pushing his life force into me. I tried to shake him off, but I was weak and my survival instincts were not.

Bones mended. Skin knit back together. Strength came back to me.

"Stop it!" I shoved at him as soon as I could. "Why did you do that?"

Before he could answer, we heard footsteps coming down the hall.

Qillian crawled back across the room. I raised my arms, swinging the chain back into place on the hook above my head.

The door unlocked, swung open, and light filled the room. I squinted against the brightness, sagging against the concrete wall.

"Hmm." The Proxy stepped in. His eyes were a dull brown and hollow as a dry well. He was hollow too.

"I told you he wouldn't do it yet," said Blue Eyes. I think his name was Marco.

"Lochlan, Lochlan," the Proxy chided. "Not quite as smart as we thought. Or maybe just not desperate enough."

I knew what was coming. Pain. More pain than the small Magic reserve from Qillian could handle. It would all be drained into healing new injuries, new broken bones. I took a chance. Using all the Magic I had left in my body, I cast.

"Mair nartha ditiun," I whispered.

"What did you just—" the Proxy started, but Marco cut him off.

"He's using Magic," Marco put his full weight behind his fist, and the hit had my head snapping to the side and bouncing off the wall. My head ached instantly and my vision blurred.

"Naughty, naughty," the Proxy shook his head. "We can't have that."

I felt deflated, empty. But I had strength enough to smile.

"You're a puppet." I looked up at the Proxy. In the dim light, I saw a sneer twist his plain face. "Let me see you dance for my grandfather."

He obliged.

I don't know how long Qillian yelled, screamed, pleaded for the Proxy to stop.

Poor Qillian, he wasn't used to this level of brutality. I was. This wasn't the first broken arm the Proxy had stomped on again and again. It wasn't the first concussion. Or second. Or tenth. This wasn't the first time the Proxy dislocated my fingers one by one. Marco took great pleasure in setting them for the Proxy to dislocate them again.

I knew it would all go black soon enough. I knew the worse it got, the sooner I would see her. And the pain would be less there.

Even though it wouldn't last.

CHAPTER SIX
Zemila

"Lochlan." Zemila jolted up off her Intelliglass desk and looked around her office. She scanned the room, then shook her head, mentally chiding herself.

Of course, he isn't here.

It was a dream. Again. And he was hurt. Again. She never saw him, but when he was hurt like that, he came to her.

Zemila tapped a pattern into the corner of her desk. The frosted glass of her office wall cleared and her assistant, Diana, looked up. Zemila waved her in.

"Ms. Alkevic," she said.

Zemila rolled her eyes and groaned. "Diana."

"Zemila," she smiled, settling in the chair crammed in the corner of the small office. "Did you have a late night?" Diana tossed her straight black hair over her shoulder. Zemila shot daggers at her.

"Well," Diana shrugged, her upturned eyes twinkling with mischief. "It's been a while since you've taken a nap at work."

"You don't know I was taking a nap," Zemila said.

Diana blinked once.

"Well, you don't knoooooow." Zemila dragged out the "o" for effect. "You're making an assumption."

"What can I do for you, Ms. Alkevic?"

"Did anyone stop by while I was not napping?"

"I printed these for you, from Rabski's office." Diana slid over a folder. "And Maha sent back your piece on the housing problem in Lowtown with a couple notes. Questions mostly."

"You're the best, Diana." She reached across the table for the file.

"And we got confirmation of your virtual with Kennedy Virtue this afterno—"

"Are you fuckin' kidding me, Alkevic!" The door burst open and a red-faced Dick Rabski stood in the entrance to her office. "Why the fuck are you meeting with Virtue?"

"It's for my piece on art conservation and general access," she said, her heart racing. Diana had her hand on her chest, looking affronted. "I'm interviewing all the private collectors on the short list."

"I know he's on the goddamn short list," Rabski spat out, his wide chest heaving in anger. "I've been trying to get an interview with him since the list leaked last week."

Zemila forced an expression of calm and blinked at him. Diana smoothed her navy pencil skirt and re-crossed her legs.

"Well?" Rabski practically yelled.

"Well, what, Dick?" Zemila said. "I didn't know you were trying to get in with him. I would be happy to—"

Rabski took two steps forward and slammed his palms on her desk.

"Whoa!" Zemila pushed her chair back. The bitter tang of panic hit the back of her tongue and a wave of nausea rolled through her as she tried to stay present.

"Hey," Zemila heard Diana say, but all she could see was an angry face; all she could feel was panic. "Hey!" Diana said again.

Zemila's vision swam with a haze of unshed tears. Diana dragging Rabski out of the office by his collar. Diana was saying something as she shook a finger at him, then shoved him in the chest. Zemila turned in her chair and put her head between her knees.

"Breathe, Zemi," she said aloud. "Just breathe."

Zemila stayed like that until she heard the click of her office door and soft footsteps.

"Hey, here you go." A tissue was placed under her nose. Zemila took it.

"He's going to tell everyone he made me cry," she said.

"He won't." Diana's tone was smug.

Zemila looked up at her and she was surprised to feel a grin pulling at the corner of her mouth. "What do you have on him?"

"Well, if I told you," Diana said smugly, "I wouldn't have it anymore."

"Oh, Diana." Zemila shook her head, still smiling, the panic ebbing away with Diana's soothing presence.

"It's not that I don't trust you, boss," she said standing and returning to her chair. Zemila sat up and wiped at her face. "I do trust you. It's just, the assistants have a code."

"Fine," Zemila laughed a little and wiped her eyes. "Thank you. I owe you big time."

Zemila didn't have a car anymore. Not since Ida, her blue Volkswagon Golf, had been crushed under the large letter "V" of the Heaven casino sign last summer.

She'd thought about getting another beater. Maybe an electric car. In the end, she'd decided on public transit. Staying at Lochlan's made the choice easier. The route from her office to his home wasn't bad, though initially, it presented problems.

For the first three weeks, she was on the verge of a panic attack every time a stranger sat down beside her. It was slowly getting better.

"Different route today?" Zemila heard from behind her when she turned left for the subway instead of right for the bus. She nearly jumped out of her skin.

"Jesus Christ, Billy," she hissed, grabbing him by the arm as he stumbled backward. Still shaken from her encounter with Rabski, Zemila had unconsciously pressed out with her gift and pushed Billy off his feet. "Don't sneak up on me like that."

Zemila released him and looked him over. Billy wore a dress shirt and slacks. He had a fresh haircut and what looked like newly shined shoes.

"Billy?" Zemila asked, barely recognizing her old informant.

"You got time?" He angled his head in the direction of a small alleyway between a couple buildings.

"For you," she said, "always."

Following Billy into the alcove, Zemila reached into her bag for a couple cigarettes and her wallet.

"Nah," Billy said when he saw what she was doing. "Nah, none of that between us anymore."

"Billy, come on," she said.

He'd never been comfortable with Zemila paying for information. Since she got him an opportunity with the Justal outreach program, he'd outright refused to take her money. She forced the issue every time.

"I'm serious this time," he said. Then he nodded at the box of cigarettes, "Anyway, I quit."

Her eyebrows popped up.

"So . . ." He put his arms out to the side and turned on the spot. "What do ya think?"

A smiled curved the corner of her mouth.

"You got it," she almost squealed in excitement. After finishing the Justal program, Billy had applied to work in the office of King Capitol Construction. He'd been on probation before officially being hired full-time.

"I got it," he said. "KCC has full benefits too, and it's all down to you. So, no more of this payin' me for information."

"You did this," Zemila said, smiling big and punching Billy in the arm.

The man who stood before Zemila now was a different one than she'd met three years ago. Back then, his hair had been long and matted, his skin gray, and his hands shaky. Now, Billy had full cheeks, rosy complexion, and close-cropped hair. Zemila wouldn't have recognized him if he hadn't spoken to her.

"And I got this." He flipped her a chip. She caught it out of the air.

"One year sober," she read, tears stinging her eyes. "I'm proud of you."

Billy blushed when she handed the chip back.

"I owe you, Zemila, I really do," he said. "I remember that first day you talked to me. You talked to me like I was a person. You looked me in the eye, treated me like an equal, reminded me I'm still Human, you know? Don't think I could ever repay that."

"Nothing to repay. You did this," she repeated. "But thanks for saying that."

"Yeah, well," he said. "New gig means I'm hearing less and, uh, different information, I guess."

"Oh yeah?" Zemila's interest peaked.

"Yeah," Billy said. "I'm trying to stay away from the old life, you know? But rubbing shoulders with construction workers keeps me in a little. Now having management on the other side, you hear things."

"What kind of things?"

"Things like Candle has an anabolic steroid and a creatine concentrate in it."

"What?" Zemila repeated. "Why?"

"Candle gives you wings." Billy flapped his hands in the air, and Zemila humored him with a smile. "I also heard Maggie Cartwrytte wasn't supposed to be home. She wasn't the target. They were looking for something."

"Looking for what?"

"No idea," Billy shrugged. "But she surprised them. Someone paid for a robbery and got a hit."

Zemila's mouth opened in a silent "oh." Her mind was racing.

"I thought you might like that," Billy smirked. "Now, I gotta go, I got a hot date with a couple rascals."

"Your kids," Zemila beamed.

"Supervised visits for now, but a review is coming up next month. Emma even asked me to stay for dinner last week."

"Go get'em, tiger," Zemila smiled as they stepped out of the alcove and back onto the busy street.

"You need me to walk you anywhere?" he asked. "I'm taking the subway to Arlington, then up to the kids."

"You're the best, Billy," she said, happy for the company.

φ

"They were looking for . . . what?" Jenner turned to look at her.

"I thought that might get your attention," Zemila said.

His eyes moved from her face to the carton of cigarettes in her hand. Zemila shoved the small box in her shoulder bag. Behind Jenner, the whirr of images had stopped on a face she recognized.

The photo looked like it was from a barbeque. Zemila's eyes were stuck on the hunched man in the left corner of the photo. She still heard his voice in her nightmares, his screams as he died. Greg Simmons and a man in a low baseball cap stood in line for a hot dog. Aaron Cartwrytte wore an apron over his collared shirt behind the barbeque.

Tick-tock, tick-tock, stick-rock.

She squeezed her eyes shut and turned away from the image.

"Sorry," Jenner cleared the screen.

"It's okay." Zemila shook out her hands.

"I'll do some looking around on what the Cartwryttes might have that's so valuable." Jenner turned back to his projection. "And I sent you some information on the APECA Committee."

"Have you eaten?" Zemila asked, but he was lost in his work. She sighed, turned, and walked to the kitchen.

Zemila heated some left-over lasagna and tried to keep her hands steady. After barely fending off a full meltdown in her office today and her therapy appointment with Dr. Janson, she was exhausted.

She ate quickly, then she brought a plate of lasagna to Jenner before heading upstairs. Quickly stripping off her clothes, she got into the shower and turned the water to hot. Zemila reached for her hairbrush. Before she could touch it, it flew into her hand.

She froze . . . took a breath. That made two times today. She'd been doing better at not inadvertently using her gift, but she was losing control. She was out of control. She was—

No, said that soft familiar voice in her mind.

"No?" she said aloud. "What do you mean no?"

Who am I talking to?

She squeezed her eyes shut and focused on the feel of water on her skin.

You're okay, she told herself, opening her eyes and turning the water as hot as she could handle. You're going to be okay.

CHAPTER SEVEN

Lochlan

I shoved Qillian off me. Again.

"Stop doing that." I put as much force as I could behind the words. "Danu, that is not how we get out of here."

"We? We aren't getting out of here, Lochlan. But you can," Qillian said in a voice sounding far older than his years. "I've made my peace. I can ensure you are able to make it through this place. I can save you for battles to come."

"Gods Below, Qillian." I shook my head.

"Queen Anne said—"

"I care not what Inanna sermonized," I snapped. "I will not allow you to trade your life for mine."

"You can't stop me," he said, lifting his chin.

"I can," I said. "I can block it."

"You don't have the strength for that."

Too smart for his own good. And far too kind for this world.

"I can resist," I told him.

"You know that after they're through with you," he leaned forward, "you won't have the strength for that."

I thought of the last thing I saw before blacking out. A dagger thrust into my chest. The hilt being twisted.

I looked up slowly at Qillian, his deep brown eyes just visible in the darkness.

"What did you do?" I asked.

"I prayed." He said it so simply. So peacefully. He said it with a confidence I envied. "They stabbed you, they were standing around you, so I couldn't really see, but when they left, I prayed."

"Is it too personal for me to ask your birthname?"

Qillian stood and reached for my hands. Shooting pain in my shoulders had my eyes flying open as he gently lifted the chain off the hook over my head.

"I'll trade you for it," Qillian said, sitting beside me. He lightly pressed his shoulder against mine. It was warm. "Why haven't they taken you before now?"

"Anti-tracking spells," I breathed through the pain in my limbs. "On me, on my house. I cast certain spells into the foundation of any place I live. I made a basement in my house and cast there to keep the bonds strong."

"Made?" he interrupted. "You made a basement?"

"I'm hard to locate if you're not a friend," I said, not wanting to get into the details of protection spells. "Let's leave it at that. Your turn. What is your birthname, Qillian?"

"Kareem," he said. "Kareem bin Aziz."

"The Most Generous son of All Mighty," I nodded.

"How do you—"

"You pick up a few things here and there in a life as long as mine."

"I don't know if He healed you, or if you healed yourself, or if it happened at the same time," Kareem bin Aziz said with a deep sigh. "I just prayed. You were bleeding out. I didn't know what else to do."

I touched the new hole in my shirt, the fresh blood stain.

"Aye," I said. "He's done that a few times now. I think he likes seeing my body go limp. Almost like I've died."

"How are you so calm about this?" Qillian looked over at me.

"He can't kill me that way," I shrugged and pain shot through my shoulder. "And I've survived much worse."

"Oh?" he said.

There was a long pause and I took the time to survey my body. I don't know how Qillian did what he did or why it worked so well. My shoulder was still dislocated, and I was still starving, but my leg seemed to be healed, and my hand too. I thought a toe might have still been broken but—

I cautiously wiggled it.

No, that's healed now too.

Qillian had done a marvellous job. His faith was strong, which prompted me to ask—

"Which name would you like me to call you?"

"I—" He paused. "I'm still working on that." I waited. Then he shrugged. "Qillian still, I guess."

"Will you tell me about why you changed it?"

"Right now?" he asked, surprised. "We have to figure out a way out of here."

"I have a way out," I said. "Your faith has hastened the process."

The Proxy, the cartel, any other minions Balor had at his beck and call, he had taught them poorly. They did not understand Magic as I did. They would not have put someone so devout in here with me if they had. They wanted me to kill whoever was placed here with me. To eat their Spark. To turn, as if it would be that easy.

"Already tainted and easily turned," the Famorian Simmons had said in the back of a dark warehouse. I'd used Dark Magic that night. But no. No, I was stronger than that now. I was smarter than when Lugh died. I could resist that pull.

"Easily turned," the Famorian hissed in my memory.

"Lochlan?" Qillian asked.

"I have a way out," I repeated. "But I need to focus."

"Do you want me to be quiet—"

"No," I shook my head. "No, it has been quiet for too long. The quiet makes me . . ." I paused. I didn't want to tell him I saw my grandfather when it got too quiet. When I was so hungry and weak. That's when I saw him. That's when he tempted me.

"You want me to talk?"

"Yes," I said. "Please, tell me about why you changed your name or . . . or anything else."

"Okay." He took a deep breath. "Okay."

"It was my great-grandfather on my mother's side who converted to Islam," Qillian said. "Nation of Islam, during the Civil Rights movement. He converted and he met my great-grandmother. They had my grandfather. My grandfather met my grandmother in college. After they graduated, they had my mom."

As he spoke, I let my head fall to the hard wall at my back.

"My mother grew up poor, as her parents had. They had a little success, but you know how it is here. The system sees Black folks rising up, and it finds a way to beat them back down."

Soon I was lost in Qillian's words. I held the metal cuff on my right wrist and tried to make my mind as blank as possible. I tried to not let Balor or the Proxy interrupt the rhythm of Qillian's words.

"I was tired of being broke and hungry. I was tired of being bullied for dating men. I was tired of the looks my grandmother gave me. And my mom . . . God, I was tired of watching her struggle. I could have gotten a job without changing my name, but I wanted to try something new. Dad said I was shaming Allah. I was tired of that too. I got a job. In a kitchen. It wasn't enough."

Magic began to pulse within me. It was low and slow at first. I would never have been able to attempt this without Qillian's help, without his faith. He had healed more of me than I thought possible. And that healing allowed me to focus.

"I went to Heaven. I started working as a bouncer. I moved up. Queen Anne was good to me. She's good to all of us. Some guys still call me 'Kareem.' Not many, just a couple from the old neighborhood."

I breathed, I listened, I focused. And all the while I drew a small pattern on the metal cuff holding my right wrist. Over and over again, the same circle and knot.

"I couldn't take the guilt trip from my dad. Once I started making enough money to have a small place, I moved out. Around then's when I stopped going to Mosque, stopped praying every day. I just . . . stopped," he sighed.

Circle, knot, circle, knot. The cuff grew hot under my touch and power surged.

"But when you meet a literal god, it makes you question things, you know?" Qillian went on.

Circle, knot, circle, knot.

"I have a new understanding now. A different one. When I had no hope in this place, when I was falling asleep to screams, when I was hungry and alone, I found Him again."

Clink!

The cuffs around my wrists and ankles popped open. I stood to my full height and, ignoring the pain in my chest, I lifted my right hand.

"I would have thought meeting a god would have assured you."

I heard the Old World thick in my voice as a ball of light flared in my palm. "We're all real."

CHAPTER EIGHT
Zemila

Zemila looked out the window above the kitchen sink. She watched the sky shift color as the sun set. Blues turned to hues of orange and purple behind Llowellyn's work shed in the back yard. She sipped her wine and let herself think about Lochlan—and about the dream she'd had. How he hadn't been alone, how he'd had hope, and she'd let herself hope too.

Zemila started to make dinner. It was Thursday, so Llowellyn was with Mrs. Abernathy. He'd started visiting her after Lochlan had been taken. Zemila wasn't sure how much Mrs. Abernathy knew, but the time together made both Llowellyn and Mrs. Abernathy feel better.

"Cooking?" Jenner asked, walking into the kitchen.

"Jenner." Zemila jumped, nearly dropping the plate she was holding. "You scared me."

Jenner looked sheepishly at her, his arms full of dishes, most still with food on them.

"Llowellyn is next door, and Nemo is at your place. I asked him to come here but," Jenner shrugged again, "he said no."

Zemila hurried to help him, and Jenner let her take a few plates and cups out of his hands.

"I told him Llowellyn was out," Jenner said, putting the rest beside the sink, and turning the kettle on. "He still said no."

"Did he tell you why he's like that about Llow?" Zemila asked Jenner. Nemo seemed to hate Llowellyn more every time they saw each other.

"Well, they didn't start off great." Jenner emptied the sink and put the stopper in. "The whole face-punching thing?"

"Yeah," Zemila said. "I'm pretty sure Llowellyn let him do that."

"Oh, I am very sure," Jenner turned on the faucet. "And I am equally sure that made it worse. But I have no idea why Nemo hates him so much."

The sound of water filling the kitchen sink stretched between them. It gave her time to wonder what the hell was going on. Jenner hadn't talked to her this much in months.

And he's about to do the dishes? she thought. Something's wrong.

The kettle whistled. Jenner turned off the tap filling the sink, took a bright pink mug off a high shelf, put in a tea bag, and filled it with hot water.

"Zemila, um . . . okay." Jenner set the tea aside, took a deep breath, then let it out slow. "I am not so great at this because usually I am a perfect friend and roommate. But I know you have been upset with me. I wanted to talk about it."

Zemila blinked rapidly, trying to hide her shock.

"Zemila, I—— dios mío, Zemila, don't look at me like that."

"Jenner," she said, her tone serious. She cautiously, stepped toward him and poked him in the arm. "Have you been body-snatched?"

"Shut up!" he snapped. "Let me say this before I remember that you Luman Ninja Turtles are actually freaks who don't deserve me."

Zemila squinted at him.

"Zemila," he tried again. "I am sorry I have been a bad friend. Distant and unavailable. I have been so focused on finding Lochlan that nothing else mattered. That was not okay. I did not see that you were hurting too, and maybe you needed something else from me. Something more than just the best, most attractive search engine in the whole world."

Jenner had been delivering this monologue to his avocado patterned socks, but he looked up at her and said, "I am truly sorry for my part in making this harder for you. You shouldn't have had to take care of me the way you did. Thank you, Zemila. I am sorry."

Zemila blinked again, then said, "I accept your apology."

"Bueno," Jenner nodded and started the dishes.

"Jen," Zemila said, approaching him like a horse she didn't want to spook. "The body-snatching question wasn't rhetorical."

"Ay, She-Devil, take the win!"

"Who the hell are you?" She pointed at him and clutched her non-existent pearls. "And what have you done with my roommate?"

Jenner pulled a hand from the dishwater and flicked bubbles in her direction. "Don't make a big deal of this or I will never apologize for anything ever again."

"I didn't know you knew how to wash dishes," Zemila smiled.

"I wash dishes," he said. "You, maybe, are not around when I wash dishes, but I wash dishes."

"With a dishwasher?" she asked.

"She. Devil." He glared at her. "Do you want me to stop?"

"Of course not," she laughed, pulling a tea towel from where it hung on the oven door. "But really, what's going on? What prompted this?"

Jenner sighed and handed her a clean plate. Zemila dried it and waited for his answer.

"I missed Marianna's birthday," he said. "I had a few missed calls from my parents and—"

"Was she upset?" Zemila asked.

"No," Jenner shook his head. "No, if she was upset it would have been easier. She was so happy I called."

Zemila had seen Jenner and Cam's older sister, Marianna, only a few times during video calls. Jenner and Cam went home to San Diego to visit her often. Or, at least, Jenner used to.

"And I realized how long it had been since I'd been home," Jenner went on. "Mama said she's been pointing at my picture. She does that when she hasn't seen us in a while. I remember her doing that a lot when Cam first left for Stanford. I just . . . I just got lost in it, you know?"

"I know," Zemila nodded, because she did. She took the clean bowl out of Jenner's hands, dried it and put it away.

"And you're smoking," he said.

"What?" she turned to face him.

"Three tonight," he shrugged. "New high. It really made me see how much stress I am adding to your life."

Zemila had started smoking when she was working as a server in Baltimore during college. It was social, at first.

"My smoking," Zemila said.

"And my sister," Jenner nodded. "The smoking thing helped me realize other people are hurting too, as stupid as that sounds."

Zemila took another plate from the drying rack.

"You should probably quit . . . again," he said.

"Let's go back to talking about your sister," Zemila deflected.

"I miss her," Jenner obliged. "People don't really understand the relationship. They think because she is disabled, because she's non-verbal, we don't communicate. But that's not true."

"I know," Zemila reassured.

"I feel so much guilt," Jenner said. "I know her medication manages the epilepsy now, but when we were younger . . . it was so bad. She was in and out of the hospital all the time. My father was working so much, and my mother . . ." Jenner handed Zemila a clean mug to dry. "Well, they both did the best they could, but with all Marianna's care—anyway, that's why Cam and I grew up in Mexico with our grandparents."

He looked sideways at Zemila, handing her the last plate. "Cam told you all this, huh?"

"Cam told me her story," Zemila said. "I'd like to hear yours, if you'd like to share."

Jenner nodded and fished around in the soapy water for any missed dishes. Then he pulled the plug at the bottom of the sink and watched the water drain.

"I'm kind of hungry," Jenner said.

"There's some shepherd's pie in the fridge." Zemila nodded over her shoulder as she dried the cups left in the rack. "And I was going to make a chicken salad."

"My abuela convinced my mom that my dad shouldn't take time off. That he should work to be a high-priced lawyer, so they could hire help," Jenner grinned. "She just wanted her grandbabies around, but in the end, she was right."

"Because your dad is a high-priced lawyer?" Zemila asked.

"Exactly," Jenner smiled. "And she never lets us forget it was her who made it happen. I try to go home once a month. I've been bad recently and I've—"

A loud thud on the other side of the kitchen wall interrupted him.

"Mrs. Abernathy." Jenner stepped towards the connecting wall.

There was a muffled cry and Zemila straightened.

Jenner started tapping on his watch. "Call Louise Abernathy," he said. A ringing filled the room.

"Come on, come on," Jenner muttered.

"I'm going to go over," Zemila stepped toward the kitchen wall. "I'll just go over, okay?"

"*Louise Abernathy,*" the androgynous home system announced.

The banging on the front door had Zemila racing down the hall. She pulled open the door to find little old Mrs. Abernathy standing before her. Her rich brown skin was pale and chalky, and her hands shook as she raised them.

"Oh dear," her Southern drawl had a panicked tremor Zemila had never heard before. "Llowellyn, he collapsed. He started shaking. Started talking about Lochlan." She pointed at her front door.

Zemila was on the move.

She hopped the small wall dividing Mrs. Abernathy's porch from Lochlan's. Wrenching open the door, Zemila raced down the narrow hall to the back of the house. Llowellyn was curled in a ball, shaking. Zemila crouched beside him.

"Llow," she said. Jenner knelt by her side, and Mrs. Abernathy followed close behind him. "Llowellyn, what's happening? What can we do?"

"L–Lochlan," he said. "I know where he is."

"What?" Zemila's heartrate picked up. She tried to temper her reaction, to dampen her hope, to understand the words Llowellyn had said. "What does that mean?"

Llowellyn groaned in response and Zemila knelt down. Jenner did too and together they hoisted Llowellyn's big body off the kitchen floor. He was shaking, but they managed to maneuver him down the hall and on to a paisley-patterned couch in the living room. Unlike Lochlan's house, where everything looked like it was second-hand and well-used, Mrs. Abernathy's living room had a matching yet eclectic look that suited her personality.

"I'll get some water for Llowellyn," Mrs. Abernathy said. "Jenny-Love, come help me."

Jenner swiftly left the room. Zemila focused her attention on Llowellyn.

"What do you mean you know where Lochlan is?" she asked.

"He–he spoke to me," Llowellyn said, sitting up and tapping his temple with a finger. "He still is, and—ahh." He clutched his head. "Danu, it hurts."

"He is speaking to you now?" Zemila knelt down beside him. "What is he saying? Why does it hurt?"

"I don't know." Llowellyn cradled his head in his hands.

"What's going on?" she asked.

"I don't know," he answered.

"Is he okay?" She was frantic.

"I don't know!" Llowellyn stood.

Zemila fell back from her crouched position and hit the coffee table. She saw the swell of Magic as Llowellyn's heavy breathing moved his chest up and down.

"I just . . ." His voice was too small for such a man. He rubbed his chest, below his ribs. His face screwed up in pain. "It just, it just hurts . . ."

He swayed dangerously on the spot, then started to fall. Without thinking, Zemila raised her hands and caught his big body with her gift. She strained to control his weight but was able to lower him back to the couch.

"Water?" Jenner said from the doorway. He looked nervous.

"And I have tea," Mrs. Abernathy said.

She didn't see anything, Zemila told herself, not able to have that conversation right now.

"Thank you." Zemila stood and took the glass from Jenner. She handed it to Llowellyn who swallowed it in one go.

"We need a car," Llowellyn said. "He's calling me."

Zemila's eyes shifted to Mrs. Abernathy. Llowellyn was in too much pain to think of what exposure here would mean. He clutched his head again with a groan of pain.

"Calling you," Zemila said. "Right."

Zemila knew Lochlan and Llowellyn could communicate telepathically. She thought they had to be physically close. Maybe that meant Lochlan was nearby, or at least free from the cartel.

But if Llowellyn was in this much pain from a mental connection, what kind of shape was Lochlan in?

Zemila tapped her watch. "Call Nemo."

"Mrs. Abernathy," Jenner said as Zemila waited for her brother to pick up. "I'm sorry about all this. I—"

"Oh hush," Mrs. Abernathy cut him off. "It's okay, I wish I could help. But I don't have a car anymore."

Zemila wasn't sure if Mrs. Abernathy was ignoring some of the stranger things happening here, or if she was oblivious to them.

"Mila, what's up?" Nemo said from Zemila's watch and she left the living room.

"I need you to come get us."

"Who is us?" Nemo asked, "And why?"

"Me, Jenner, and Llowell—"

"I'm not coming to—" Nemo interrupted.

"He knows where Lochlan is," she cut in. "We need a car."

There was a beat of silence. Zemila stared at the stunned image of her brother.

"I'll be there as soon as I can," he said, and hung up.

CHAPTER NINE
Lochlan

The ball of light felt strong in my hand. Stronger than the pulsing irritation under my sternum. The Magic I'd slowly siphoned into the metal cuff over the last months pulsed through my body, healing as it went. Without Qillian, it would have taken me years to store enough Magic for an escape.

The most generous, indeed.

The illumination cast in my hand lit the gray concrete walls and the blood-stained floors. There were chains along the wall and a gutter in the center of the room. I turned to Qillian and focused on his Spark. It had expanded back to its original size. I scratched my chest before offering my hand to Qillian and pulling him to his feet.

"Avery?" he said, hope lighting his eyes. "Maybe we can find her on our way out."

In this light, I saw Qillian better too. His skin was dry and dirty, his dreadlocks were grown out. He was thin, and pale, but his eyes were bright, and his spirit strong.

"I don't know how long this strength will hold," I said. "But we can try to find her."

Okay," Qillian nodded.

"The guards are waiting for me." I moved over to the door. "A different me.

"Different?" he repeated.

I ignored him. He need not know how lucky he was to be alive. I need not dwell on the path I might have taken.

"Nasgadh chaidil," I said.

"Lochlan," Qillian said, but I held up a hand. The spell took more effort than I'd expected. I rubbed at my chest. After some twenty seconds of stillness, Qillian asked, "What are we waiting for?"

Five successive thuds answered his question. I pulled open the cell door. The guards were sprawled on the ground. The hallway had gray concrete walls and metal doors. Hanging florescent bulbs cast an eerie dimness.

"No windows," I said.

"I had a window, a small one. I was brought down in an elevator," Qillian said. "No idea how many floors up it was, though. Will they wake up if I touch them?" He gestured to the sleeping guards.

"They'll wake up in thirty minutes," I said. "Not before, unless their lives are in imminent danger."

"That's part of the spell?" Qillian asked, grabbing a key card from one guard and a ring of keys from another.

"Stipulations like that are why Dark Magic is easier," I explained as Qillian jogged down the hall, opening doors as he went. "More powerful."

"No Avery," Qillian said, kneeling back down and relieving a guard of his weapons. "I guess it would be too easy if she was in the cell next to ours."

Qillian stripped a guard of his bulletproof vest and handed it to me.

"You take it," I said. "I don't need it."

"Lochlan." His tone was exasperated. "For my peace of mind, please. I'll take one of the others."

I remembered the feel of his body shaking against mine as he took bullets meant for me.

"You know a gun can't kill me, right?" I took the vest and pulled it on. It rubbed painfully against my sternum.

"Can it slow you down?" he asked, taking a vest off another sleeping guard, and putting it on.

"Fair point," I conceded.

"I know you need to survive," Qillian said. "That's enough for me."

"I am going to kill Inanna," I said under my breath.

Qillian handed me a SIG Sauer and a pistol I didn't recognize from the third guard. He'd already stripped all the weapons of the first two for himself.

"You know how to use this, right, Gramps?" he smirked.

"Knowing how to use and needing to use are not the same thing."

"Yeah, yeah." He looked up and down the hall. "Right or left?"

"Your guess is as good as mine." I half-shrugged, then stopped when I felt the pain in my shoulder.

"Are you sure?" Qillian turned to me.

"That I don't know where I'm going?" I said. "Aye, I'm sure."

I threw a small spell right and left. It came back to me a moment later. "There are guards to the right."

"Just guards? No one else?" Qillian asked.

"The spell can't tell the difference. I'm sorry."

"So, you don't know they are guards, just people," Qillian said. "The spell could be revealing prisoners?"

"Correct," I nodded. "My instinct is to avoid all people."

"My instinct is to look for my friend," Qillian said.

I nodded stiffly, starting to mentally catalogue my few remaining injuries, and my strength, what I needed, and what I could spare as we looked for Avery.

"But—" Qillian interrupted my thoughts. I looked at him. "Is the chance of finding her worth the risk of getting caught?"

His kind eyes met my cold ones. I offered no guidance. This wasn't my choice to make. If he wanted to look for her, I would look. No question. I owed him that.

"What do you think?" he asked.

"I don't know," I said, and I didn't.

I didn't know who this girl was, what their relationship was. If it was Zemila, if it was Jenner, or Nemo, if it had been Cam, or my brother, I would burn the world to find them. If this girl was that for Qillian, I would follow his lead.

"Promise me," Qillian said, and it looked like it pained him to speak these words. "Promise me we will come back for her. Promise me when we get out of here, we will send people back, we won't abandon her."

"I swear it," I said. A zing of Magic flew through the air.

"What was that?" Qillian asked.

"A bonded promise," I told him. "Doesn't usually happen with Humans."

"Will you tell me about it later?" he asked. I nodded. "Then we go left."

We jogged down the dark concrete hallway. I sent another revealing cast ahead of us, breathing through the effort of casting, the pressure building in my chest. I stopped where the corridor turned.

"Two people here, three more down the hall. I can't use the same spell as last time. It doesn't have the same range . . . well, it could, but body Magic is challenging, unless its Dark. The—"

"Stipulations," Qillian finished. "Okay, what do we do?"

"Depends on the goal. Do they deserve death?" I asked Qillian as much as I asked myself.

"I don't know," he said. "I don't think so."

"I don't think so either." I placed a hand on his shoulder. "Dorcha tothaim."

As shadows, Qillian and I jogged side by side. The first two guards were stationed on either side of the hall. We had to move directly between them to get by. And while the spell camouflaged, it didn't make us invisible.

Using the extra Magic needed for a non-verbal spell, I cast. The fluorescent lights flickered and died.

"What the hell?" one of the guards said as we silently turned the corner.

"Call up top and—hey, don't shove me?" said the second.

"Get over yourself, I didn't shove you."

"Yes, you did."

"Call up top to, oh . . ." The second guard trailed off as the lights flickered back on.

"What's going on down there?" said someone from up ahead.

I followed Qillian out of that hallway and into a stairwell. After two flights of stairs, I still had no idea how far underground we were. We had little choice but to keep moving.

"Almost out, I think," Qillian said. "The air is different here."

He was right. It was lighter, less dank. We climbed yet another flight of metal stairs before hitting a dead end and I said, "This place is a labyrinth."

"We need help getting out," Qillian vocalized my thoughts. "We're going to need someone to show us the way. Unless you have a spell for that."

"I don't know where we are," I said. I was weakening. Magic was hard, and I didn't know why, but it hurt. "Any spell like that would need—"

"Hey!"

I turned to see a pair of guards sprinting toward us.

"Shit," Qillian said, half-raising his gun.

He hesitated. I knew he didn't want to kill. Mayhap he wasn't a good enough shot to solely wound.

I was.

"Gada-tothaim." I pushed my hands in the direction of the two men. A small ball of light hit each of them in the chest. I guided the spell, and the men collapsed.

There was a beat of silence as Qillian lowered his gun.

I wobbled on my feet and Qillian's arm shot out to steady me. I shook him off quickly, not wanting to take more of his Spark. I was stronger than I'd been in months, but Magic could only do so much in a moment. I wouldn't be back to full strength for weeks.

Not unless I . . . my gaze drifted to the two men down the hall.

"Wake one up so they can lead us out," Qillian said.

"Aye."

We moved down the hall more slowly than I liked. I stumbled once before Qillian put a hand to my neck and muttered words in Arabic too quiet for me to hear. My body surged with energy and the pain in my chest diminished.

I grit my teeth, annoyed. "I am going to—"

"You're gonna what?" Qillian asked. "Say 'thank you'?"

I glared at him, then looked down at the two slumped bodies. A light buzzing came from one of their earpieces.

"Report, report," the tinny sound echoed.

"Dúisigh," I muttered over one of them men, then adjusted my vest. The man's dark hazel eyes snapped open. "Tell them it was a false alarm, then lead us outside."

"All clear here," the man said into his comms. He stood and started jogging down the corridor. Light footsteps and heavy breathing filled the hall as Qillian and I followed. My bulletproof vest was hot and uncomfortable. I scratched my chest and tried to adjust it. Every time I cast a reveal spell, or put another guard to sleep, the discomfort increased.

"Yang, report," said a familiar voice. The Proxy.

The voice came in clear and cold through the earpiece I had taken off a fallen guard. I scratched at my chest and listened.

"Yang," said the Proxy. "Report."

Yang, the guard leading us out, opened his mouth and paused. I pressed my spell deeper into his mind, pushing him to say there was a bug in the system and he was working on fixing it.

Yang's eyes cleared and swung from me to Qillian. A panicked expression crossed his face. My vision blurred. I spoke my spell words again, but stumbled over the phrase. I tried to shake off the heat in my chest, the fear in my heart, but I could hear the squeak of small wheels.

"Eyes here, Lochlan." I could feel the long thin rod being driven into my chest. "You know I like to see when it happens."

"Yang, Yang," the Proxy said.

"Lochlan, you good?" Qillian asked.

Heat flared under my vest. I scratched at it again, trying to pull myself back to the present, to the hallway. To the cast. But I couldn't. I tried to give Yang a command.

Qillian placed a hand on my neck.

"Lochlan," Qillian said, I could feel him pushing his Spark into my body, but it wasn't enough.

"Lochlan," the Proxy said from my memories.

"Give him a command."

"Give me what I want."

My legs felt weak. Qillian tried to grab my shoulders. All too quickly, the ground came up to meet me.

"Lochlan," Qillian said. "Snap out of it, man, I need you."

"He's out, he's out, he's out," I heard frantically in my ear and over my head.

I blinked slowly and lifted my cheek off the cold wet concrete. Qillian tackled Yang. They wrestled for a moment and Yang ended up on top. After landing a solid blow to Qillian's head, Yang disentangled himself and sprinted down the hall.

"I'm in the south end," Yang shouted into his device. "Near Exit 33. Get down here, they're escaping."

"Near Exit 33," Qillian said, pulling me to my feet. "I want to know you're okay, but I really need you to wake up and help us get out of here.

That must be the exit he was talking about?" He pointed in the direction Yang had run. "You good?"

"I'll manage," I said. "Let's go."

We moved as fast as we could, as fast as I could, down the hall after Yang. Where he had turned left, we went right. The air was less dank here, less musty. I was sure we were getting close to the surface.

"There," Qillian yelled, and pointed as we careened around a corner. There were two sets of large security doors. Qillian grabbed my hand. Spark charged through my body, my survival instincts pulling at Qillian. Heat burned unbearably in my chest. Qillian stumbled and released my hand. I got weak, like something was draining my strength. It felt like something was sucking out everything Qillian had poured into me.

"Come on, man." Qillian half-dragged me through the first set of doors. The second set was closed and needed a fingerprint to get through. "Shit," he said.

I reached up from my collapsed position on the floor.

"Oscailte."

The heavy door opened a few inches, then stuck.

"Ar oscailt," I said, calling Magic, pleading. But it was too hot, too much, too—

"Lochlan!" My name boomed down the hall. The Proxy, flanked by several guards, walked toward us. "You think I didn't take precautions against this?"

Behind me, Qillian wedged his fingers through the small opening between wall and door. He grunted with the effort, and kept fighting to open the door.

"Of course, I did," the Proxy said.

I tried to cast and pain exploded in my chest, and I screamed.

"Lochlan!" Qillian yelled. "Hold on, Loch, it's moving."

Inch by inch, Qillian pried the door opened.

"Everything has a cost," the Proxy said, getting closer. "And the price for your Magic is pain."

I fumbled with my bulletproof vest, tearing it off, trying to get to whatever was on fire in my chest.

"Your pain, your Magic," the Proxy stared at me with dead eyes. "It fuels me."

As if by his words, my fingers went numb. It felt like Magic was being pulled from my limbs to my chest. I threw the vest aside and looked down. There was a fine line where a very sharp scalpel had cut skin. So fine I had never seen it. I would have never noticed this scar below my ribs if something behind it hadn't been burning.

"Almost there, almost there," Qillian said.

The Proxy was too close. The second door wouldn't be open in time. I had to get this thing, whatever it was, out of me.

"Ditiun-balla," I cried. Pain ripped through me, and only feet away, the Proxy slammed into a glinting blue wall of energy.

"Oscailte." I grit my teeth as I ran a finger over the thin line in my skin. Blood spilled over my chest as the scar reopened.

"God, Lochlan," Qillian said. "What are you doing?"

But he didn't know, he couldn't feel it. Qillian couldn't feel the thing buried inside my chest. The Proxy and his men pounded on the protective barrier. The ground beneath me shook. Cold dead eyes looked at me, head tilted to the side. It was like he was a cat, watching a mouse trying to escape an impossible trap.

"Tarraingt!" I screamed through gritted teeth and fought the desire to pass out from the pain. "Ag mo caitheamh, ar oscailte mair tarraingt."

"Holy shit," Qillian breathed, still fighting with the door.

"Ag mo caitheamh, ar oscailte mair tarraingt," I repeated.

Skin and muscle parted and tore as I pulled at the thing in my chest that pulled Magic out of me. The Proxy's lip twisted in rage and he pounded on the barrier again. It flicked, and almost died. He pushed at the wall, and it bent under his hands.

It was going to fall. I was captured again. I couldn't—

Hands on my back, my body being dragged. *Pop! Pop! Pop!* And the first set of doors slammed closed on the snarling face of the Proxy. I wrenched a small black orb out of my chest and looked up to where Qillian stood, feet planted, gun in hand.

Replacing the gun at his hip, he pushed the second door open wide enough to drag me through.

"How— how did you do that?" I asked, trying to carry my own weight.

"I shot the control panel," he said, pulling my good arm around his shoulders.

"That— I— That actually worked?"

"I saw it in a movie once and took a chance," Qillian said, then stumbled when I unintentionally pulled at his Spark.

"Sorry," I said. "I didn't mean to do that."

"It's okay," Qillian said, helping me up the concrete stairs into cold open air. "Of course, it's okay. Take what you need. I'll be fine."

It was overcast, but daytime. We were in a small clearing. We were surrounded by tall trees, just beyond the in-ground stairwell we'd come up. I stumbled over a rock or tree root. My vision was dark around the edges. We moved slowly, too slowly, away from the underground compound. I had no idea where we were but the red maples and white oaks told me we were still on the East Coast.

The air was clean and cold and I could reach Llowellyn from here.

Gods willing, and with Qillian's help, I could reach Llowellyn from here.

"Stop," I said, when I couldn't go any further.

"We have to keep moving, Loch," he said.

"I have to call my brother." I leaned against a large tree and slid to the earth. I gave one last plea to Magic, one last pull.

I clutched Qillian's hand. I heard him gasp. I knew I took too much. I knew I danced too close to the edge, but as he pushed his Spark into me, I ignored the thrum of dark power and pushed it all into the spell. The word. The name.

Llowellyn.

CHAPTER TEN
Zemila

Zemila paced across Mrs. Abernathy's front porch. As frigid air blew her dark waves over her face, she ripped the black hair tie off her wrist. She pulled her long hair into a tight ponytail and started to pace again.

"Easy, Zemi," Zemila told herself. It had only been ten minutes since she'd called Nemo, but it felt longer. Llowellyn was incoherent, Jenner was panicked, but thank God for Mrs. Abernathy, the voice of calm.

Zemila's head snapped up at the sound of a car and she vaulted off the front porch. By the time she threw open the gate, Nemo was pulling up in front of the house. Zemila wrenched open the SUV's passenger door and looked at her brother. His hair was shorter than usual, and his black suit hugged his wide shoulders.

"We need you inside," she said. "He can't say much, and he's having trouble moving."

Nemo got out. "If he can't say much, then how the hell is he gonna tell us where Lochlan is?"

"Срање, Nemanja, I don't know."

"I hate it when you call me that," he said.

"He knows where Lochlan is," Zemila said over her shoulder as they flew up the front porch steps. "Isn't that enough?"

Llowellyn was hunched over, on the couch. Jenner sat cross-legged on the floor looking at a projection of the city traffic cams.

"Mrs. Abernathy." Zemila stepped into the living room. "You remember my brother—he's here to help us."

"Of course, hello, dear." Mrs. Abernathy put down the glass of water she'd been holding for Llowellyn. Nemo nodded to her. "My, you are all so very tall!"

"Get up, asshole." Nemo pulled Llowellyn's arm around his shoulder and hoisted him to his feet.

"Fuck you," Llowellyn squinted in pain at Nemo.

"Language!" Mrs. Abernathy glared at them.

"See, Zemi," Nemo said. "He can talk fine. He's being a little bi—"

"Young man!" Mrs. Abernathy's tone was sharp and the room stilled. Nemo turned slightly to face Mrs. Abernathy. "Are you here to help? Or bicker?"

"Uhh . . . um," Nemo stuttered and readjusted Llowellyn.

"Because I was told you're here to help," Mrs. Abernathy nodded to Zemila. "Right now, my very good friend Lochlan needs you—we all do—to bring him back to us."

There was a beat of silence. Even Jenner stopped typing to look up at the odd tableau. The very small Mrs. Abernathy, hands on hips, scolded the two men towering over her, and they were cowed.

"Now, I don't know what's going on here," she continued. "Frankly, I don't want to know. I just want my friend back." She looked up at

Nemo, waiting. "Are you going to help or let whatever other issue you have waste this moment? A moment we don't know when we'll get again."

"I'm here to help," Nemo said. "I'm sorry."

"I'm sorry, Louise," Llowellyn said.

"Go now," she said, releasing them from her glare. Nemo nodded and helped Llowellyn outside.

"You are such a badass," Jenner whispered to her as he passed.

"Language," she called after him, then turned to Zemila.

They stood alone in the living room. Mrs. Abernathy took a step forward, reached out, and squeezed Zemila's hand.

"Bring him back now, y'all hear?" she said, the South thick in her words.

"Yes, ma'am," Zemila said and turned. Jenner was holding the front door open for her.

"What's up, Jen?" Zemila asked. They walked to the SUV, where Nemo was helping Llowellyn into the passenger seat.

"While you were outside," Jenner said, "Llow told me some things he's seeing, what he is feeling, from Lochlan."

"Okay," Zemila said, opening the white gate. Jenner pulled her to a stop. "Jen, what?"

"It wasn't good, Zemila," he said, worry pulling his dark brows together. "If we find Loch—"

"When we find him," she corrected.

"Sí," Jenner inclined his head. "When we find him, he'll be in rough shape. Prepare for that."

Jenner stepped past her and into the SUV's back seat. Zemila got in behind the driver's seat, thinking of Lochlan, thinking of the dreams.

She knew he was being hurt. She'd known it for a long time.

Houses turned to highways and highways turned to trees as they drove. The SUV was large but seemed to shrink in the tense silence. Every five or ten minutes, Llowellyn would try to give directions, and Jenner would try and clarify.

Zemila reached out with her senses. She wanted to find Lochlan the way she sometimes could in her dreams. All she could think of was her own fear, her own lack of control.

"Well, I can't go that way," Zemila heard Nemo say. "You're pointing at trees."

Llowellyn clutched his chest, his breaths came short and fast. "That's what I feel!"

"Go straight, there should be a path on your left, in about a mile," Jenner said.

Zemila refocused on her surroundings. A strong wind forced the tall trees to sway, making the last light of day dance on the narrow gravel road.

"Jenner, I swear to God," Nemo muttered. "We've been driving in a circle for fifteen minutes."

"Just do it," Jenner said.

"Where are we?" Zemila asked, checking her watch. They'd been in the car for well over an hour. Maybe two—she'd zoned out.

"Near Blure Lake Park," Jenner said.

"Near the base?" she asked.

"Near a campground too," Jenner said, then whispered, "You okay?"

"Yeah," she lied.

"Left here," Jenner said to Nemo at a road Zemila would have missed.

"Closer, we're getting closer," Llowellyn said after the sharp turn.

"Where now?" Nemo asked.

"Stop, stop, stop!" Llowellyn yelled. Nemo slammed on the brakes and Zemila was thrown forward in her seat. "Back up, I think."

"You think?" Nemo glared at Llowellyn.

"That way," Llowellyn pointed into the dense trees barely lit by the last rays of the sun.

"There is no road that way." Jenner looked up from his projection.

Llowellyn threw open the door and sprinted into the woods. Zemila felt a pull in her chest. Hope flared to life and she jumped out of the SUV after Llowellyn.

Was this the connection she'd been hoping for? The link she thought she imagined?

"Close, close," Llowellyn muttered as she caught up. They moved through the brush, into the trees, pushing branches aside.

"Right behind you," Zemila said when he paused. She touched Llowellyn's back. He seemed to relax under her finger tips.

"That helps." He reached a hand out behind him. She took it and the pull inside her grew stronger.

Nemo caught up and asked, "Why are we stopping?"

"Magic something-something, I think," Jenner answered.

"That helps," Llowellyn repeated. He took in a deep breath and let it out slow. "Think of him," he instructed. "He is thinking of you."

She did. Together in the dying light, surrounded by trees, Zemila and Llowellyn breathed as one.

"This way," Llowellyn said, changing course.

Zemila let go of Llowellyn's hand when his pace was too much. Nemo had no trouble keeping up with him and soon overtook her. Then, it was just her and Jenner, trying to keep Llowellyn and Nemo in their sights. Branches tore at her skin and caught in her hair as she ran through the trees.

Tension pulled at her insides when Llowellyn and Nemo disappeared in the trees. She tried to keep up, to follow the trail of broken branches. The thick woods blocked the hazy gray-orange sky making it difficult to see, but she managed.

"This way," Zemila pulled on the back of Jenner's hoodie, when he veered off course.

"Are you sure?" he asked.

Zemila's breaths were heavy, and blood pounded in her ears. A howl of frustration, anger, and fear was muffled in the dense wood.

"I'm sure," Zemila said.

Moments later, they broke into a small clearing and Zemila stumbled to a stop.

"Lochlan," she whispered.

His limp form was half-pulled onto Llowellyn's lap. Zemila covered her mouth with a hand, trying to keep the scream inside of her as she looked at Lochlan.

Dark brown and bright red stains covered his clothes. A patchy blood-matted beard covered his gaunt and bruised face. She'd known he was being hurt, but to see him emaciated, his skin covered in scabs and fresh wounds . . . she'd thought she was prepared for this. She'd thought she was strong enough to stay composed, to be useful, to help.

She'd thought wrong.

"Little One, Little Lochlan, open your eyes." Llowellyn shook Lochlan's shoulders lightly, and all Zemila could do was watch. Llowellyn dug one hand into the earth and placed the other on Lochlan's chest.

"Ag mo breatha, aire cagair-gada, beannachd nartha, beannachd nartha," Llowellyn chanted. The forest swam before Zemila's eyes as she tried to blink away her tears.

"Mine, mine, mine-mine-mine," Zemila heard the whisper behind her. She whipped around hands raised, but no one was there.

"Ag mo breatha, aire cagair-gada, beannachd nartha, beannachd nartha," Llowellyn continued. Zemila could barely hear him.

"Tick-tock, stick-rock," the rasping voice of the Famorian Simmons whispered in her mind.

"Ag mo breatha," Lochlan's voice came back to her in waves. "Ag grà mas grà, nasgadh corp a anam, nasgadh breatha a breatha."

She squeezed her eyes shut. A pool of blood surrounded her. Lochlan knelt, a hand on the ground, fingers extended in the deep red liquid.

No, no, no, she told herself. Simmons isn't here. He is dead. He died in a cloud of dust.

She opened her eyes.

"Aire cagair-gada, beannachd nartha," Llowellyn chanted, and the woods swam again.

"I would only slow you down," the Lochlan of her nightmares said. The one she'd left behind as Heaven fell.

"I need you," she'd told him.

"You don't," he'd lied.

Lochlan was bleeding out on the floor in the hallway of Heaven as the building shook. Lochlan was bleeding out lying in his bed as a crow cawed and scratched at the window. Lochlan was dying on the forest floor and there was nothing she could do to help him. Even the connection she'd felt before had flickered and died. Had she imagined it this whole time? Doubt, terror, and self-loathing stoked the fire of worthlessness that always burned her inside.

Nothing, NOTHING!

Fear, pain, and helplessness exploded out of her. She screamed.

The earth shook as Zemila folded in on herself, clutching at her stomach, her clothes, clenching her fists and pulling at her hair. Llowellyn's chanting faltered. Jenner stumbled and fell. Nemo threw his hands up, shielding Lochlan and Llowellyn from a falling tree with a blast of telekinetic energy.

Zemila screamed and screamed and couldn't stop the flood of emotion pouring out of her in waves. Her knees landed on the cold ground and her fingers dug deep into the earth.

Helpless. Worthless. Powerless. Everyone she loves leaves her. He is going to die, he is going to leave her. Again. The scream of anguish, despair, and failure convulsed through her. She let it.

"Zemila!" Jenner yelled.

"Zemila!" Llowellyn tried.

"Zemi," a voice hissed in her ear.

Hands on her shoulders, lifting her up and pulling her tight to a broad chest.

"Zemi," he said again. "Right here."

Her brother, the only voice that broke through her grief when their mother died. The voice that broke through when their father left and she couldn't stop crying. The voice she'd needed so much over the last few months, and now he was here. He hadn't left her. Not really.

"Right here," Nemo said. "You're right here, with me. And I've got you. Okay? I've got you."

Zemila clutched him as her screams turned to sobs.

"Come on, Zemi," he said. "Come here, I've got you."

Nemo pulled her around, still tucked to his side, and knelt down beside Lochlan. She saw Nemo and Llowellyn exchange a look, then Llowellyn stepped away and Nemo put her hand on Lochlan's chest.

"I can't," she sobbed. "I can't, I can't feel him, I can't do anything. I'm nothing!"

Nemo looked up at Llowellyn then back to Zemila.

"You can do it, Zemi," he said. The nickname Nemo only used when he was pissed. The one he used now with such love, such patience. "You can do it."

"I can't," she said. "I'm nothing!"

No, said the foreign but familiar voice. The soft voice. One that was hers, but not hers. One she heard from time to time.

Zemila thought of that day in her apartment. She thought of Lochlan's hands on her skin. The glow she felt in her chest, the stir she felt in her gut. She thought of the soft kiss she pressed to his lips while he slept. She thought of how perfectly he seemed to fit her. How he made her feel like she was perfect all on her own.

The glowing feeling grew and grew until all she knew was love, and light, and Lochlan. Her vision went bright gold as the world seemed to float and expand.

Then it all went black.

"He's breathing," someone said. "So is the other one."

"How's she?"

"Is she okay?"

"Zemila?"

Wake up, said the familiar voice.

Zemila's eyes flickered open. She looked around. They were still in the woods.

"You okay?" Nemo asked. She was kneeling, still beside Lochlan, with her hand on his chest. "That was . . . incredible."

Nemo held her up. Llowellyn was a few feet away, kneeling over a figure she hadn't noticed before. Sitting back on her heels, she blinked rapidly and asked, "What happened?"

Before Nemo could answer, Llowellyn was back. Jenner was helping the other figure lying in the brush.

"Little One," Llowellyn said. "Lochlan, Little Lochlan, I need you to open your eyes now."

Llowellyn closed his eyes and Zemila knew, by the look on his face, that he was communicating to Lochlan through their telepathic link.

"Ugh," Lochlan groaned. "Didn't . . . miss that."

"Lochlan!" Llowellyn said and threw his arms around his brother. "Gods Below, Lochlan, I thought I was alone."

"Qillian?" Lochlan rasped. "Where . . . Qillian?"

"Qillian?" Nemo repeated. "What are you . . . oh, my God." Nemo pushed up and rushed over to where Jenner was kneeling.

"Lochlan." Zemila tried to stop the tears rolling down her cheeks, she tried to keep her voice steady.

"Mila," he said, lifting a hand and clasping it with hers.

CHAPTER ELEVEN

Lochlan

Lochlan sat leaning against the hard-stone wall of the castle with no king. He sniffed, wiped his nose. The slow burn of rage heated his skin.

"I must speak with the Dagda," Llowellyn had told him. "He will know of his father's plans. I am not certain of our safety here. I—" Llowellyn had shot him a glance and Lochlan had read it all too well. "Little One, don't stray."

"Don't stray," Lochlan spat out to the empty hallway of the empty castle. He'd heard the rumours. That one of Lugh's wives had been unfaithful. That her lover had been killed. He'd heard the rumors of revenge.

A bitter dark tang filled his mouth. It tasted like power, like rage, like purpose.

You can avenge him, a dark voice in Lochlan's mind whispered. The voice was cold and familiar. It filled him with a righteous anger.

"Disloyalty," Lochlan hissed through clenched teeth. They should have known better. The woman and her lover. They should have been faithful to their king.

And I, he thought. I should have been there. I should have known.

The rumors of assassination were just that, rumors . . . until they weren't.

You can be there now, the dark voice said. You can avenge your king, now. Take his place, now. You can ensure this never happens again.

"Disloyalty," Lochlan said again, throwing his head back to smack against the hard stone.

The pain mixed with rage. Had he too not been disloyal for his lack of action? In his arrogance, he thought them too powerful to be challenged by mere mortals. Too righteous to be harmed.

He had looked into the threat, as he did every time. He knew the three sons of the man Lugh had put to death were displeased. Were upset. But Lugh had assured him this time was like all the others. Empty. He had been wrong.

And now Lochlan's king was dead.

You can prove your loyalty now, the dark voice said again.

Vengeance and rage mingled in his blood. Anger boiled hot and deep. A flood of excess power shot red sparks between his fingers. He knew where the three sons lived.

He stood. With purpose.

φ

Lochlan left the dark stone home and began to walk. Where to, he did not know. Only that he was being pulled, being taken, being guided.

His bare shins and leather boots were stained in blood. His linen shirt was red and wet and he cared not for the lives he had taken. For the Spark he had eaten. Power radiated off him and rage still coursed through his veins. He wanted to burn the wretched home he left behind him with three dead men inside. He wanted to burn the world.

Lochlan kept walking, kept following that pull in his gut, that call to greatness. The darkness was singing to him and it matched the rich power of stolen Spark now running through his body.

Wait, the dark voice in his head told him.

Lochlan stopped walking.

Listen.

Drunk on Dark Magic, Lochlan closed his eyes and listened to the call. When he opened his eyes again, he was no longer in a field.

There was no light to see, but he could hear movement. A slither, a rasp, the sound of stone on stone, then skin on skin. The hoarse rhythm matched the call in his chest. It was a song, rich and powerful, dark and grotesque. And it was for him.

"Igna," he whispered. A ball of light appeared in his upturned palm.

He was at the mouth of a cavern. The writhing melody came from inside. The sound of stone on stone grew louder as he stepped forward. He sent the ball of light through the opening in the black grotto. As it traveled forward, the heat in his veins grew. The cavern was full. Full of bodies, of soldiers, demons, woken by their new king.

He had found Balor's hidden Famorian army.

φ

"Little One," Llowellyn said, calling me back from the darkness. Pulling me from the memory of an irredeemable path.

"Lochlan, Little Lochlan, I need you to open your eyes now. It's time to come back."

I didn't know if I could. I didn't know if I wanted to. I'd done so much damage, caused so much pain. I did not deserve the salvation my brother offered.

Little One, I heard in my mind. Little Lochlan, I need you now. Please.

She's here, so I must be dreaming. Her scent filled my senses and I longed for it to stay forever. I lay there. Soft ground beneath me and the smell of sweet earth and something else just out of my reach.

"Open your eyes," my brother said again.

Soft ground? I'm not in that cell. I left. I got away. Qillian. Qillian helped me.

"Come back to us, Lochlan."

Lochlan! Llowellyn yelled in my mind.

"Ugh," I groaned at the pain. "Didn't . . . miss that." I lied, elated this was real.

"Lochlan!" he said, flattening me with a bear hug. "Gods Below, Lochlan, I thought I was alone."

"Qillian?" I rasped. "Where . . . Qillian?"

"Qillian," said a familiar voice. Nemo. "What are you . . . oh, my God." I blinked open my eyes in time to see Nemo rush away.

Thank the Gods Nemo was safe. I'd feared all our efforts at Heaven had been for nothing, but if he and Llowellyn were here, they must all be all right.

"Lochlan?"

My eyes shifted to the most beautiful being I'd ever seen. The true salvation I didn't deserve. The hope that led me out of the hell of that place. My safe haven.

"Lochlan," she said again, and her voice cracked on my name.

"Mila," I said, lifting my hand in her direction. She grasped it, and I felt the darkness ebb away at her touch. "Mila, don't cry."

I wanted to wipe the tear slowly rolling down her cheek, to tell her everything would be okay. I wanted to tell her I loved her. I wanted to believe that was enough. I wanted to sit up, to hold her, but even the small movement of reaching for her exhausted me.

"Dios mío, Lochlan, you're all right. I would have killed you if you'd been dead."

I smiled as Jenner's tear-stained face swam into view above me.

"I missed you too, Jen," I croaked.

"I'll get you back for this," Jenner promised. "As soon as you are healthy, I am putting laxatives in your coffee."

I laughed, then coughed, and tried to sit up again. Llowellyn fiddled with something at his collar, then pulled out our necklace. He looped the gold chain around my neck and tucked the stone under my shirt.

"Your turn again," he said, a hand on my shoulder. "May it help your strength."

I nodded my thanks and felt a small surge of energy. Whether it was the stone, or contact with my kin, I didn't know.

"We should go," Qillian said.

I looked up at him, relieved he was safe. The right side of his face was slightly swollen and he had a cut above his left eye. He gave me a weak smile that I returned.

We were free from that place now.

"Nartha." My brother pressed Magic into my chest above the gash. He pulled my arm over his shoulder.

The walk through the woods was painful and exhausting. There wasn't enough room for Zemila to be beside me, but every so often, I felt her hand on my back, or my shoulder. As if assuring me she was still there.

Every touch lifted me. Lifted my spirits and gave me more energy, more momentum. Whether it was real or imagined, her touch made me stronger.

Finally, a black SUV came into view through the trees.

"Is that—" Qillian started to ask as we stepped on the dirt road.

"Yeah," Nemo answered. "I've been working for Queen Anne for the last few months."

"You've what?" I said, stunned into stillness.

"Oof." Zemila bumped into me in the dark.

"You work for—"

"Not now, Lochlan," Zemila said softly, putting her hand on my waist. "You were gone a long time."

"You must go back for—" I tried to turn to Qillian.

"Avery," Qillian said, and the bonded promise swelled then diminished.

"Now?" Jenner said from the tree line.

"Not now," Qillian said. "But soon."

Nemo popped the trunk of the SUV and pulled up the third row of seats. Jenner climbed in the very back and Llowellyn helped me into the middle row with Zemila and Qillian. It wasn't until we pulled onto I-66, with the windows open and the fresh air blowing around me, that my body truly started to relax.

CHAPTER TWELVE
Zemila

"I'm going to take the morning off," Zemila said as Llowellyn carried Lochlan up the stairs.

He's back, she told herself. He's safe.

The drive back had seemed so surreal. After not having Lochlan for so long, after only seeing shadows of him in her dreams, he was here. Right in front of her. She'd run her hands over him as he slept. She'd needed the contact. She still needed it.

"Maybe more than the morning. Maybe—" She stopped moving. She stopped speaking. She was right behind Llowellyn. Too close. She knew that.

Zemila forced herself to wait as he moved a few stairs ahead of her.

"The covers," Llowellyn said once they were in Lochlan's room. He nodded at the bed.

"Oh," Zemila rushed forward. She pulled the covers down and stepped back. "Don't you think we should—"

"Yes," Llowellyn said. "I was going to put him here while I draw a bath."

"I'll do that," Zemila said. "I'll start that, and then I can change the sheets when you—"

Lochlan groaned in his sleep as Llowellyn put him down. She paused. Stared. Swallowed.

His body was harsh angles and sunken flesh. His hair was dirty and matted, his cheeks were bruised and unshaven. Through a rip in his shirt, she could see the deep grooves between his ribs, and his eyes. His green eyes, usually so bright, were lost and dull when they fluttered open then shut.

"I–I . . ." She didn't know how to help, what to do. Any Magic she and Llowellyn had already poured into him, anything that had allowed him to speak, to stand, was gone now.

And she didn't know how to help.

"I'll take the week off."

Why do I keep saying that? Go start the bath! Stop staring. You're not helping here.

"I—" she tried.

"You don't have to do that, Zemila," Llowellyn said. "The morning would be great but—"

"Don't." She stepped back, feeling a soft touch of his Magic. "No, don't waste that on me." She turned to leave the room. "Give that to him. I'll start the bath."

When the bath was drawn, she knocked lightly on the bedroom door. Llowellyn half dragged, half carried Lochlan to the bathroom. Lochlan was awake, but barely. As soon as the bathroom door closed, Zemila hurried to Lochlan's room and stripped the bed. Though he'd only lain on them for a few minutes, the sharp pungent scent had soaked into the material.

How had he survived? Would he be different now? She would be. She would be so changed after an experience like that. Had this happened to him before?

Questions chased each other around in her mind as she took the sheets to the washing machine at the end of the hall. She set the cycle to double wash and went to the kitchen for a garbage bag. The tattered clothes Lochlan had been wearing weren't worth saving. She held her breath as she scooped them up, and knotted the garbage bag as soon as she could. Zemila quickly made the bed with fresh sheets before hurrying outside.

It was dark and cold as she went around to the side of the house where Lochlan kept the large black garbage bins. She threw out the bag of clothes, closed the lid of the bin, and burst into tears.

The cold night air made it harder to breathe. Harsh, ragged, breaths ripped through her. She turned around to lean against the red brick of the house and covered her mouth with both hands in an attempt to keep quiet. She slid to a crouch on the ground, arms over her face, muffling the sound of crying. She tried to breathe, to calm down, to think.

But she couldn't.

Her nose was cold. Her fingertips tingled in the frigid late February air. She ignored it. Huddled against the house, she tried again and again to gain her composure. All she could do was think of how helpless she was. How helpless she had always been.

She clutched at her mouth with her hands, shaking with the force of her sobs. She hadn't been able to do anything to bring Lochlan home, and now there was nothing she could do to help take his pain away.

"Zemila, baby girl," said a soft Southern drawl.

Zemila jolted and looked up.

"Oh, what's wrong?" Mrs. Abernathy stood, slightly hunched, with a pink bonnet over her gray-black curls. She wore a winter coat over her flannel pajamas and a scarf wrapped haphazardly around her neck. "Lovey, you don't even have a coat on!"

"Oh, Mrs. Abernathy," Zemila said through her tears. "Did I wake you? I am so sorry."

"You might have woken up the president, baby, let alone the neighbourhood—"

"Oh, God—"

"But I was already awake, so never you mind that." Mrs. Abernathy bent down and pulled Zemila to her feet. "Come now," she said. "Let's get you inside. You'll catch your death of cold out here. Come, I'll make you some tea."

φ

"Llowellyn will be looking for me," Zemila said when Mrs. Abernathy handed her a mug of mint tea.

"He knows you're here," she said. "Sugar?"

"No, thank you." Zemila sipped her tea. "He knows?"

"Hmm." Mrs. Abernathy left the kitchen and returned a moment later with a blanket that had large roses in the center. She draped it around Zemila's shoulders. Though it wasn't very thick, it was heavy and the weight was a comfort.

"I sent him a message when I found you. Told him you would be here for a little while before I returned you."

"Oh," Zemila whispered.

"Do you want to talk?" she said. "Or not talk."

"You were already awake?" Zemila asked.

"Well, after what happened earlier, I could hardly fall asleep until I knew you were all back," Mrs. Abernathy said.

"God, that was tonight," Zemila put down her mug and caught her head in her hands. "Seems like so long ago."

"Mmm-hmm," Mrs. Abernathy nodded and sat down beside Zemila.

"We didn't even think to tell you." Zemila said, her eyes on her mint tea.

"Oh, I dare say you had your hands full. Y'all left maybe five or six hours ago. Came back forty minutes ago, and you were out there crowing like a rooster for some fifteen minutes before I came to collect you."

"What?" Zemila looked up sharply.

"I'm kidding." Mrs. Abernathy's smile was wicked. "I just thought that might get your attention."

Zemila gave a weak laugh. "You're bad."

"It's more fun that way," she shrugged and pulled her blue housecoat tight around her. "And it was only a couple minutes. I put my coat on as soon as I heard you."

"Thank you," Zemila said. "Thank you for . . . everything?"

"Is that a question?" Mrs. Abernathy asked.

"No," Zemila gave her a tired smiled. "I don't know how to encompass all the things you've helped us with."

"That's what neighbors are for," she nodded. "The good ones, anyways. Now baby, why are you crying?"

"I, um, Mrs. Abernathy, I don't—"

"Child." Mrs. Abernathy's look was stern. "I may be old, but I ain't stupid. You think I don't know there is something special 'bout all you?"

Zemila blinked, not sure what to say.

"Think I haven't known that boy's not all he seems to be?" she went on. "No twenty-three-year-old lives the way he does, speaks the way he does. Thinks he's so slick," she chuckled. The sound was warm and full of affection. "But he's not. I see him. Maybe not everybody does, but I do."

"Ha," Zemila breathed.

"I know I can't know all that's going on. I don't want to know all that's going on. I just want to know what I need to, to help him, and help you. That's it. As it has been for going on five years now."

"He must really trust you," Zemila said. "He must really feel safe with you. Otherwise you would have never noticed a thing. Otherwise you might never have seen him at all."

"I thought as much," Mrs. Abernathy smiled. "The way he seems, I thought he mustn't even have noticed he dropped his guard. But enough about him. How are you?"

"I'm scared," Zemila said, and despite her better efforts, tears filled her eyes again. "And I'm happy he's back. And I am so, so worried about what's coming."

Zemila took a deep breath and let it out slow. Mrs. Abernathy waited for her to continue.

"We found him, Lochlan, tonight." Zemila looked to gauge her reaction.

"I saw you all bring him in," she said. "He looked in a bad way."

Zemila nodded, swallowed. "It'll take him time to recover. I'm not sure how long. I want to help, but I don't know how. I want to take off work, but, but—"

Mrs. Abernathy handed her a box of tissues. Zemila took it. "I feel so helpless!"

Zemila breathed heavily and tried to shove down the emotion thick in her throat, the self-loathing and the second guessing. It didn't work.

"I'm helpless in this, in my life. I feel like a passenger on a ride I didn't buy a ticket for and I can't get off. My life's not my own anymore." Zemila put down the tissue box before she crushed it in her hands.

"I don't know if it ever was mine. But these last few years, God—I try, I work hard, and it's never, never enough. I'm never enough. I'm always running, running, running trying to catch something, or, or to catch up to something, and I don't even know what it is! I don't even know what I'm chasing.

"I leave Baltimore for a job, then Tyler, then Tiffany's murdered, and I got engaged." Zemila stood and started pacing. She clenched her fists, pressing them against her temples. "As if getting engaged would fix something, would give me stability, make me worthy! God! Why?"

I'd never been invested in Tyler, not really. He was a warm body at the right time, she thought, disgusted with herself. And then . . . Tiffany's wide smile and blue eyes flashed in her mind.

"I miss my friend." Zemila pounded at her chest, at the spot that ached when she thought of Tiffany. She missed their movie nights and their morning coffees. The venting sessions and the gossip sessions. "I miss her and I never talk about her. I miss her and I never think about her because it–it hu—"

She stilled and laid her palm flat on her chest, fighting to hold tears, trying to regulate her breathing.

"I just repeat a pattern." Breath. "Paris." Breath. "And the break-up." Breath. "Simmons." Breath. "Then Nemo." Breath. "Then Lochlan!" Breath. "God!"

She was helpless. She was useless. Her Magic was out of control. Her job was beating her down. Her family was in danger, constant danger, and she could do nothing to help.

She couldn't even catch her breath.

Zemila flopped back down on the couch.

"God." She shook her head, clutched at her hair, at her chest.

"I want off, off this ride. I want my— friends to be safe. I want—to not— be so afraid all the time. Not be so worried all the time. So helpless, all the time. I hate, hate it. I hate it!"

"Child," Mrs. Abernathy said, placing one hand on Zemila's chest and the other on her shoulder. She took a long slow deep breath, and Zemila copied her. She did it again, and again. Zemila mimicked the action. A few moments later, Zemila could breathe on her own.

"I'm sorry," Zemila said sheepishly.

"Do not apologize," Mrs. Abernathy told her, sitting beside her on the couch.

"I don't know if that made sense, if I was making sense."

"I got the gist," Mrs. Abernathy nodded. "Can I tell you something? Something you might not fully grasp until you're an old woman like me?" Her smile was soft and warm.

"Please," Zemila said. "Tell me."

"We are all helpless in a way," Mrs. Abernathy said. "We are all worried about what's to come. We are helpless against time, and against change. We are helpless in the face of other people's choices and how those choices might affect our lives. And we can worry about that. It's only natural to worry about that.

"But . . ." Mrs. Abernathy reached over and with two fingers under Zemila's chin, forced their eyes to meet. "We are not helpless in our choices, in our minds. You, child, have a vastness you have yet to perceive. And with that vastness may come a sense of worry, a sense of helplessness. But know this, we are resilient beyond our wildest imaginings. And though we may lose our way, feel lost and alone, helpless and worried, remember, we control the ride. We have but to grab the wheel, and steer."

CHAPTER THIRTEEN
Lochlan

I woke slowly, feeling unusually warm. I kept my eyes shut and scanned my body for new injuries. I catalogued what had healed and what would be broken next. There was a softness beneath me I wasn't used to, a heavy blanket on top of me, and a new yet familiar weight around my neck.

Was I still dreaming?

No. No, I got out. They found me.

Memories came rushing back. Qillian, the Proxy, the hot black sphere in my chest. Then Llowellyn, and Lugh's stone. Zemila's fingers laced tightly into mine the whole ride home.

A warm body lay beside me. The smell of sweet earth and something else pressed into my senses. I blinked my eyes open. My brother sat in an old arm chair far too small for him. My armchair. My room. We were back in my house. My home.

"How are you feeling?" he asked me.

"Empty," I said, shifting slowly onto my side and then sitting up. I tried not to jostle Zemila who was sleeping next me. "Like I have no strength, no Magic."

Llowellyn's brows drew together.

"What time is it? What day is it?" I asked.

"You have been in and out for a while," Llowellyn said.

I remembered drinking slowly and trying to eat. Llowellyn taking me to the bathroom and Zemila shaving my face. Qillian coming to see me, Nemo hurriedly leaving when Llowellyn walked in.

"How long was I . . ." I didn't know how to finish the question.

"Almost eight months, Little Lochlan, since Heaven collapsed. It's March now. March 12, 2048."

The words hit like a physical blow. Zemila made a soft sound and I looked down at her.

"I hoped it hadn't been that long." I moved a lock of her hair behind her ear. My shoulder ached at the small movement, but I wanted to see her face without obstruction. "It felt like longer."

"It always does," Llowellyn said with the darkness of someone who knew intimately how poorly Time moved when paired with torture.

"Hmm," I said, rubbing a spot on my chest. My shoulder protested the gesture and I switched arms.

"You must be hungry," my brother said. "You've been keeping things down a bit more over the last couple days."

"I'll try something," I said, with confidence. "I can eat."

I was wrong. I could barely swallow the oatmeal Llowellyn brought me.

Good thing no one else is awake for this, Llowellyn thought to me.

Why? I asked. Even though the idea of Zemila watching me fail to eat, seeing me this weak was mortifying.

Llowellyn grinned.

Exactly, he thought, reading my emotions.

"We will try again in a couple hours. Sleep, Little Lochlan," he said aloud. "And I will sleep too, knowing you're safe."

My eyes blinked open and I looked around my bedroom. I was alone but for the fairy creatures on the poster Jenner had pinned up a couple weeks after he'd moved in.

As I had done every time I'd woken up over the last two weeks, I stretched my mind. My telepathic ability with Llowellyn had returned immediately, but everything else felt just out of reach. I could feel my brother downstairs, and a moment later, his voice drifted up to me. The muffled singing was low, and I couldn't hear the words. My eyes flicked back up to the ceiling. To the water damage I'd been ignoring.

Mayhap Llow will fix it for me. He was always the better carpenter.

A soft knock at my bedroom door interrupted my thoughts.

"Awake?" a voice whispered from the hallway.

"Yes, Mila, come in," I said. The door opened slowly and Zemila stepped into the room. "You don't have to knock. This is your room too, if you'd like it to be."

We'd never really talked about us, about what we were. I knew she'd been staying here, living here.

"I'd like that," she said and my shoulders relaxed. I wanted to wake up to her every morning and fall asleep next to her every night. I wouldn't waste time being coy.

"Can you try and eat?" she asked.

"For you," I gave her a wolfish grin. "Anytime."

"Uh-huh." Zemila smirked and walked in the room.

I straightened in the bed as much as I could. She put the bowl of what looked like broth and noodles on the side table, then leaned forward to help adjust the pillows at my back. I closed my eyes and breathed her in. Her nearness sent an electric charge through me and my body radiated with the desire to touch her.

"Thanks," I turned my face to hers. She paused, her rich brown eyes falling to my mouth. My eyes followed her tongue as it traveled across her bottom lip.

"Hi," I said, tilting my chin up and brushing the tip of my nose against hers.

"Hi," she whispered, and her smile lit her eyes.

We were only an inch apart. It was nothing to close the distance. I lightly pressed my lips to hers, tentative at first. But when I pulled back, she came with me. I raised my good hand to cup her cheek, wanting more of her. She rubbed her full lips slowly against mine before opening.

My tongue met hers and she moaned. My hand on her cheek moved to tangle in her hair. Gently, I pulled, tilting her head and—

"Ahem," Llowellyn cleared his throat and Zemila jumped up in surprise. Her speed jostled the bed and pain exploded through my hip, shoulder, and chest.

"Christ, Llowellyn," Zemila said.

"Danu," I grit out. "That hurt."

"Not the first part, though, right?" Llowellyn smirked.

"Walk into . . ." I took a deep breath. ". . . a black hole."

"Glad to see you're feeling a bit better, Little Lochlan," my brother taunted.

"Black. Hole," I repeated.

"Food," Zemila said, and I stopped glaring at my brother. "Are you actually going to try?"

"I'll try," I said.

"You said that yesterday," Llowellyn squinted at me. "I made chicken soup today."

"Mrs. Abernathy's chicken soup?" I asked.

"My inferior version of it," he said. "It doesn't have that . . . thing . . . hers has because she refuses to give me the recipe."

He muttered the last part to himself. I grinned. I had been after her sweet tea recipe for five years and there was nothing for it.

"Y'all stop comin' by if I give it to you," she'd say, though I knew she didn't believe that.

"Smells good, though," I said. "Not as good as hers but—"

"Be nice," Zemila chided, positioning herself on the edge of the bed.

I reached for the bowl and spoon but missed and nearly spilt it in Zemila's lap.

"Okay," she said. "Shoulder's still wonky. At least you can move it today."

I was annoyed and embarrassed I wasn't able to use Magic to heal myself. I was a low-level healer on the best of days, but even when Llowellyn tried, it hadn't worked. My Magic was so depleted that any spell was diverted to the bottomless pit where my connection used to be.

Zemila brought a spoon of the broth and chicken to my lips. I stared at her.

"You need to eat," she said. "Your body needs the fuel."

I frowned as I thought how to articulate my feelings.

"He's embarrassed," Llowellyn said from the doorway. "He doesn't like the idea of you feeding him. He doesn't like you seeing him weak."

Zemila whipped around to look at my brother.

"You're joking," she said. Then she turned back to me. "You're joking."

Llowellyn tapped his temple.

Can you do it? I thought to my brother. I don't want her to—

Down with the patriarchy, Little One, Llowellyn thought back, then he laughed and went down stairs.

"You can't be serious, Lochlan," Zemila said. "Come on."

Begrudgingly, I opened my mouth. "This is infantilizing," I said, annoyed.

"This is what needs to be done," she replied.

"I can use my good arm to do it," I protested.

"Fine, you don't want my help? Fine," she said, standing and balancing the bowl on my lap. "You want to be a big strong man who doesn't need anyone, great, have at it."

Well . . . no. No, I don't want that either.

Shame and guilt warred with my pride as I watched her walk toward the door.

"I'm sorry," I forced out. Zemila's hand rested on the doorframe. "I don't like feeling helpless. I am taking that out on you. I am sorry."

I reached for the spoon with my good hand and brought it to my lips. The piece of carrot splashed back into the bowl. I put the spoon down and looked up at her.

"Did that tiny drop of soup taste good?" she asked, leaning in the doorway, arms crossed.

"I couldn't keep enough on the spoon to tell," I whined.

Zemila huffed out a laugh.

"Hang on," she said. "I'll be right back."

Zemila turned and walked away. I tried again to eat without sloshing chicken on my lap, and I managed three or four spoonfuls with only one large noodle falling back into the bowl and splashing onto my glasses.

"It's a comfort thing now, huh?" Zemila said, walking into the room as I tried to clean my glasses with one hand. She put a large mug full of soup on my bedside table and sat down on the edge of the bed. "Give them here."

She cleaned my glasses on her dark auburn shirt and gave them back to me. Then, she pointed to the mug at the same time as she took the bowl off my lap.

"I should have given you a mug to begin with," she said, taking a spoonful from my bowl. "I think Llowellyn wanted to see you struggle a bit."

Zemila reached over to my bedside table and handed me the mug of chicken soup.

"That sounds like him," I looked in the mug and saw she'd cut everything up into smaller chunks. "I love you," I said, bringing the mug to my lips with my good arm. Then I paused. I'd meant "thank you" but "I love you" just came out.

No time for coy, I reminded myself. Besides, she's known I've been in love with her for years.

Zemila laughed a little and said, "You're welcome."

We ate in comfortable silence. I almost finished the full mug, before the effort of sitting up became too great. Zemila helped me lie down, pressed her lips to my temple, and I was asleep.

It went on like that for the next couple weeks. I would wake up. Sometimes alone, most times with a beautiful woman curled around me, or an enormous demigod asleep in a small armchair nearby, his feet propped up on the bed. My access to Magic seemed to come and go. Some days, I felt like I was almost able to cast, to touch my Magic, and others I would wake up as empty as if the Proxy had just used his device on me.

After what felt like years since they had found me in that forest, I could feed myself again, thank the Gods. In reality it had been about a month, but I was getting impatient.

"Shoulders are stupid," I told the empty room as I slowly sat up and reached for the water glass on my bedside table. After the repeated dislocations, the muscles must have torn completely. It hurt to extend my left arm, but I was determined.

"Almost there," I muttered as pain exploded in my shoulder. "Almost."

I gritted through my teeth. I was so close. My fingertips brushed the edge of the glass, I leaned sideways and—

I gasped as the glass fell, water sloshing up the side and out. On instinct I lunged forward, and hissed in pain at the speed of my movement.

But the glass didn't crash to the floor. It hung in mid-air, the sloshing water frozen in time. Both were surrounded by a haze of bright sand gold.

"What in the—"

"You know what they say about pride." The accented voice came from the far corner of my room.

I knew that voice. I didn't turn.

"It goeth before the fall."

"Are you here to taunt me, Inanna?" I said, eyes still on the floating glass.

She'd gotten through my protection spells. My protection spells made this house near impossible to enter if one meant me harm.

The sandy haze guided the water back to the cup, and the cup to my lips. Using my less injured right hand, I cautiously took the water glass and drank. Then I turned to see a short, curvy, frighteningly dangerous woman step out of the shadows.

"Of course not, Ethinnson," the Sumerian Goddess said, her thick eyebrows pulling together in mock concern. "Just to check in on you. To . . ." she paused, her cold dark eyes roaming over my weak form. "To see how you are doing."

"To see if I'm dead, you mean."

"If only I could be so lucky." She examined her gold-painted fingernails.

Inanna didn't lie, but she did amazing things with the truth.

She was a friend, I realized. Or, at least, she thought of me as one. Whether that thought was conscious or unconscious, I didn't know, but she meant me no harm.

"I would have known if you were dead." She smoothed her cream-colored pencil skirt and straightened the matching blazer. The golden-brown inlay on the suit perfectly matched her skin. "Qillian would have informed me. Nemo would have too."

I laughed bitterly, and it took all my strength not to show the pain it cost me to remain seated and awake. "From victim to employee. Is that a common route your workers take?"

"I came to see how badly you were hurt," she said, ignoring my jab. "And to talk."

"About what?" I asked.

"The past." Her tone was lazy and she took a step forward. "The future. The plans you have for your grandfather and my part to play in it."

"Why on earth would I believe you want to help, Inanna?" I said, wondering if she knew how much she revealed by coming here. "I am not my brothers. We've too much history to pretend."

"There is a fine line between hate and lust, Lochlan." She drew out my name on a purr and the sound dripped with intention. "Don't tempt me."

"Get over yourself." I rolled my eyes. "You entered a home—my home—that is protected against enemies."

She sucked in a long breath and let it out slowly.

"There is a God in my domain flooding the streets with drugs, Balorson, and I want him out," she said, ignoring my comment. "Get off your high horse. I know your secrets too, don't forget. I know what happened the last time he got to you. I have no interest in seeing that repeated. Not here. Not in my city."

"No." I shook my head. The small movement sent pain shooting down my arm.

"No?" she asked.

"That's not why you're here," I said, knowing there was more to her visit.

"You think I do not care that there is—"

"Oh, Inanna," I said, derision dripping from my words. "I know you care about him. I have never been a real threat to you. Not on my own." I scoffed. "That's why I hated you so much."

"How kind of you to use the past tense," she mocked.

"I can't," I stopped and took a deep breath. "I barely have the energy for this conversation. I can barely do anything on my own." I nodded to the glass in my hand. "As you've seen. So, cut the act, Inanna. What are you really doing here?"

"Well," she said, wiping her hands against each other as if brushing away my words. "Since you are being so rude. Qillian spoke of something that interests me."

"Avery?" I asked. I knew she must have sent a group to look for her. The pull of my bonded promise was weaker than it should have been. Though I had not fulfilled it, some part of it had been done.

"Nemo took care of that," she nodded. "The facility was abandoned. We are still looking but that isn't why I came to speak with you."

I scratched my chest with my good arm and winced at the movement.

"Yes," she said, tilting her head in my direction. "Of that. He told me of that."

"Of what?" I asked. Her gaze was fixed on my chest.

"Of an item implanted into your body. An item that stole your Magic."

CHAPTER FOURTEEN
Zemila

"Mr. Virtue, hello." Zemila leaned back in her office chair and tapped her Intelliglass desk.

"Ms. Alkevic, yes?" Kennedy Virtue's voice came through Zemila's earpiece. "This is about the Gala short list?"

"Among other things." Zemila nodded, even though the call was voice not video.

"Yes, of course. Well, Hale and I have run in the same circles for years, sweetheart, and I can tell you, there is no finer man anywhere."

Zemila raised her eyebrows. The gala was a month away, a replacement for Clemens had yet to be solidified, and Lochlan was still weak. He had filled out some over the last two months, but Zemila was still concerned.

"Since you brought up Mr. Clemens," Zemila said, "what are your opinions on how the loss of his rather impressive personal collection will affect the success of the gala? Many are speculating his collection is one of a kind."

"Is that so?" Virtue asked.

"I try to work off facts, Mr. Virtue," Zemila said. "And the fact, among the art historians and collectors I've spoken to, is that he has several unique personal pieces he was going to unveil at the gala."

"Which collectors said that?" he asked.

"I'm sure you're not asking me to reveal my sources, sir." She let her voice go light, flirtatious, then paused long enough for Virtue to process the information.

"It is my understanding," she went on, "that everyone on the short list of replacements have made great strides for Art Inclusion. That, Mr. Virtue," she said his name slowly, "is the real reason I am hoping to steal just a few minutes of your time." She paused again. "To talk about your outreach projects. If the board chooses your collection to be shown, I can only hope it will garner at least some of the buzz of Mr. Clemens' art . . . for the outreach programs."

Zemila waited.

"I am happy to talk about my outreach programs with you, Ms. Alkevic." Virtue's tone shifted, matching her flirtation. "Happy to," he repeated. "My organizations have worked with several schools, here in Austria and at home in the States, to try and incorporate as much art history and art appreciation as we can. I will set you up with my assistant Lucy. She'll connect you with the right people for that conversation."

"That would be excellent, thank you," Zemila said.

"Now, as for the Day Dream Ball . . ." Virtue seemed to search for his words, and Zemila held her breath. "I will be in attendance. I do think I have several pieces that could bring attention, more attention than anything in the Clemens collection." Then he muttered, "I may have to remind the board about that."

Zemila grinned, thankful she wasn't on a video call. Keeping her voice neutral, she said, "Oh really?"

"What do you know," Kennedy Virtue asked, "about the Lance of Longinus?"

φ

"The Lance of what?" Jenner said from his childhood bedroom in San Diego. Old movie posters papered the wall behind him. Llowellyn and Zemila sat in Lochlan's living room, looking up at Jenner projected on the opposite wall. "Did you just say the Lance of Vaginas?"

Llowellyn spat out the water he was drinking and Zemila rolled her eyes.

"Christ, Jenner. Long, Longinus." Zemila leaned forward and grabbed a tissue from the coffee table.

"Oh, dios mío, thank God," Jenner said. "Because me and vaginas are like firecrackers and thunder storms.

Zemila and Llowellyn exchanged a look. Llowellyn put his water down and accepted the tissue.

"Because you don't work properly in them?" Llowellyn asked, slowly trying to piece together what Jenner meant. "No, that can't be right."

"Sometimes I wonder if you're a himbo," Jenner said. "Where is the other pretty one?"

Zemila squinted at the projection. "Lochlan?"

"Eww." Jenner wrinkled his nose in disgust. "No, Nemo. I thought he was staying at the house this weekend."

"He won't be here until the weekend," Zemila said.

Ember was coming for a few days. Zemila had suggested Llowellyn and Ember stay at her bachelor apartment, and Nemo stay here.

"Nemo can call me a firecracker anytime." Jenner waggled his eyebrows.

"Please stop," Zemila raised a hand.

"I kid, I kid," Jenner said. "I know him too well now. The mystique of his over-hanging forehead is gone."

"It's—" Llowellyn blinked rapidly as if to clear away his confusion. "It's a fancy way of saying the Spear of Destiny."

"Nemo's forehead?" Jenner started. "Or Nemo's—"

"The Lance of Longinus." Llowellyn shook his head, sat forward on the couch, and put his elbows on his knees. "Virtue thinks he has the Spear of Destiny."

"Not only that," Zemila said. "He thinks he has Gungir, and Gáe Bulg."

"You're joking," Llowellyn scoffed.

"Gungir," Jenner said. Zemila could hear the thudding sound of his fingers typing. "Norse mythological spear belonging to Odin, and gay bulge, a Mexican-American magical spear belonging to me!" Jenner said proudly.

"Jenner." Zemila let her face fall into her hands.

"I am so sorry, but it was right there. I could not help myself." He started typing again.

"I'm really sure you could," she said.

"It would more likely belong to me," Llowellyn said.

"Jenner's spear?" Zemila looked up confused.

"In his dreams, maybe," Llowellyn said.

"I do dream of that." Jenner's tone was airy.

"I can't with you two, sometimes." Zemila shook her head. But it was a lie. One she knew neither of them believed.

Since Lochlan had been back, the tone in the house had changed from the verge of tears and walking on eggshells to light and easy. Lochlan was recovering, though he was still too thin, Jenner was out of his funk, and Nemo—still avoiding Llowellyn like the plague—had been more present.

Zemila hadn't figured that one out yet, but she was happy for the time he'd be spending with her over the next week.

"I mean," Llowellyn explained. "Gáe Bulg is Irish."

"And which one of Virtue's collection is the one we want?" Jenner asked.

"That's what I need you to find out," Zemila said. "I'm not sure which he thinks our spear is, but he had a collection of 'powerfully magical'—according to him—weaponry."

"What else does he think he has, Excalibur?" Llowellyn snorted.

"The Sword of Light, I think," Zemila said.

"They're kind of the same." Llowellyn looked a little annoyed.

"Oh my God, Excalibur is real?" Jenner asked.

Llowellyn smirked.

"Oh my God, did you make Excalibur?!" Jenner screeched from the spot on the wall.

"Yes and no," the demigod shrugged. "It really depends who you ask."

Jenner rolled his eyes and said, "I so don't have time for this. Me and Marianna are going for ice cream—you frighteningly gorgeous creatures have five more minutes of my time."

"Virtue still has to be chosen by the board," Zemila said. "He really took the bait on how popular the Clemens exhibit was going to be. I think he will make a personal appeal but maybe, Jen, you can give the board a little push?"

"I have something for that," Jenner said and Zemila could hear the dull *thunk thunk thunk* of his fingers typing. "I will start a few message boards about his collection, make him look more appealing. I am also working on rescheduling Mickelson's daughter's engagement party so he will drop out—Oye, hermana, quieres conocer a mis amigos?"

Marianna walked slowly into the back frame of Jenner's image. She had warm brown skin, wide set eyes, and a curious expression that changed into a broad smile.

"Marianna, this is—"

"Haaaaaaaa," she interrupted him and moved towards the camera and screen. She seemed to get as close to the image of Llowellyn and Zemila as possible.

"Hello, Marianna," Llowellyn said in a dreamy voice. Zemila felt a wave of affection ripple through the room and she turned to stare at Llowellyn. He was standing and walking towards her image on the wall.

"Mmm," Marianna said and sighed.

"Yeah," Llowellyn said.

Marianna laughed.

"Yes," he nodded, completely enamored.

Zemila looked back and forth between Marianna and Llowellyn. Marianna made a sound and Llowellyn laughed and stepped forward.

"Llowellyn, no," Zemila said. "Any further and she won't be able to see you."

"What?" He looked at Zemila, confused.

"You'll be too close to the camera," she explained.

"Oh." He looked back to the screen. "Right."

Marianna didn't care how close to the camera she was. Her eyes and forehead filled the projection as she gazed at Llowellyn.

"Que demonios está pasando ahora?" Jenner said before joining his sister in the frame. "Marianna, mamá te está hablando."

Marianna made a sound of protest but stopped when Llowellyn spoke.

"Goodbye, Marianna," he said, and she smiled at him again. Zemila heard Jenner's mother in the background, and with a last look at Llowellyn, Marianna was gone.

"I am not sure what the hell that was," Jenner said, "but you keep those dreamy eyes to yourself, lover-boy."

Zemila tried to stifle her snicker as Llowellyn blinked and looked a little sheepish.

"Marianna has very strong empathic qualities for a Human," Llowellyn said. "Many with her differences do."

"I don't care what she has. Hands off, she's mine!" Jenner spat at Llowellyn, then promptly hung up.

Zemila threw back her head and laughed.

"Stop that," Llowellyn said, smiling. "You'll wake up Lochlan."

"I'm sorry." Zemila covered her mouth, still giggling. "I've never seen Jenner like that, so . . ."

"Jealous?" Llowellyn asked. "If only he could feel how much she loves him."

Zemila's eyebrows went up. "Over a call? I didn't think your Magic worked that way."

"It usually doesn't," he said. "But sometimes, technology and Magic work beautifully together, and this city . . ."

"This city . . ." Zemila prompted.

"There's a lot of power in this city," Llowellyn said. "Inanna says there is a door here."

"A door to what?" Zemila asked.

"That is the question." He smiled and his eyes lit up in a way she recognized. Lochlan's eyes did the same thing when a topic excited him. "There are many theories as to where Magic, where life, comes from. Each one as far-fetched as the last."

"But . . ." Zemila said, knowing there was more.

"The Anima Mundi," Llowellyn said. "The world soul is the one most of us believe."

"Hang on," Zemila squinted at him. "Like, even the Gods—all the Gods—don't know why things are the way they are?"

Llowellyn laughed, "Of course we don't. Gods are—"

"If you say people too—" she cut in.

"Well," Llowellyn shrugged. "We didn't make ourselves."

"So, this door thing?" Zemila said.

"Some believe that the veins of the Anima Mundi run through every world, every dimension, every plane. In some places, the veins are deep. Some, they are shallow."

"Queen Anne thinks the veins—" Zemila thought out loud. "She thinks there is a door to the world soul in DC?"

"The door is a bit of a metaphor. Not an actual door."

"Hmm," Zemila said.

"I would imagine Inanna believes the veins of the Anima Mundi are close to the surface here."

There was a moment of silence as Zemila absorbed this new information. She thought back over her life, over her gift. It was too easy to say her abilities started to change when she came to this city. Too simple to say the proximity to the Anima Mundi was why.

"Does that affect us? Our Magic?"

"I'm not sure. I started crafting the second spear as soon as Sahrias left the mountains. Working on it here has felt the same, except I had Ember there."

"Well, you're about to have her again."

"Yes," Llowellyn's smile was shy. "Her gift will help. Does Nemo?"

"He'll come here after work on Friday. You two will have the place to yourself."

"Ember wants to see you the night she gets in," Llowellyn said.

"I'll have dinner waiting," Zemila said. "It will give me the week to figure out what I'm going to make for the two of you. And I'll have some good snuggle time with Oriole without Nemo around, before you two get there."

"She has some information from her grandfather on Elementals."

"Oh," Zemila said. "Okay."

The more Zemila thought about her gift, and how it was changing, the more she realized it wasn't her ability that was changing at all.

No, said the soft voice in her head.

No, Zemila thought. It wasn't her gift changing. It was her willingness to use it.

CHAPTER FIFTEEN
Zemila

Zemila was ready for the weekend when she left work and headed to her apartment. And she missed her dog. After putting the tulips she bought on the way home in a yellow vase, she spent fifteen minutes on the fire escape brushing Oriole. The smell of her downstairs neighbors' pink and yellow rhododendrons wafted up as the sun began to set.

She spent the next fifteen minutes vacuuming, then lint-rolling her couch and the armchair trying to get rid of all the dog hair Nemo had ignored. Then, finally, she lay on the floor in the living space of her bachelor apartment, lazily playing tug of war with her puppy.

The fluffy black Akita mix had been so excited when she'd walked in. Zemila had been too. Though Nemo neglected her apartment's upkeep, Oriole felt like she had been brushed almost every day. Regardless, Zemila made the decision to bring the dog to Lochlan's . . . assuming Oriole would go.

"You'll be good," Zemila said. "For me, won't you?"

The look Oriole gave her was as clear as any verbalized "no."

"Please, Ori!" Zemila whined and scratched her dog's belly. Oriole immediately rolled onto her back.

"You're such a suck," Zemila whispered at the same time she heard a key in the lock. "Hey, Ember," Zemila called. "How was your flight?"

Ember and Llowellyn climbed the narrow stairs to her apartment.

"Good," Ember said. Her flame-colored hair was in two neat cornrow braids. Llowellyn carried a bright yellow suitcase behind her. "Easy, how are you? How are things here?"

Zemila got up, despite Oriole's look of disappointment. She grabbed a lint brush and quickly rolled the front of her clothing before giving Ember a hug.

"Better," Zemila said. "Now that Lochlan's back."

"Yeah," Ember nodded, releasing her. "I'll come by first thing tomorrow."

"He'll like that," Zemila said.

"Umm . . ." Llowellyn stood awkwardly in the middle of the living space and kitchen area.

"Oh, sorry," Zemila said. She pointed at a curtain that made a wall hiding the bed from view. "It's all one room, so that curtain makes the bedroom, closet is that door on the left, and the bathroom is just there."

"Huge bachelor," Ember observed.

"But it would be a tiny one-bedroom," Zemila said. "The bed area is sacrificed for the kitchen."

"I approve," Ember nodded as a timer went off.

"That's the meatballs," Zemila said, moving around the white marble kitchen island and over to the stove.

"I'll just—" Ember started.

"Go for it," Zemila said as she added pasta to the boiling water and heard the bathroom door close.

Zemila grabbed her apple-pie-patterned oven mitt from its hook near the fridge and pulled the meatballs from the oven. By the time the last one was in the tomato sauce, Llowellyn was crouched in the living room.

"Hiya, puppy," he said.

"Oh, I wouldn't—oh," Zemila said, rushing around the island and peaking over her couch. "Oooo, your brother's gonna hate you."

"Why?" Llowellyn said as he scratched behind Oriole's small pointed ears.

"This dog can't stand him," Zemila said. "I try not to even say his name around her."

"Really?" Llowellyn asked.

"No," Zemila laughed, turning back to the pasta. "Not really. I don't think she knows his name."

"Lochlan," Llowellyn said, and a soft growl filled the room.

"Are you kidding me?" Zemila whipped around. Llowellyn laughed. "Well, she's going to really hate it when I force her to live with him."

"She'll appreciate that back yard," Llowellyn said. "Why has she been here?"

"I felt like Nemo needed the unconditional external validation more than I did," Zemila said, perhaps too honestly.

"Hmm." Llowellyn walked over to Zemila. "What can I do to help?"

"Pasta bowls are in that cupboard." Zemila gestured with a tilt of the head.

While Zemila finished the sauce, and put some fresh basil in a bowl, Llowellyn set the island for three. Ember came out just as Zemila was straining the spaghetti.

"It smells amazing." Ember settled on a bar stool at the white marble island. There was a black spiral-bound sketchbook near an empty fruit bowl. Ember pulled it towards her. "You draw?" she asked as she opened it.

"My brother does." Zemila dished out pasta, meatballs, and sauce into three bowls.

"He's good." Llowellyn peeked over Ember's shoulder before pouring three glasses of wine.

"Lots of the same face," Ember observed. "And a few landscapes."

"The girl is probably Camile, and the landscapes . . ." Zemila looked at the sketchbook as she brought over their dinner. "Oh, uh . . . that's—that's home."

"Home?" Llowellyn asked.

"Serbia," Zemila sniffed and straightened a little before sitting down in front of her spaghetti. "My father had a country house. We would spend the summers there. That's the view." She pointed to Nemo's sketch of rolling hills and farm houses.

She missed that house. Her father rarely visited them in the summers. It was an escape with her mother and brother. It was peaceful.

"Here," Ember said, bringing Zemila back to the present and sliding a small journal towards her.

"What's this?" she asked.

"From Pa," Ember explained. "He thought this would be the best way to communicate what he knows, short of your going to Toronto for a visit."

Llowellyn reached for the journal.

"Hands off," Ember playfully slapped his hand away. "The Elemental gets first look at the Elemental handbook."

"Ouch," Llowellyn rolled his eyes, reaching for his wine instead.

"Is that what this is?" Zemila ignored Ember's assessment of her abilities.

"That's what Pa says it is." Ember picked up a fork and large spoon and started twirling her pasta. "He also said maybe I was a little . . ."

She paused in her twirling, ". . . harsh with you up there."

"No," Zemila told her.

She knew more now. Understood more now. Even though it had only been a few months since they'd been in the mountains, Zemila could see how resistant she had been.

"You were right to be harsh in that moment," Zemila said, meeting Ember's eyes. They were brown, like hers, but somehow orange too. "I wouldn't have been able to push past the things I needed to. You and Llowellyn helped me with that."

"And the gala." Ember looked between the two of them. "I heard Kennedy was chosen."

"Yes," Llowellyn nodded. "That was announced yesterday."

"Dyson's POS maker came through." Ember took a bite of pasta.

"Ember," Zemila chastised.

"What?" she said through a mouthful of spaghetti.

"All we can do now is hope Virtue brings Lugh's spear as a part of his collection," Zemila said.

Ember swallowed and asked, "Does he know what he has?"

"I doubt it." Llowellyn shook his head. "But there is an old piece of stone inside the spear. Impressively old. I think he will bring it for that."

"I hope you're right." Zemila sipped her wine.

"And our project?" Ember asked.

"The replica spear is almost done," Llowellyn said, changing the topic. "My abilities are more controlled."

"Have you been practicing?" Ember asked.

"Honestly," Zemila sighed. "I have been working on not moving things when I don't mean to move them. It no longer seems to matter what the thing is made of, though I have most control over Earth-derived objects. Glass, marble, wood . . ."

"Hmm." Ember slid a finger along a crack in the island top before going back to her pasta.

There were a few moments of silence while everyone ate. Zemila tried to not think about the journal at her elbow.

"Maybe you're telekinetic, like your brother?" Llowellyn said.

Ember shook her head. "Telekinetics can't move fire."

"Most can't," Llowellyn corrected.

"Fire is different," Ember said. "Telekinetics can move things around the fire, which may move the fire, but they don't move the actual fire.

"She"—Ember pointed a finger at Zemila— "pulls the element. I feel her moving my element."

"I don't really use that element," he said, squeezing Ember's knee under the table. "I will defer to your expertise."

"You two are adorable," Zemila said, looking between Ember and Llowellyn. "I've missed this."

"I missed you too, babes," Ember said. "How's Lochlan?"

"Still weak, still . . ." Zemila trailed off.

"What's that look for?" Ember's molten eyes moved between Llowellyn and Zemila.

"He won't be at full strength at the gala," Llowellyn said.

"It's still a month away," Ember said.

"He doesn't need to be involved," Llowellyn said immediately.

"Do you think he sees it that way?" Ember asked.

Zemila agreed. She knew it would take a miracle to get Lochlan to stay home, regardless of his recovery.

"Pa said you might need an accelerant, but I am not sure what he meant by that if your Magic isn't helping," she nodded to Llowellyn.

An accelerant, Zemila thought, and an idea popped into her head. She knew who to call.

φ

Zemila had taken a cab to her apartment, but since she was taking Oriole, Llowellyn told her to use his car.

"We'll cab over tomorrow?" he'd said.

"You two haven't seen each other in a while," she'd said with a smirk. "I'll see you when I see you."

Oriole had been cautious upon entering Lochlan's house, but when the dog realized Nemo was in the first-floor bedroom, that's where she ran.

"Still my dog," Zemila said to her brother, when what she meant to say was, "I'm so happy you're here."

"Sure, it is," he laughed and stepped into the hallway. But what she heard was, "I'm happy too."

"How's our boy?" Zemila asked as Nemo walked towards her. "Was he able to keep anything down?"

"A bit," Nemo said. "He's sleeping, but he looked better today. Qillian came by. I think that helped."

"Okay," Zemila nodded and hugged her brother. "Good night."

"Night, sis." Nemo didn't let her go right away. Then he kissed the top of her head, and she went upstairs. "Go to sleep," he called after her. "Don't work."

Lochlan was asleep when Zemila sat down beside him. She looked at him, then hit the call button on her phone. He was thin, he looked frail, but some of his color was coming back.

Her eyes moved to the journal Ember had brought her. Could her answers be in there? Was she brave enough to look, to accept, to know what she really was?

You're scared, a voice sounding suspiciously like Ember's said in the back of her mind.

Zemila was scared of what might happen if she really leaned in. If she really let go. If she really dug deep and reached whatever she had connected with when they'd found Lochlan. But every time she tried, Greg Simmons' screams filled her ears. The image of blood being pulled from Otto's face filled her sight. She feared that Elemental Magic was boundless. That her abilities were boundless.

When her call was picked up, relief filled her.

"Hey," she said. "Lochlan's not healing. We need your help."

CHAPTER SIXTEEN
Lochlan

"Bio-locks," Jenner told us from my living room wall. He would be home in a few days, but had requested we meet in the "bat cave" for his discovery. "Virtue needs to be near the artifact to power down the security system immediately around it."

"We have to get him close to the Spear?" Zemila asked.

"We basically have to get him to pick it up and hand it to us," Jenner said. "That's how close he has to be."

"I can get him close," Zemila said with a confidence I didn't feel.

The gala was a few weeks away. Kennedy Virtue had announced his list of items for display and the Spear was on it. Everything seemed to be falling into place. Everything except my recovery. I still felt empty, and only a whisper of my Magic had returned. Was Inanna right? Was the Proxy trying to steal my Magic? Did he succeed?

"How are you going to get him that close?" Nemo asked. "He has to basically sit on the thing."

Having Nemo back in the house for the weekend while Llowellyn was with Ember was great. I knew he would disappear when Ember and

Llowellyn came over this afternoon, as he'd done all week when they were around. I decided to enjoy what I had and not ask for more.

"I can do it," Zemila repeated. "I'll get him to show me his collection and I'll get him close."

"I mean, he's not going to walk you right up to the Spear," Nemo squinted at her. "He knows how the security system works. You think he's stupid."

"I think he's a man," Zemila said. "And that he doesn't actually know what he has."

"Zemi," Nemo scoffed. "Not all men—"

"Cam called me about you yesterday," Jenner said, the tall mullet of David Bowie on a movie poster visible behind him.

"Ab—about me?" Nemo stammered.

"Are you going to be around more, or are you still scared of Llowellyn?" Jenner asked.

"No, I'm, wha—did she ask that? Are you asking? I can come around, to her. Is she here a lot?"

"He's trying to prove a point, Nemo," I said.

"What?" he looked from me to Jenner. "So, she didn't talk to you about me?"

Jenner shook his head with a devilish grin.

"But, like," Nemo stammered, "does she want to see me more?"

"Virtue will follow me," Zemila said, through a half-laugh. "And I'll get him close to the Spear."

"I thought she was seeing someone," Nemo grumbled.

"She may be, but we are moving on now, sweetie," Jenner said.

Jenner took us through the rest of the security system and what the exit strategy would be. "Assuming everything works as simply as that," he concluded. "Lochlan, you do have somewhere to keep the Spear?"

"The basement," I said. "It's protected."

"This place has a basement?" Nemo turned, brows pulled together, and looked at me.

"I installed it when I moved it," I said. "To protect the house. It was exhausting."

It had been a risk then, to use so much Magic at once, but it had been worth it. This house was nearly impossible for enemies to find, and if they did find it, they'd never be able to get in.

"You aren't zoned for a basement," Jenner said.

"Now, why would you know a thing like that?" I was both shocked and completely unsurprised.

"Do you think?" Jenner looked at me like I'd asked if he liked computers. "I wouldn't thoroughly research a place before I moved into it?"

"So, the plan is pretty straight forward," Nemo said, bringing us back on-topic. "We can talk about Lochlan's secret lair later."

"Plan A is," Jenner said.

"Is there a plan B?" Zemila asked.

"Grab the money and run?" Nemo suggested.

"Ha, ha." Zemila shoved her brother.

"If plan A doesn't work," Jenner said, "the Magic people take over."

"Hmm . . ." I had ten days to get back in shape, Magically speaking. I had no idea if that was possible.

I needed help, and I didn't know who to ask.

φ

I sat in my backyard on a lawn chair, with a blanket over my lap, and a beer in my hand. Ember leaned forward in her Muskoka chair, listening to Llowellyn show Qillian the renovations he'd made to my back shed.

"This hooks into place." Llowellyn pointed to where the side wall lifted and created a covered workspace. "What was a five-by-ten-foot area is now some fifteen-by-ten."

"You have no way of heating the space now," Qillian observed.

"I had no space before," Llowellyn said, pushing Oriole out of the way and pulling out one of the benches to create the L-shaped workstation. "Plus, I have her," he gestured at Ember.

"Fair enough." Qillian shrugged.

The dog repositioned herself under the work bench and glared at me.

"Babes." Ember settled in her chair. "You know I live in Toronto, right?"

"For now," Llowellyn smirked as she rolled her eyes. Then he muttered, "I'm also a demigod, I can heat my own space."

"And the replica is done?" Qillian asked, picking up his club soda, and sitting in the empty chair beside me.

"It's done," Llowellyn said. "I don't know how it will carbon date, and the original has a piece of stone in the center of the head I couldn't replicate, but to the naked eye—"

"They're identical," Ember said. "It's brilliant work."

"Thanks, love." Llowellyn's mouth pulled up at the corner.

"Then why are we out here freezing our butts off?" Qillian asked.

"It's summer," I tilted my head back to take in the sun.

"It's spring," Qillian corrected. "And it's cold today."

The May air was cool, but the sun on my skin was too wonderful to pass up. I nodded toward Ember. "Well, we have her."

"Here," Ember said standing and walking over to Qillian's chair. "Stand up for a second."

When he did, she pressed a hand to the seat and back cushion in turn, then took a blanket from the bin. She gestured for Qillian to sit.

"Ohh," he sighed and she threw the blanket over him. "This is amazing. Please move here?"

"Not a chance," she laughed. Then she moved to touch a few melon sized-stones on shelves and on the ground of Llowellyn's workspace. She scratched Oriole behind the ear and the dog yawned happily as heat radiated around us.

"Another reason we're out here is because I want to finish my shoe rack," Llowellyn said. "And maybe start on a dagger."

"I'll take a dagger," I said, raising my hand.

"And when will you be well enough to use it?" Qillian asked. I looked at the dog, and Qillian laughed.

"It's that bad, huh?" he asked.

"I think she's sweet," Ember said.

"She doesn't like me," I said. "She thinks I'm dangerous."

"Well, you are looking at Ori like you want to skin her," Llowellyn pointed out. "Even though you barely have the strength to stand."

"Ori?" I scoffed. "I would never actually hurt her, I'm just, just—" I didn't want to tell them I was jealous the dog liked them and not me. Or that I thought the dog was right, and I was dangerous. "Anyway, I'm getting better."

"Your recovery is very slow," Qillian said. "Maybe if I just—"

"No," I told him. "It's too risky."

"I don't know that it is," Llowellyn said, measuring out where the shelves would sit on a piece of wood. "Especially if you insist on coming to the gala."

"Aren't you Human?" Ember asked Qillian.

"Yes!" Llowellyn turned, eyes bright. "It's fascinating. I am sure there is a connection between true belief and the Anima—"

As Llowellyn, Qillian, and Ember discussed the possibility and intricacies of how faith may increase the natural ability of Human Spark, I zoned out. After going back and forth on whether or not true belief can manifest in an ability, the conversation turned back to me.

"Someone is too worried I'll deplete myself." Qillian hooked a thumb in my direction.

"Maybe," Ember said. "But it doesn't seem likely."

"He already did once," I said. I'd pulled so much from him when I called to Llowellyn after we escaped. Too much. "Or did you two leave out that part of the story?"

"I've recovered faster than you," Qillian said jutting his chin towards me with a laugh.

I rolled my eyes. "I still have a month before the gala."

"Twenty-four days—" Llowellyn corrected.

"Your concern is noted," I said, annoyed. And ignored, I added silently.

I heard that, Llowellyn said in my mind, and Oriole yipped.

"You too, huh?" I asked her. She got up and walked over to Qillian, the hair on her back slightly raised.

"I still think we should try," Qillian shrugged. "What's the worst that could happen?"

"I could eat your Spark, then kill you," I said, flatly. Oriole growled. "Oh, calm down." I waved a hand at the dog.

"I have faith you would not." Qillian's voice was so cheerful, it made it hard to keep a straight face. "Plus, Llowellyn wouldn't let you."

"He might not be able to stop me," I said, trying to relay the gravity of what Qillian was asking.

"Uh-huh," Llowellyn said casually. "Sure, I wouldn't, Little One."

"It would help," Ember said. "But I am not sure how much. Did Zemila tell you what Pa thinks is going on?"

"Dry soil." I looked down at my beer.

"Our very own wilting shrub," Llowellyn smiled. I threw the cap of my beer at him.

After their dinner last week, Zemila had filled me in on what Ember's grandfather, Thavaindor of the First Line, had theorized. I was like dry potsoil. The Magic going into my body was flowing right through. I was so dry, so limited in my connection, my body was only able to absorb small amounts of Magic at a time. After learning this, I'd given my brother's stone back to Llowellyn in fear I would somehow drain its power.

Thav didn't know how long it would take for me to recover, but it was a comfort to know I would.

"How are things with Inanna, at Heaven?" I asked, changing the subject.

"Fine," Qillian relented as he reached down to pet Oriole. "We still have no idea where Avery is."

I searched for something to say as the low hum of the bonded promise made itself known. "I'm—"

"Don't apologize, Lochlan," he said. "We wouldn't have made it out of there if we'd looked for her."

I shivered at the memory and Ember took my hand. Warmth spread through my body.

"Avery is powerful," Qillian went on. "A good kid, a rare ability."

Llowellyn looked up from where he marked a piece of wood with a pencil. "How do you know she didn't—"

"Die in the blast?" Qillian finished.

Llowellyn half nodded, half shrugged, then to my surprise, reached for a tape measure.

I remembered when he'd started to cut without measuring. It was infuriating. The number of times Lugh and I would measure to ensure we were cutting the right length, and Llowellyn would smugly wait for us to catch up.

"Tape measure is a sixteenth of an inch off," he muttered.

"Unbelievable." I grinned and shook my head.

"We lost more than a few people when Heaven fell," Qillian explained. "Too many families buried empty coffins. Add to that, Candle is still getting into the casino, into Lowtown. Queen Anne is angry, but we know Avery is alive."

"How?" Ember asked.

"She is a null," Qillian stated.

"Gods." Llowellyn looked up and Ember sucked in a breath. "I understand Inanna's interest."

Qillian was right when he said Avery had a rare ability. To nullify Magic of any kind took strength. To nullify all Magic around you with a thought was almost unheard of.

"We think they keep moving her," Qillian told us.

"How could you know . . ." I started. "You can't feel her gift, can you?"

"No," Qillian said. "But a few of our Gifter staff have been reporting . . ." he paused, searched for his words. ". . . roaming brownouts, I guess you could call it."

"Brownouts?" I asked.

"Not a full blackout or nullification of Magic, not what it's like to be near her when she's using her gift," Qillian explained and I thought of how the whisper of Magic I could feel, the drops at the bottom of a well, would come and go. "Or so I'm told. But a power dip."

"That's worrisome," Ember said, leaning forward and fixing her brown-orange gaze on Qillian.

"Yes," Qillian said. "The Queen is very concerned about the long-term implications."

"I'm sorry about your friend," I said, knowing that, while Inanna was concerned about the implications, Qillian's concern was for Avery.

"Thanks," Qillian said. "Now give me your hand."

Qillian put down his empty glass and extended his hand to me.

"You're not going to let this go, are you?" I asked him.

"Nope," he said.

"I'll be here if Lochlan goes on a rampage," Llowellyn smiled.

"Me too," Ember said, releasing my other hand—but not before sending a burst of heat into my palm.

"OW!" I scowled, blowing on the palm Ember had practically singed. Then I took Qillian's hand and tried to relax.

CHAPTER SEVENTEEN
Lochlan

"Lochlan." Zemila planted a soft kiss on the shell of my ear. I kept my eyes shut and sighed at the contact. I didn't want to get up.

Zemila's lips met my cheek and I turned to capture her mouth with mine. She let me, but pulled away after far too short a time. "Can you make it downstairs? Someone is here to see you."

"Who?" I asked. With my protection spells, only friends could find the house, let alone come inside.

Zemila raised her eyebrows and smiled. The dark circles under her eyes were lighter than they'd been a month ago, but still there. She'd been in full caretaker-mode for months with Jenner—and now me. She needed to be taken care of too. I needed to be stronger, better, so she could rest, so the worry wouldn't crease the space between her brows when she looked at me.

"He's downstairs," she said, kissing my lips again. I leaned into her. For a moment, all I wanted was to drag her down on to the bed with me. I tried to push myself up, to be closer to her, but my shoulder gave out and I cursed.

"Danu," I growled in frustration. Three weeks until the gala and I was still weak. "I hate this."

"I can see that." Zemila stepped towards the door, then paused. "Maybe change. He has a very good sense of smell."

"Do I smell?" I lifted an arm.

The last time bathing on my own had been a major accomplishment was a year after I'd been crushed in a landslide. I'd had to relearn how to walk, how to write, how to do everything. It was painfully slow and, Gods Below, I was lucky I'd been taken in by someone who understood the art of healing.

He kept me in his home, a small hut in the jungle, and he nursed me back to health. I never understood why. And I didn't know how to repay him.

"Be good," he'd said to me when I'd left some seventeen years later. I'd stayed and worked his lands once I'd healed. Built a small hut of my own near his. When villagers started to get suspicious about a mysterious white man who didn't age, I knew it was time to move on.

The feeling of independence, after weeks of not being able to shower alone, and months of not being allowed to do it at all, was intoxicating. I could have stayed in that shower all day, but as soon as I was clean, I stepped out, curious as to who was downstairs. I hadn't heard the home system announce anyone.

I wondered aloud at Zemila's words. "Good sense of smell?"

Light laughter and a soft suave voice I hadn't heard in a decade wafted down the front hallway. I smiled and picked up my pace as much as I could.

"Sahrias?" I said, stepping into the kitchen. The long body of a dark-haired, dark-skinned vampire leaned on my counter. "What are you doing here?"

"Lochlan." Sahrias pushed off the counter and closed the distance between us. He stopped several feet away. "It has been too long."

"Aye, it ha—"

"Before you say anything, Lochlan," Zemila cut me off, "I think it's really important to keep an open mind about other people's perspectives."

"What?" I squinted at her.

"I know you are probably very upset, but Si has his experiences too." Zemila faltered at my look of confusion. "I mean, you don't have a lot of energy so maybe don't yell at him."

"Why would I yell at him?" I asked.

"Lochlan," Zemila crossed her arms. "You know what I mean."

"I really don't," I said.

"I think," Sahrias cut in, "that Zemila must not have told you how Ember took my presence at the BC house."

"You met Ember?" I turned back to Si, pity in my gaze. I wish I'd known that when she was here on the weekend. "What happened?"

"She was . . ." Zemila paused, looking at me strangely. ". . . less forgiving."

"Because of your conflict with Dyson." I looked back and forth between the two of them.

"Well, yes," Zemila said, her eyes searching my face.

"That has nothing to do with me. Sahrias and I have no issues, as far as I'm aware."

"No." He shook his head. "No hard feelings, of course. But I will confess to being a little nervous you shared the same sentiments as Ember and Dyson, considering—"

"Considering you left with her," Zemila interrupted. Her words were colder than they'd needed to be. Colder than I thought she meant them. Mayhap I still had work to do there. Still had amends to make.

I looked at her bright brown eyes and saw a lingering hurt. I wasn't sure she even knew it was there, but for the first time I truly realized how loaded every lie had been between us. Every half-truth. Zemila had been twelve when her mother died and her father left. She'd been lost. Adrift. Then, some ten years later, I'd abandoned her too.

"Mila," I said softly. But she shook her head.

"Not now," she whispered. "We can have that conversation later. Si is here to help."

"I envy you two," Sahrias said. "Finding each other after all this time."

We turned to him.

"You mean since school?" Zemila asked.

"Ahh," Sahrias looked back and forth between the two of us. "Something like that, but as Zemila said, that is not why I'm here. Shall we sit?"

Zemila gestured for the three of us to sit at the square table pushed up against the kitchen wall.

"What are you doing here?" I asked as I sat. "I'm happy to see you, but it has been a long time."

"I trust everything is in place for the gala?" Sahrias said, taking the seat across from me. "I saw Virtue was selected."

"I don't know how you did that," Zemila told him, "but thank you."

"Of course." Sahrias inclined his head. "And to your other request, my dear…"

Sahrias pulled two small jars from a bag.

"Blood?" I raised my eyebrows.

"Zemila reached out to me," Sahrias said. "I thought I would be able to help. I did a little research on Magic depletion. There is limited science on it, but some. I think the device that the . . ."

"Proxy," Zemila supplied.

"The Proxy placed inside you," Sahrias nodded at my chest, "must have left a residue."

I rubbed the spot under my ribs. The memory of that rod being shoved into me, the paralyzing pain, the sucking sensation that left my body empty of Magic and of will—it started to overpower me.

"Lochlan," Zemila placed her hand on my shoulder. I blinked up at her.

"How long do you think the object was there?" Sahrias asked.

"I'm not sure. It felt like he was pulling the Magic out of me every time he used . . . or maybe that was an effect of my injuries. It's hard to tell. The thing he used . . ."

"It left that mark on your chest?" Zemila guessed.

I dropped my hand from the spot I'd unconsciously been rubbing. Then I pulled up my gray T-shirt to show Sahrias the coin-sized scabbed and scarred mark in the center of my chest.

"Indeed." Sahrias raised an eyebrow. "I believe it left some kind of infection, for lack of a better word. My blood should, or perhaps could, eradicate that infection. But it is to be taken in very small amounts," he warned, "as I am not completely sure how it will react to your own Magic."

"Right," I whispered, remembering everything leading to when Dyson and I left Erroin. "Your gift."

"Our curse," Sahrias corrected.

"I can relate to that," I said, thinking of my own curses.

"Your blood could be dangerous to him?" Zemila asked.

"Perhaps 'unpredictable' is a better word," Sahrias explained. "It carries a mixing of Magics that should not be mixed. But that also makes this—" He laid a hand on one of the small jars. "All the more powerful."

"Do you have a gift?" I asked Sahrias.

While at Erroin, Dyson began to manifest an extra ability. The gift originated from the curse in Dyson's line, in Sahrias's line.

"Alas, no," Sahrias said. "Just the pull."

I nodded.

"My blood should accelerate your healing," Si said, dark eyes flicking to the jars on my kitchen table, then between Zemila and I. "It should help a great deal."

"What are the odds I'm back to normal in three weeks?" I asked.

"Not high," Sahrias said, the corner of his mouth turning up. "But you should be stronger than you are now. I hope there will be no other side effects from the Ankhian Magic."

"Small doses," I repeated and pushed away from the table.

"What do you need?" Zemila asked. "I'll get it."

"A teaspoon please," I said. Sahrias opened the jar. Mayhap this would allow me to be strong enough to protect my people when they needed me.

"I'm sorry I can't stay." Sahrias rose. "Please don't tell Dyson I was here."

"Why?" I asked.

"I'm not going to lie to her, Si," Zemila said.

"I am not asking you to lie." He looked at Zemila.

"Then what are you asking?" She crossed her arms. "Isn't this exactly the behavior that led to your estrangement?"

Sahrias sighed, "Indeed. As Dyson always said, old habits die hard. I just— I—" He took a breath, and turned to me. "I am here for you, Lochlan."

"I know that, Si," I said. "And I know you two will also find your way to each other again. One day."

I stood. Sahrias hugged Zemila, then me. We followed him down the hall. Just as he was pulling open the front door, Zemila said, "Hey, Si?"

"Hmm?" He turned back to her.

"What did you mean, before, when you said you're glad we found each other after all this time? You didn't mean since school."

"No," he said. "Prophecy is a funny thing. There are many of them, and most never come to fruition. Most get told and forgotten, or misunderstood. You have been featured in more prophecies than you will ever know." He gestured to me. "And I think you know a few?"

"Two," I said. "One about my grandfather. One about a future war."

"It's a funny thing, prophecy," Sahrias said, stepping out into the darkness. A dark green sedan waited for him in front of the house. "Some are so small, insignificant. Some are merely a meeting of two people. I heard one once that started lifetimes ago and has a happy ending, once everything was said and done. I choose to believe it was about the two of you."

I tilted my head in thought as Sahrias left us in the doorway. He walked down the few steps and along the path to my front gate.

"It's strange," I said, stepping out onto the porch. Zemila followed me. "Fascinating, really."

"What is?" Sahrias asked, turning back to us asked.

"Well," I squinted at the vampire, considering him. "If you are thinking of the same prophecy I am . . . from the book of Ohtli." Sahrias nodded and I continued. "It is fascinating to me you think it may be us."

"Why is that?" Sahrias asked.

"Because after I met Dyson, after I learned about Rayyan . . . I thought it was about you."

His mouth parted in a look of surprise and I saw the light of a new idea spark behind his dark gaze.

"I—" He took a step toward us. Paused. Thought. Inclined his head. "I had never considered that. Well then, let us make our own fate. Prophecy rarely brings good times. Let us fight for the small victories, the quiet moments, the days not prophesized. Let us be more than fate makes us out to be. Let us live whole and free and honest lives.

"Thank you for that reminder today, my dear." Sahrias gave Zemila a small salute. "And for the idea of a better tomorrow." He nodded to me. "When you speak to Dyson, if she asks, please tell her I wish to regain her trust. That I hope one day, I will."

Then Sahrias Gillrana pulled open the gate, walked to the back door of a dark green sedan, and was gone.

CHAPTER EIGHTEEN
Lochlan

"Well, isn't it nice to see you heading out somewhere." Mrs. Abernathy leaned around her screen door. "I was worried tea on the porch was all you did."

"I still get tea on the porch, though, right?" I asked, unzipping my jacket. The air was warm enough that I wasn't sure I needed it.

"Oh, of course, deary," she smiled. "But you've been having so many visitors."

"Are you keeping tabs on me, then?" I grinned, walking over to sit on the little wall separating our porches.

"Lochlan, dear." She waved a wrinkled hand at a planter attached to her porch railing. "I have been outside enjoying my garden. Am I not supposed to notice you still look mighty skinny? Or all the comings and goings at your home? I've got to keep an eye out for my favorite neighbor."

"I might tell Jenner on you for that," Nemo called from the street. He walked around his black SUV.

"Nemo." Mrs. Abernathy smiled wide. Nemo jogged up to my porch and took my gym bag. "Jenner knows Lochlan is too skinny, dear, but you can tell him if you like."

"I can carry my own bag," I muttered.

I'd taken two teaspoons of Sahrias's blood every morning and night for the past ten days. I was feeling more myself, and strong enough to try a swim.

"Hush," Nemo said to me, then turned to my neighbor and ran a hand through his hair. "Mrs. A, Jenner will be devastated to learn he's not your favorite. I'm a little heartbroken too."

"Jenner cannot expect that, and you don't even live here anymore, and—oh, don't look at me like that, young man." Mrs. Abernathy made a shooing motion with her hand.

Nemo looked up at her through his lashes. I shook my head and couldn't help the smile.

"Mrs. A." Nemo looked down and stepped towards her. "I am sure we both know what Jenner expects."

I rolled my eyes, having seen this routine many, many times over our college years.

"Ohh," she smiled. "Stop flirting with me, you and your haircut. I could be your grandmother."

"You noticed," Nemo ran a hand through his hair. "Lochlan never notices."

"I notice," I said. "I just don't care."

The truth was, I did care. The shoulder-length, carefree waves Nemo used to sport had been replaced with a near military-short haircut. It had happened while I was away. It had happened when he started working for Inanna.

"Age is but a number, Mrs. A." Nemo clutched his heart. "I'm still waiting for you to notice me."

"I'll tell Jenner you said that," she retorted.

"Ha!" Nemo barked out a laugh.

He seemed lighter, more confident. I'd loved having him back in the house, even though it was temporary. I still didn't know what Nemo's issue with Llowellyn was, but I hoped to learn today.

"Where are you two fine gentlemen off to?" Mrs. Abernathy asked.

"Gonna see if I can get this one into the water." Nemo nodded in my direction. "It's been a while."

"Too long," I said. Water carries its own Magic, as the River Shannon continued to teach me. Hopefully it would help my recovery. "And don't let him lie to you, Mrs. Abernathy. I had to positively beg him to take me."

"I doubt you've forgotten how to swim, lovey," Mrs. Abernathy said. "You two have fun now."

"Thank you," I stood.

"Buh-bye, Mrs. A. I'll be thinking of you." Nemo wiggled his fingers at her and Mrs. Abernathy made another shooing motion before slipping back inside.

"How much does she know?" Nemo asked, eyes still on her front door.

"I'm not sure," I answered honestly, pushing off my seat. I stepped slowly down the porch stairs. The limp was gone, but I still felt unstable. "Llowellyn was with her when I called him. He collapsed—no, come on, Nemo. It is spring, the sun is out, the birds are—" I waved a hand at a nearby tree. "Chirping. Let's walk."

"Walk?" he asked, still moving towards the black SUV. "It's a thirty-minute walk."

"I am aware." I turned in the direction of the community center. "I dare say, I have made this trip more times than you."

"I dare say?" Nemo repeated, in a horrible imitation of an Irish accent.

"Nemo," I groaned. I wanted my routine, my normal life. Whatever that was anymore.

"I dare say," he said losing the accent, "that you should get your ass in this car. I highly doubt you will be able to walk all the way and have energy to spare."

I dropped my head, not wanting to admit he was right. Not wanting him to be right.

"Fine," I turned around slowly and walked to the SUV. "But I hate you, and because of this, we're going to make a small detour."

"Whatever, Gramps," he said. "Let's go."

φ

"It's . . . a tree." Nemo blinked at me a few minutes later. "It's a nice tree . . . a nice . . . big . . . tree."

"Gods, you're a jerk," I shoved him and turned my eyes back to the wide old oak, where a steely blue barn swallow had landed on a branch full of the lush green leaves. "I took Llowellyn here when he first came." I noticed Nemo stiffen at my brother's name. "I hoped he would see the same thing I do."

"Why?" Nemo said, glaring at the tree.

"It reminds me of a time long past. It feels like a connection to the Old World."

"Hmm." He was still glaring.

"So, I guess we have two hard conversations on the docket today."

"Two?" Nemo turned his dark eyes to me. "I didn't even know we had one."

"You knew we had one, Nemo," I said. "You made me promise to have one if you ever," I paused. He sighed and dropped his head. "If you ever got back into that life."

"Lochlan," he groaned, and banged his head lightly on the steering wheel. "I think the circumstances of the last few months were beyond what university prepared me for."

"You made me promise if you ever got back into any criminal activity—"

"I know, I know." He waved his hand at me, without looking. "I remember. I hoped you didn't." He sighed again and looked up. "What's the second tough conversation?"

Nemo turned the key in the ignition, checked his blind spots, and pulled onto the street.

"Oh, so we aren't having the first one now?" I asked.

"We just did," Nemo said, looking heavenward as if for patience. "What's the other conversation?"

"What is going on between you and Llowellyn?"

"Jesus, Lochlan." He turned left.

"I said they were both tough." I shrugged, glad my shoulder didn't ache anymore.

There was a long moment of silence, and under different circumstances, I might have waited for Nemo to be ready. But sometimes he needed to be coaxed. To know that no matter what, he was still important.

"You know, if we were walking, I wouldn't have the energy to talk," I said.

"You're such an asshole," he said, trying not to smile.

"You also know that no matter what choices you made, or who you have tension with, you're my brother too. You know that, don't you?"

I looked at him. His eyes were glued to the road. He blinked rapidly, then fumbled around for his sunglasses.

"That never changed," I said to him. "Even if I wasn't the friend to you I should have been. It never changed."

Nemo gave a small nod, then cleared his throat.

"I knew an Empath once," he said. "It didn't go well. He . . ."

This time I did wait. I waited while silence filled the car and Nemo searched for his words.

"Honestly, Lochlan, I am not really ready to talk about him. Hell, I haven't even told Zemila, but— but it was bad. It was really bad and it messed me up."

"Okay," I said, prompting him to continue.

"It wasn't long after you'd disappeared, Zemila was all cold and different and he just— Christ. He made me feel like I was okay again. Does that make sense?" Nemo looked at me before returning his eyes to the road. "He made me feel like I was worth something."

"That makes sense," I nodded.

"And then he— it was bad after, Lochlan. I felt like I couldn't trust myself. Anyway," he went on. "Rationally, I know Llowellyn is not that guy, that Empath. But in here—" He tapped his chest. "I can't help it.

I'm scared he'll make me feel something that isn't real. That isn't there. I can't trust him, and I don't want to be around him."

"Okay," I nodded. "Well, if you think of something he or I can do or say to make you more comfortable, let us know."

Nemo pulled into a parking spot at the community center. "I think I need time. These past months have been . . . so stressful. It was all I could do to keep my head above water."

"I'm sorry for that," I said.

"It's not your fault," he answered quickly. Nemo turned off the car, took off his sunglasses and looked at me. "Man, you were at Heaven because of me. Balor's actions, the cartel's actions, they aren't your fault."

"This was supposed to be a conversation about you." I smiled.

"Ha." Nemo's tone was sarcastic. "You think I'd miss an opportunity to turn this around when I know the 'you-need-to-get-out-of -the-life' is going to happen again."

"You do need to get out of—"

"You need to get out of this car," Nemo cut me off. "Let's swim."

The panic that overtook my body as I sank slowly into the pool was a familiar comfort. Nemo and I stood together in the shallow end and I slowly sank into the water. There was lane swim along one side of the pool, and a sleeping teenager on lifeguard duty in a chair near the deep end.

"It's pretty messed up that you like this." Nemo stared at me with a half-confused, half-disgusted expression. "Is this, like, the demigod version of cutting?"

I tilted my head to the side.

"Huh?" I said. I had started swimming after my brother died. It was my means of self-regulation. It still was.

"Jesus, Lochlan, you can't be serious."

"No, really. I have never thought about it that way before." I blinked at him. "But I suppose it is."

"I'm going to the hot tub." He shook his head at me and turned away from me. Avoiding a pair of toddlers in water wings and their parents about to start a swimming lesson, he yelled, "Don't drown!" This earned a reproachful look from the instructor.

"I haven't yet," I called back.

"Jesus Christ," Nemo muttered as he walked to the pool steps.

I smiled, took in a breath, and fully submerged myself. I stayed under the water and held my breath. I felt my heart rate increase. I came up for air and started to swim slowly. It was hard work and I stayed close to the wall.

The demigod version of cutting. Was this self-harm?

I had started swimming after Lugh died. After I had so much anger and Dark Magic coursing through my body that it was all Llowellyn could do to bring me back to myself. Then, after Llowellyn and I went our separate ways, it was swimming that kept me grounded. The blind panic and fear of dying the way Lugh had, drove everything else out of my mind.

Was that the same as pain? Did it matter? Did I care?

I paused, holding onto the wall and trying to stay out of the way. Lane swimmers passed me as I gulped in air. The pain, the measured breathing, the relief. It was all still there. I didn't care how much it hurt if it kept me sane. If it kept the people around me safe.

"I haven't seen you in a while," said a smooth baritone as I slid into the hot tub next to the pool. Nemo had left to shower. I'd told him I would follow in five.

"I've been away. Nice to see you, Tim," I said.

"Well, vacation didn't suit you. You look skinny," he said.

"How's Usman?"

"He would feed you if he saw you in this state," Tim chuckled. "But he's good. We started pottery. I like it."

Tim had been going to the community center pool as long as I had. Longer, I was sure. He would arrive right when they opened, would swim, and leave. That is, until his husband Usman told him he had to slow down. Slowing down meant stretching and art classes and complaining to me when we saw each other.

I didn't realize how much I'd missed it until this moment.

"Pottery? How long had that been going on?" I asked.

"I see you have no desire to talk about what's happened to you. I can understand that. I've lived a hard life too." I opened my mouth to speak but Tim cut me off.

"I hope," he said. "I hope you don't let it eat at your soul. The road is long, and it's harder alone."

CHAPTER NINETEEN
Zemila

Bright white lights crisscrossed in the sky, calling on wayward travelers—
the downtrodden, and high rollers alike. Illuminated wing-tipped white
letters spelled 'Heaven' over the entrance. Stone lions with the same eight-
pointed star on their chests guarded the door.

It was impressive how fast construction had happened, and it was
eerie how similar this re-built casino was to the original. Right down to
the statue of Queen Anne riding a lion and crushing the head of
Hammurabi, everything was the same.

"Business as usual," Zemila had muttered the first time she'd visited
the new location six months ago.

"It is very much Inanna's way," Llowellyn had told her then.

She looked up at him now. He stood beside her in the lobby of the
casino where they waited. His hair was half-up, and his eyes pensive.

"Ms. Alkevic, Mr. MacEthan," said a security guard walking up to
them. "If you could follow me."

They walked through the wide lobby to a large entryway draped in
soft cream-colored fabric.

"Right through here and down the stairs. Qillian will meet you at the bottom."

"Thank you." Zemila nodded and stepped through the curtain and onto an escalator.

"Welcome," said an androgynous voice, as Zemila was moved forward. "Welcome to Heaven."

She steadied her mind, as she did every time she came here. The mix of Magic and the specific scent in the air made Zemila feel comfortable and at home. Something she knew she shouldn't feel, especially here.

"We're all right," Llowellyn said, feeling her unease.

"Are you all right?" she asked. He didn't have time to answer before they were at the bottom of the escalator.

Zemila smiled. "Hey, Qill."

"Hey, you." Qillian hugged her.

"How are you?" Zemila asked when the hug lasted a little longer than expected.

"Busy." Qillian released her. "The brownouts are getting worse. No progress on . . . well." His eyes shifted, taking in the people around him. He gestured for them to follow him across the casino floor. "The Queen doesn't want any external help with this one."

They walked in silence past the slot machines and poker tables. Qillian stopped at a door and scanned his palm, then his eye. It beeped once, then clicked open. Zemila and Llowellyn followed him into a beige hallway. "I've already said too much."

"We've got you," Llowellyn said as they turned down a hallway ending in a carved oak door. "You know that, right?"

"Yes," Qillian nodded. "I know that."

Qillian pulled open the thick wooden door of Queen Anne's office and stepped back, letting them in.

The office was small, cozy, and a complete contrast to the Goddess of War. Queen Anne pushed back from her desk as they walked in. She stood and put her hands on her round hips. Her black pencil skirt and black silk blouse gave her the hour-glass figure of Marilyn Monroe.

"Shouldn't that be at the Louvre?" Zemila pointed at the painting behind Queen Anne's desk. It was all blacks, whites, fiery reds, and oranges. A horned figure stood in the foreground, on a rock, arms raised, one hand holding a spear and shield. A river of lava flowed between the man and the massive building painted in the architectural style of fascist Rome.

"It's a print," Queen Anne shrugged.

"Liar." Zemila squinted at her.

"Thank you, Qillian." Queen Anne waved her hand, long gold nails glinting in the light. "You may go."

Qillian gave a small bow and left.

"You still refuse our help with your null," Llowellyn said when the door shut.

"Do I look like I need your help?" Her tone was sharp. "You are here for my help, are you not?"

"We can help each other," Llowellyn said.

"You are not so special, Balorson." She walked around the small desk. The slight upward tilt of his chin was the only displeasure Llowellyn showed at the name. Queen Anne leaned back and placed her hands on the desk. "Perhaps you don't know me as well as you think you do."

The Goddess of Heaven and the grandson of a Demon King stared at each other. Some silent conversation Zemila didn't understand passed between them. When Llowellyn looked away, Queen Anne sagged slightly, then straightened.

"Would you be so kind," she said to Zemila, pointing to a kettle in the corner of the room. Her tone was softer than it had been a moment ago.

Zemila turned on the kettle then sat on the loveseat tucked against a wall of the small office.

"I am glad you have come to me, Llowellyn," Queen Anne said with a devious glint in her eye and all former animosity gone.

"Don't get any ideas, Inanna," Llowellyn said, smiling. "I am spoken for."

"Forgive me, Ethinnson," she sniffed, examining her perfect nails. "When did I give you the impression I was interested in monogamy?"

"Inanna," he said in a warning tone, sitting down next to Zemila.

"You used to be more fun," she pouted at him.

"And you used to be sleeping with half the Western deities," he shot back.

"We want what we can't have." She leaned forward and exhaled in a way that made it clear Queen Anne was a goddess of love.

"Queen Anne," Zemila said more harshly than she'd meant to. The queen looked sharply at her, and fear shivered down Zemila's spine. "Is this why you asked me to bring Llowellyn? One would imagine you wouldn't need a wingman."

"You are fascinating to me," the Queen whispered. "I can feel your fear, yet you hide it so well. I wonder what else you are hiding, little Luman girl . . . if that is even what you are."

"Say what you want to say." Zemila squinted at her. She hadn't read Thav's journal yet. She wasn't ready for that information.

"I suspect you have some kind of mental block," Queen Anne said to Zemila. "I believe Llowellyn can help you remove it."

"That's dangerous work, Inanna," he said. "The block is there for a reason."

"She may not even know what that reason is," Queen Anne retorted.

"She is protecting herself from something," Llowellyn said.

Zemila sat back on the couch, and thought of her last session with Dr. Janson.

"Self-protection is often a mask for self-sabotage," her therapist had said. "If you protect yourself by building walls, you can't experience anything new. You never learn. You never grow. Safety, self-protection— it can be a powerful illusion. But it is just that: an illusion."

"Yes," Zemila said, cutting off the back and forth. She might not be able to open that journal yet, but this—this she could do.

"Zemila," Llowellyn cautioned.

"No, she's right." Zemila nodded to Queen Anne. The gala was in six days. Lochlan was stronger, but not strong enough. "I need to try."

Queen Anne smiled.

"If you're sure," Llowellyn said, shifting in a chair beside her.

Zemila gave a stiff nod.

"Okay. Once we're linked," Llowellyn leaned his big body forward in his seat, placing his elbows on his knees, "I will be able to feel where your resistance is.

"You have some kind of emotional block," Queen Anne explained. "You will think through the same meditative pattern we have been working on in our other sessions. But instead of verbally guiding you, I will use Llowellyn as a booster of sorts and, ahh—" The Queen smiled. "Look around."

Zemila didn't like the sound of that, but it was what she had asked for. She knew there was something holding her back and she couldn't figure it out on her own.

"Okay," she said. "Let's do it."

Zemila tried to keep her mind blank as Queen Anne and Llowellyn poked and prodded her. The mental energy was intense and she felt a trickle of sweat run down her forehead.

Moments from her childhood flashed in her mind. Her mother falling to the floor, her brother banging on a locked door, her father looming large in front of her. And with each flash of memory, a force, a presence, a resistance was there.

"No," the strange yet familiar voice had said all those years ago when her father yelled and her mother cried.

"Interesting," Queen Anne muttered.

"I felt that too," Llowellyn said.

"No," the voice said, and Zemila remembered something. Something that seemed like another life.

"Most interesting," Queen Anne said. "Zemila, think of that, whatever just happened, whatever pushed back, think of that."

An hour later, Zemila was exhausted and drenched in sweat.

."Otto," Queen Anne said, after hitting a button on the phone on her desk.

Old school, Zemila thought. I guess that fits.

"Please bring Zemila a change of clothing and escort her to a private shower," the Queen said.

Zemila stood from the cross-legged position she had been in for the last forty-five minutes. "That was—that was intense."

"Are you all right?" Llowellyn helped her to her feet.

"I'm fine," Zemila said. "Just tired. Demoralized, but fine."

"Don't be," the Queen shook a finger at her. "Your resistance is a show of your strength, and we made progress today. Very interesting progress."

Zemila wasn't sure what that meant.

There was a soft knock and the door of the office opened. Otto was there with a towel and a small bag.

"Ms. Alkevic?" he nodded to Zemila.

"Go," Queen Anne commanded. "I have things to discuss with this one." She nodded to Llowellyn.

Zemila flicked her eyes to Llowellyn who raised a brow at her. She took that as a dismissal and left. When she was in the hallway, and the office door was shut behind her, she sagged against the wall.

"You shaved your head," Zemila observed.

"Thanks for noticing." Otto ran his hand over his smooth olive skin.

"How could I not?" Zemila asked from against the wall. Otto used to have a short buzz cut. Zemila didn't know which was scarier. But the broad shoulders, dark eyes, and shaved head definitely suited the man.

Otto smiled wide and it changed his face. Made him softer, younger maybe.

Yep, Zemila thought. The shaved head is working for him.

"She must have really done a number on you today, huh?"

"If you tell her that I—"

"I'm a vault, Ms. Alkevic."

"Zemila," she corrected, pushing off the wall.

"Zemila." He nodded. "I know the Queen can be a lot. She uses weakness to her advantage. It's pretty incredible how you keep it together when you're in front of her. We talk about it sometimes."

"Oh, yeah?" Zemila asked as they turned a corner and headed down a hallway towards a door marked EXIT.

"Yeah," Otto said at the same time as Nemo pulled open the exterior door.

"You're done," her brother said. "Finally, I have to get back to work soon."

Tired though she was, Zemila ran the last few steps and flung herself into her brother's arms.

"God, you need a shower, Zemi," Nemo said, not letting her go.

"Shut up." She smiled and pushed him away.

"Are you okay?" he asked.

"It was. . ."

"A lot?" Otto filled in, then handed Nemo the bag of clothing and the towel.

Zemila only had energy to nod.

"Thanks," Nemo said, taking the bag.

"No problem, Kev," Otto said, then he tossed a small box into the air in Zemila's direction. "Since I know he won't give you any."

Nemo tried to catch it in the air, tried to pull with his telekinesis, but Zemila was motivated. She pulled the white and blue box towards her with her gift, ignoring how little effort it took and how that scared her.

"You have about twenty minutes," Otto said, turning away.

Zemila flipped the box over in her hand. "Thank you," she called after Otto, blowing him a kiss.

"You really should quit," Nemo said, holding open the door for Zemila. The night air was warm as she walked onto a loading dock and pulled out a cigarette.

"I did quit," she said. Peering into the box, she saw there was a lighter in there too.

God, I love Otto, she thought.

"I thought you had," Nemo said. "I didn't see you smoke at all the week I was at the house."

"It's circumstantial," she said, lighting up. "I'll quit again."

That first drag was everything she needed in that moment. She kept her eyes closed as she exhaled, then breathed in deeply through her nose. After one more deep drag, she scratched the cigarette out on the wall beside the door before sliding it back into the box.

"Happy?" She raised her eyebrows at her brother. She put the box in the bag with her fresh clothing, then sat down on the end of the loading dock. Nemo followed her. "Things felt easy when you were at the house, better. It was like a week in someone else's life, you know?"

"Yeah," Nemo scratched the back of his head before sitting down next to her. "Yeah, it was nice. The apartment feels weird without Oriole."

"You can see her anytime you want to come by." Zemila bumped her shoulder into his.

"How are you?" he said, ignoring the comment's implications. "How was that? It looked— you look—"

"Thanks," she said with a wry smile. "It was . . . tough. It was tough, but good, I think."

"Tell me about it?" Nemo asked.

"You remember how it felt, when Dad was angry?" Zemila tried to explain. "How there was, like, this pressure that settled in the room? How

Mom would shrink down and you would shrink down and he would look at me and say—"

"My strong girl," Nemo finished. "Unbreakable."

"Yeah," Zemila sighed, wishing she hadn't put the cigarette out. Wishing she could take the pained look out of Nemo's eyes. "It felt like that. It felt like how I had to push back and be happy at the same time all the time. But more."

Nemo nodded. "What were they doing?"

"I'm not sure," Zemila said. "Queen Anne says there is a barrier in my mind. A wall I have to take down. The queen explained some stuff to me about mental blocks, and power control, then she had me sit on the ground while she and Llowellyn just . . . just . . ." Zemila looked up at Nemo, and his dark eyes were hard, detached. "It felt like they were hammering at something inside my brain."

Nemo blinked and the hard look was gone.

"Maybe a wall Dad forced you to put up?" Nemo asked.

Zemila looked at him, confused. "How could—"

"Like some defense mechanism you created?" he said quickly.

"Maybe," she nodded. Their father was Human.

Is Human, Zemila corrected herself. The bastard is still out there somewhere. She knew they weren't lucky enough for him to be dead.

"Maybe," she said again.

Nemo showed Zemila to the private change rooms and all too soon she was back in the tiny office with Llowellyn and Queen Anne.

"The gala," Queen Anne said.

"The gala," Llowellyn repeated.

"I would like Nemo to go with your group," she said. "He will be in communication with my team."

"But—" Zemila started, but the Queen held up a hand.

"They are already hired by the catering and security company." Queen Anne reached under the table then produced a small duffle. "This is for you, Ethinnson. You have also been hired. You're welcome."

"You're so helpful," Llowellyn said, inspecting the contents of the bag. Zemila saw a security pass and a server's uniform. "Why?"

"I have been given a warning from a friend," Queen Anne said. "I do not think we need worry yet, but . . ."

"That doesn't answer my question," Llowellyn said.

"Do you not want my help?" she challenged. Llowellyn inclined his head. "The Shield is active again."

"The Shield," Zemila said. The name stirred something in her memory. Something about Dyson. "Luman Law Keepers."

"In the most draconian sense." Llowellyn's eyes were dark.

"They have been dormant, of late," Queen Anne explained. "Watching, mostly. The last time they stepped into something was the late twenties, maybe. The nineteen-twenties," she said, for Zemila's benefit. "Perhaps the thirties. Torturing some poor soul to see what would happen if they did."

"What?" Zemila asked. "They just . . . tortured someone for the fun of it?"

"Power is revealed in desperation." Queen Anne tilted her head, observing Zemila as she spoke.

Zemila fought the urge to lean back, to get away from her.

"They wanted to see what he would do."

"And what did he do?" Zemila asked.

"Died, mostly. Anyways, that was over a hundred years ago. They are active again, and I don't understand why. Might be a repeat with the Red Katari, but I need to know what you know here."

"Nothing," Llowellyn said.

"Who is the Red Katari?" Zemila asked.

"Never you mind," Queen Anne said, her tone changing to all business. "We need to be aware. The Robin only said—"

"The Robin?" Llowellyn leaned forward. "She was here? In this city?"

"You have met her?" Queen Anne smiled. "Should I be jealous?"

"I've never met her," Llowellyn said, his eyes shifting to Zemila and back. "But I have crossed paths with Will Scarlet . . . her presence, his, and the Shield—this is valuable information, Inanna. Thank you."

"All the stories are real," Zemila muttered.

"Just remember, Balorson," she said. Her tone harsh, all flirtation gone. "The dark corners of the world harbor creatures far worse than your grandfather."

CHAPTER TWENTY
Lochlan

"Are you sure?" Zemila said. I saw her out of the corner of my eye. "It's only been a few weeks since Sahrias—"

"I can do it," I interrupted.

I'd been taking small doses of Sahrias's blood more frequently for over the last week. I was finally able to perform small spells again. Llowellyn was also helping me heal. Was I at full strength? No. Was I strong enough to do what was needed? I thought so. Or at least that was what I told myself.

"What I can't seem to manage is this bow tie." I was standing in front of the bathroom mirror, failing with the tie for the third time.

"I can do it," she said.

"No, no," I told her, dropping my hands, and taking a breath. "It's nerves."

Was it this hard to tie last year? I thought back. Maybe Camile tied it for me then.

I was wearing the same suit I had worn to the Gala last year. Thinking back to how nervous I'd been then was surprisingly helpful.

Zemila and I had just reconnected, she was still with her ex, and I didn't know why I was getting strange visions. I didn't know Balor was still out there.

Now I knew it was him giving me those images, those thoughts, and now Zemila was going with me. I half-glanced at Zemila. "Whoa, you look amazing."

"You like?" She smiled, turning on the spot.

Wrapped in bold deep strokes of crimson, Zemila was a vision. Thin straps extended across her honeyed shoulder. The soft lines of the dress's neckline looked like she was wrapped in the petals of a rose. Her red lips perfectly matched the fabric hugging her curves, and she was almost my height in her heels.

I took in a deep breath and looked from her perfectly pinned-up hair to her bright brown eyes.

"You're fantastic," I said. "I need to take you out on a real date. I—"

"That sounds like a tomorrow thing," she said. "Tonight, we have a job to do."

"Yeah," I said, doubt creeping back into my thoughts. "It's a good plan, right? For tonight. Simple, but good. It will work."

"It will work," she echoed.

φ

Zemila and I took a cab downtown. Llowellyn had been at the venue for a few hours and Nemo was meeting us there. Camile would be in attendance with her office, and though she was a little nervous about it, Nemo was thrilled.

We passed the big bronze spider outside the white stone Parthenon of the National Art Gallery and a couple Smithsonian museums I always planned to visit but never did. When we stopped in front of the Museum of Nature, a Romanesque, medieval-style castle, Zemila pressed her thumb to the pay pad. I got out and walked around the cab to open her door and offer my hand. She took it with a wry smile and muttered, "How chivalrous of you."

The knot of tension in my chest eased and I couldn't help my grin. Though I enjoyed doing things for her, I had done this to get under her skin, and she knew it.

"I'll get the door too." I nodded toward the small flight of stairs that led to the Tudor and Gothic style museum doors.

"There is someone standing there to check our tickets and open the door," she said. "You gonna steal his job?"

"Madre de dios, you know we can all hear you, right?" Jenner said in my ear.

"Seriously," Llowellyn muttered.

"I think it's sweet," Cam said.

"Of course, you do," Nemo said, not quietly enough.

"What?" Cam asked sharply.

I fought to hide my laugh. Zemila lightly elbowed me in the ribs before taking my arm and leading me up the stairs.

Being with Zemila was so easy, I'd forgotten we had an audience. Jenner had put us on with Llowellyn and Nemo before we left. Cam must have been added to the call at some point as well.

"Sorry," I muttered.

"No, you're not," Cam said, and I could hear her grin.

"No." I looked at Zemila and knew I would never be sorry for something that made her smile. "I'm not."

"Please stop," Jenner said. "We have work to do and Llowellyn is literally hiding inside a toilet."

"I am not hiding inside a toilet, I'm behind a bar," Llowellyn growled and we heard the pop of a champagne bottle. "Jenner, we can't all be in each other's ear all night."

"I have been saying this for the last week," Nemo said.

"And now I'm agreeing with—" Llowellyn started but was cut off.

"Jenner?" Zemila asked.

"I separated them," Jenner said. "And you two. I can hear you, so please no sexy time behind the dino bones."

"Jenner," I chided.

"But no one else is on this line," he finished. "I am going to mute myself until we all need to be in communication. Behave."

There was a soft click, and I looked to Zemila.

"Show time?" she asked.

"Show time," I said.

The museum was a castle-style building with a glass tower shooting up from the center. Getting in is always the easy part, I reminded myself as we approached the doors.

I pulled two tickets out of my jacket's inner pocket. Paper tickets. The nods to a by-gone era were works of art themselves. They were hand-written in beautiful calligraphy with a gold border.

Zemila certainly made an impression on the security guard at the doors. The sweetheart neckline and her dark soft waves made her look like the heroine on a romance novel cover. I could hardly blame him. All the same, once our tickets had been taken, I not-so-subtly looped an arm around her waist and led her into the main hall.

The cathedral-style ceilings made the museum feel bigger than it was. Paintings and statues lined the walls, and well-dressed people milled around, champagne flutes in hand.

"We can get a drink, then explore?" she suggested.

I nodded stiffly, suddenly feeling tense.

"Everything all right?" she asked.

A server with a plate of hors d'oeuvres walked past us and I took one for something to do.

"I don't know. I feel off." I popped the small cracker into my mouth. It was good.

"Maybe you shouldn't have—"

"Not like that," I cut her off. "Not strength or power, just . . . off."

"Patching in Llowellyn," I heard in my ear.

"He and I don't need that," I reminded Jenner after swallowing. Then to Zemila I muttered, "Try one of those things. Fresh basil and some kind of cheese."

"Did you ever think the rest of us might like to hear what you're feeling, Magic Man?" Jenner said with the snark turned up to eleven.

"Oh," I said, keeping my eyes on Zemila, even when talking to Jenner. "Right."

Zemila smiled at me and the knot of tension building in my chest eased a little.

"I am near the bar past the Ice Age exhibit, third floor," Llowellyn said. "Come get your drink here. I can meet you."

"Coat check." Zemila pointed over my shoulder.

"The line isn't too long, Llow," I said. "Be up there soon."

Zemila and I walked to join the coat check line.

"Oh my god," Zemila said when she found the same cracker I had.

"Right?" I said, taking another one.

"Good turnout this year," said a woman, stepping in line behind us. We turned and Zemila let out a little squeal.

"Diana!" Zemila hugged the woman. "I'm happy you could come."

"I'm surprised Ms. Jace gave me a ticket," Diana said, smoothing down her sleek bun.

"Diana, this is my boyfriend, Lochlan."

Boyfriend. I don't think I'd ever been a boyfriend before. I liked it.

"Hello, Diana." I extended my hand. "A pleasure. Zemila has told me she is nothing without you."

"I hardly think that's true," Diana said modestly.

"It really is, Di," Zemila nodded.

"The way she tells it," I looked at Zemila, "you are the one who first got her onto some of the Justal stuff? Helped her with a couple articles about his outreach programs. I read them and it's important. People might not know about it otherwise."

Diana's eyes opened a little wider and her warm dark gaze shifted between me and Zemila.

"I know, right." Zemila gave Diana a grin I didn't understand. "He's the best."

"Allow me?" I asked for both of their coats. They clearly wanted to talk about me and I was only too happy to not be present when they did.

"Thank you." Diana handed me her thin pale pink jacket, and the two women moved to the side.

I smiled as I watched them, heads together and smiling. It was encouraging to see Zemila had support at work.

"Stop staring," Jenner said in my ear. "You look like an idiot and the line is moving."

"Oh," I said quietly and I took a step forward. "Right."

It took a few minutes for me to get to the front. I surveyed the crowd around me, unsure of what I was looking for.

"Separate hangers please," I said to the coat-check man, still thinking about Zemila.

"No problem," he answered. He turned away with the coats. A moment later he returned.

"This one is for the pink coat." He handed me a ticket for Diana. I reached for it. "And this one is for the girl whose name you called out in your sleep."

My hand froze on the tickets. The man hadn't let go. A chill crept up my spine.

"What did you say to me?" I looked up at him for the first time, meeting his bright blue eyes. Eyes I saw in my nightmares.

"Don't tell me you've already forgotten me, Lochlan." He pulled the tickets towards him and I stepped forward without meaning to. My muscles tensed, to fight or run, I didn't know.

"Marco," I whispered and light flared behind his empty eyes. Sparks of Magic flew between my fingers. I made a fist to contain them. The pain of the Magic burning my palm grounded me.

He smiled. It sent a chill down my spine.

"Are we here for the same thing?" Marco asked softly. "I can only imagine we are . . . a race, then. This should be fun." Then he released the tickets and at full volume said. "Enjoy the night, sir. Next."

I stumbled back a few steps. My hands were hot and I fought hold onto my Magic. My body seemed to vibrate with the desire to attack. Or flee.

"Lochlan," I heard in my ear. "Lochlan."

"Jen?" I asked. A woman in line for coat check turned as if I was speaking to her. "No, sorry," I waved her off and tried to act normal, to find my balance, to not get sucked back in to the cut flesh and dislocated fingers of my memories.

"I see you, and I see him." Jenner said at the same time as a gentle wave of calm washed over me. "There is an alcove down the hall. Turn right, yes, a few steps more, yes. Wait there. Zemila is coming."

I looked down at my hand and saw blue-black sparks zing between my fingers and across my palm. I shoved my hands in my pockets, and hurried for the alcove.

Lochlan, Llowellyn said in my mind. I'm right here. We all are. You are not alone.

I pulled in my small Magic reserves and pressed my hand against the cool marble of a stone pillar.

Llow, I thought to my brother. They're after the spear. They're planning, he's . . . they're, I don't know what I—

Another wave of calm settled my frantic thoughts.

Gods Below, I have to get my head on straight. A taunting comment shouldn't be enough to affect me like that.

"Lochlan," I heard Zemila say.

"Here," I told her. "The ticket for your friend's coat." I held it out as if it was important. "Jenner? Are we all right? Can you see everyone?"

"I'll get it to her in a bit. Are you okay?" she asked. "What happened?"

Llowellyn, I sent to my brother.

I'm okay, he sent back. But—

"I can see Cam and Nemo," Jenner said, "not Llowellyn."

"He's okay," I breathed.

"What happened?" Zemila asked again.

Lochlan, Llowellyn said in my mind.

"Jenner, can you?" I asked before turning my attention to my brother.

"Sí," he said, and started to fill Zemila in on the short conversation.

The Proxy is here, Llowellyn told me. I think I saw him.

Did you tell Jenner? I asked.

I was trying to find him, to confirm. I lost him.

"Jenner," I said aloud.

"Hold," Jenner told me. "Yes, yes, looking now."

Llowellyn must be talking to him on their channel. I turned to Zemila.

"He's here?" she asked.

"That's what Llowellyn said."

"That doesn't change anything, right?" she asked. "Except maybe Llowellyn's Plan B."

"Llowellyn has to get to the Spear first," I said.

"He's already on it," Jenner said. "The Proxy is on the guest list as Lewis Ethan. How did he get on the guest list?"

"Lewis Ethan," Llowellyn scoffed. "I hate this guy."

"He's a donor," Jenner said.

Why didn't we do that? Llowellyn thought.

Why would we draw that kind of attention to ourselves? I answered.

Like you've never created a fake identity, he responded. The banter was somehow soothing.

"Looks like he's here with a team," Jenner said. "Here for the same reason we are."

"We just have to get there first," Zemila said.

"Right," I nodded.

"Great." Zemila rolled her eyes. "He might as well be sitting at our table then."

"Sorry, you two," Jenner said. "No more playtime. We have to move everything up."

I took a deep breath.

"Okay," I nodded to Zemila. She stepped forward and pressed her lips to mine.

"Virtue is with a few people on Three." Jenner told us. "He just finished giving them a tour of his collection."

"Let's hope he's willing to give another one." Zemila reached for me.

"On my way," Llowellyn said.

I took Zemila's hand and smiled.

"Let's fight."

CHAPTER TWENTY-ONE
Zemila

"I thought you said you wanted to stop this," Lochlan hissed after Zemila as she stalked away. She whipped around and glared at him.

" 'This'?" Zemila put air-quotes around the word as best she could, holding the gin and tonic in her hand, "meaning what?"

"This." Lochlan gestured back and forth between the two of them. "Stupid argument."

"Stupid!" Zemila started to turn away from Lochlan.

"Zemila, wait." Lochlan grabbed her arm.

Once she was sure their audience was paying attention, Zemila threw the remaining contents of the glass in Lochlan's face. Turning on her heel, she walked through an archway and let out a half sob, half sigh.

"Excuse me, boys," she heard Kennedy Virtue say as she passed a small group of men.

She kept her eyes forward, walking at a brisk pace away from everyone milling around before the dinner and bidding on the silent auction.

"Ms. Alkevic?"

Zemila didn't turn at the sound of her name. She kept walking until she rounded a corner, in the direction of Kennedy Virtue's exhibit.

Placing one hand on her hip, and the other on the wall, she dropped her head and waited.

"Ms. Alkevic?" Kennedy Virtue came into view.

"Oh," Zemila looked up sharply, pretending to be surprised. "Oh, oh god, what a horrible first way to meet." She wiped under her eyes and stepped forward. "Hello, Mr. Virtue."

"Kennedy, please." His smile was kind. "We'll say the video call was our first meeting. I saw you and your—well, I saw, and then you left."

"Oh god, how embarrassing." Zemila covered her pouting lips with a hand. "I'm so sorry you—"

"No, no," Virtue said. "Don't apologize. I'm sure it was a deserved drink in the face."

Zemila gave a half laugh, half sob. Kennedy Virtue was taller than she'd expected. She looked slightly up at him through her lashes and allowed her expression to soften.

"I need a minute," she said. "I'll go back . . . in a minute. Maybe he'll . . . Maybe we'll—" She sighed and let her shoulders slump forwards a bit. "I don't know."

"Would you like to take a walk with me?" he asked. "I'd love to show you my collection."

"Oh no." She waved a hand through the air. "You were talking with—I wouldn't want to intrude. So embarrassing."

"Not at all, Ms. Alkevic," Virtue offered his arm to her, his slight drawl adding to his charm. "It would be my pleasure to take your mind off things, and it will give me a chance to show off a bit."

"Well." Zemila stepped forward, taking his arm. "Mr. Vir—Kennedy. I would enjoy that. Lead on."

The plan had been to put on this little show after dinner, but with the added pressure of the Proxy, they couldn't risk waiting. Zemila made sure she'd drunk most of her gin and tonic before tossing what was left in Lochlan's face. She'd also tried to do it out of view of most of the crowd. No need to make a real scene when you had an audience of one.

Hoping that Lochlan was dried off, she put on a doe-eyed expression as Kennedy Virtue walked her around his artifacts.

"And this," he said, stepping up to a long spear, "is the Spear of Destiny."

It looked to be made of wood and iron. Zemila reached with her gift, careful to not move the Spear, and felt the iron pulse. A band of dull gold wrapped around the space where the hilt met the blade.

Not old enough. Not the true Spear of Destiny.

The thought surprised her. How did she know that? She pushed that out of her mind and played along.

"No way," Zemila said, releasing his arm and moving forward. "Not the real one. I mean, how could you prove that it's the real one?"

She turned from the false Spear of Destiny to the man, waiting expectantly.

"Am I on or off the record?" He grinned at her. She took a few steps back. He shortened the distance between them.

"Which will get me the real answer?" Zemila's smile was coy.

"I think you know," Virtue drawled.

"Off," she sighed. "This isn't my story anymore. It was given to a colleague."

He leaned in conspiratorially. "This spear was quietly denounced by the Catholic Church."

"Quietly?" she asked, as she started circling the room, observing the other objects.

"Yes," Virtue said. Zemila could feel his eyes on her. "The last time they loudly denounced an artifact they said they had, everyone knew they were lying."

"And how about this one?" Zemila pointed at a sword in a case next to a suit of armor. She looked over her shoulder at Virtue and saw the wall move. Like a ripple in the water, the wall curved and moved as Llowellyn came towards them under a spell of camouflage.

"And this." She moved her eyes from the suit of armour to a helmet. "And this." She pointed to another spear, a broken, unassuming spear. A spear whose real power Kennedy Virtue didn't know.

"The jousting armor is of Germanic origins. I acquired it recently. The frog's-mouth helm design always interested me. But this . . ." He stepped away from the broken spear towards another sword. "This is a sword you know."

"I don't know many swords," Zemila said sweetly.

"You've heard of this one," he said, dramatically. Zemila raised an eyebrow.

"Excalibur."

There was a snort from across the room and Virtue whipped his head toward the empty archway.

"Did you hear something?" he asked Zemila.

"Hmm?" Zemila kept her eyes fixed on the small plaque in front of the sword. She could've happily punched Llowellyn in the face for nearly exposing himself.

She felt the press of guilt on her mind. An emotion she knew wasn't hers. Llowellyn's silent apology.

"Surely, if this were Excalibur, you would have that information on display somewhere," she said, drawing Virtue's attention back to her by threading an arm through his.

"The right people know," he said, moving his arm to her waist.

"Oh?" Her eyebrow raised and she used her moment of surprise to step away from him. "Like a secret society," she whispered, then laughed. Zemila moved closer to the broken spear, Lugh's spear. Virtue followed.

"Something like that," Virtue said, and Zemila turned slightly, then put a hand on his shoulder.

"Thank you," she said, taking another small step backward. He moved with her. He was close, close enough to the Spear that his biometrics key code allowed Jenner to hack into the case's security system.

"Almost Zemila," Jenner said in her ear. "Almost."

"For what?" Kennedy asked.

"For . . ." Zemila leaned into him, then shook her head and took yet another step back. Virtue stepped forward.

"For being kind to me. For," she nodded back to the doorway, "helping me take my mind off things."

Virtue moved closer, like he was going to kiss her. She reached out and held onto his jacket. She stepped back again, and pulled him towards her. The glass enclosure was cool on her back. Virtue leaned in.

"Perfect," Jenner said in her ear, and the power went out.

For a heartbeat, everything, even the exit signs went dark. Then the lights came back on.

"What was that?" Zemila said. Both she and Virtue were looking at the fully operational lights.

"I don't know." Virtue none too gently moved Zemila to the middle of the room.

Zemila looked at the Spear. It was in its case, and the ripple she knew to be Llowellyn, moved along the wall.

Virtue tapped his watch and spoke into it as he surveyed his collection. Muttering too quietly for Zemila to hear, he circled the room before returning to her side.

"Are we good?" she asked Jenner aloud.

"Of course we are, my dear," Virtue said, placing a hand on her lower back, still looking distracted. "Let's head back, shall we? I think folks are getting ready for dinner."

"Sí, sí," Jenner answered her. "Listen up, Ninja Turtles. Good job, Zemila. Virtue knows that was an attempt on something. He sent a message to his people. Llowellyn is going back in his hidey hole until Virtue exits the building."

Zemila let out a breath as Virtue offered his arm. He led her back to the dining room. The second they entered, she felt Lochlan's gaze on her. It was easy to find his sharp green eyes across the room. He waited for her to leave Virtue, then pushed off of the bar, and walked toward her.

Her gaze dropped to his lips, which turned up in a smile.

"The replica is in place," he said. "We've got it."

CHAPTER TWENTY-TWO
Lochlan

"It wasn't as hard as I thought it would be," Zemila said as she pulled me behind one of the large pillars around the edges of the dining hall.

"We're not out yet." I brought the back of her hand to my lips.

"Llowellyn?" she asked.

"In my hidey hole," he said through our comms.

"Can you stay camouflaged all night?" Zemila asked.

"I'll go back behind the bar. The spear is small enough to keep under my clothes without notice. Come visit," Llowellyn said. "I make a mean martini. Jenner, split us up until it's needed."

"Aye, Aye, Capitano," Jenner said. "Hopefully it won't be needed."

There was a clicking sound and I knew Llowellyn was gone.

"You two have made up, then?" A familiar voice spoke from behind us.

I turned.

"Rosamund will be so disappointed."

"Adrienne," I extended my hand. She shook it, then pulled me close to plant a kiss on my cheek.

"Here I thought I would be playing therapist."

"Not at all, Ms. Jace," Zemila said.

"Come." Adrienne stood between me and Zemila, linked her arms through ours to lead us towards our table. "Let's eat."

We sat at a round table with beautiful mosaic-patterned plates. Vibrant yellows and blues stood out against the cream-colored tablecloths. Zemila and Adrienne's daughter, Rosamund, whispered and giggled non-stop. Halfway through dinner, Zemila stood.

"We're going to the bathroom," Zemila said. She pushed Rosamund's wheelchair and said something in her ear. Rosamund shrieked with laughter, turning several heads when she did. I looked over to Adrienne's husband Ben, who shrugged as if to say, "But we love them, don't we?"

When the speeches and recognitions were over, the lights dimmed and the music started.

"May I?" Ben offered Adrienne his hand.

"Of course, my love," Adrienne said with a dreaminess I didn't recognize.

"Gross, Mom," Rosamund cringed. I hid a laugh before looking up at Zemila. She gave a subtle nod in Rosamund's direction.

"Do you want to dance with me?" I asked and the young girl's head snapped up.

"Who, me?" She looked between me and Zemila.

"Yes, you." I smiled. "Zemila can come too, if you like?"

She nodded, and the three of us headed to the dance floor.

The pop song bled into a ballad. A boy about Rosamund's age asked her if she wanted to go check out an exhibit with him. She flushed, nodded, and they vanished down a wide hall.

I offered a hand to Zemila.

"May I have this dance?" I said, with a small bow. Zemila put her hand in mine.

"You may." She smiled as I pulled her close.

My thumb brushed the smooth skin of her back where the dress dipped. I breathed her in and almost forgot we weren't here only to dance.

"This is nice," Zemila said in my ear. She turned her head slightly and kissed my cheek. I closed my eyes. "Almost like we're just people."

"Yes," I answered, slowly revolving on the spot. "Almost like we're just people."

Someone tapped my shoulder lightly and my eyes flew open.

"May I cut in?" said a bland cold voice.

My muscles tensed and a chill ran through me.

"Now, now, Lochlan," said the Proxy, gently pushing me aside. "You wouldn't want to make a scene in front of all these people."

Zemila clutched my hand to the point of pain. It was a reassurance. It kept me grounded, in the present.

"Come now," he offered his hand to Zemila. "People will start to notice."

"It's okay, Lochlan," Zemila said. Her gaze fixed over the Proxy's shoulder before flicking in my direction. "It's okay."

No sooner had she released my hand, did Camile show up at my side. I'd barely seen her all night.

"Lochlan," she said. "Give me your hand, Lochlan."

I made a fist, quenching the build-up of power sparking in my palm. Tearing my gaze away from my torturer pulling Zemila into the crowd of dancers, I took Camile's hand. Even in her five-inch heels, she was considerably shorter than me. That didn't stop her from leading me around the dance floor.

"Jenner," I said. "Can you hear them?"

Zemila's jaw was tense as the Proxy maneuvered her through the crowd. He whispered in her ear and I saw her flinch.

"Jenner?" I said again. Then someone lightly slapped me in the face.

"Lochlan," Cam said. "I am talking to you."

"What?" I looked down at her, tearing my gaze away from Zemila and the Proxy.

"We lost Jenner a few minutes ago," she said. "We were hoping you were still in contact. Can you get in touch with Llowellyn?"

"We lost—what?" My mind tried to focus on what Cam said while my eyes kept flicking back to Zemila.

"Can you contact Llowellyn?" Camile asked again. "I think phones are down, but most people haven't noticed yet."

Llowellyn. Llowellyn? Llowellyn, God's Below if you don't—

I'm here, Little One, my brother thought back to me, but it was faint.

Do you have Jenner? I asked him.

I . . . Lochlan? Llowellyn thought, but I could scarcely hear him.

Why do you sound so far away?

Silence.

Llowellyn?

There was nothing.

"I see Virtue," Cam said. "Can you tell Llowellyn he's here?"

"I can't," I told her, still screaming for my brother in my mind.

"He's moving," Cam said, not registering my words, my panic.

"So is the Proxy." I stopped dancing. "And I don't have Llowellyn."

My words were as hollow and empty as I felt. Losing the connection to my brother after not having it for so many months had a prickle of fear raising the hairs on my neck.

Was it actually gone?

I tried again.

"I don't have him. I'm alone again," I muttered.

"What?" Camile asked. "No. You're not."

I reached out for the little Magic I knew I had. I reached and pleaded with Magic, but it wasn't there.

I was empty. Again.

The Proxy was trying to pull Zemila off the dance floor and I was going to lose her too.

I started to move towards her. Magic or no, I could fight if I needed to. Zemila stopped the Proxy, and he stepped close to her. I saw her try to step away, but he grabbed her arm hard.

Then the lights cut out—and didn't come back on.

There was a moment of darkness. A moment of silence broken by the growing whispered confusion. An alarm sounded and the emergency evacuation lights started to flash. Screams went up around the room as panic rippled through the crowd. I pushed through toward Zemila, Cam's hand still clutched tightly in mine, my heart as loud in my ears as the persistent alarm.

"Llowellyn," I yelled out loud and in my mind, knowing it was useless, praying it wasn't. I saw the Proxy kiss the back of Zemila's hand and disappear into the chaos.

"Zemila," I said, finally getting to her. I pulled her into a tight hug, needing to feel her, to know she was there. Cam was behind me, and she gave my shoulder a squeeze. "Are you all right?" I asked Zemila, releasing her.

"I–I—" She was frazzled, rubbing the back of her hand on her dress and staring where the Proxy had disappeared. "He took it," she said, her brown eyes meeting mine. "He told me he took the Spear and asked if we were safe. Took it from Llowellyn?"

"No," I said, "but—"

"Jenner," Cam said.

"No." I shook my head. "As long as he didn't leave the house, he'll be fine. The protections are strong."

I started to turn and look for the exit, but Zemila pulled me back.

"Lochlan, I can't use my gift," she said. "I can feel it, but I can't do anything."

"Neither can I," I said, finally understanding what was happening. My panic ebbed only slightly as the pull of promise burned anew.

"Avery. The Proxy has Avery. She must be nearby. Qillian needs to know." I tapped my chest, the spot where the bonded promise pulled at me, stronger than it had before.

"Phones are down," Camile said.

"They knocked out all communication, Magic and otherwise," Zemila pulled me toward the flow of people heading for the exit.

"Llowellyn should be getting out with Virtue," I told Cam and Zemila. "He'll meet us at home. That was the plan if anything went wrong. Where's Nemo?"

"I don't know," Cam yelled over the melee of people. She looked at the turned-over tables and chairs, the broken champagne flutes and mosaic dinner plates, the swarms of people moving toward the exit. "I—"

Her words cut off and I felt a hand on my shoulder. There was an arm around my neck and pressure on my windpipe faster than I could react. Zemila and Cam were both struggling against men who, under the guise of rushing to the exit, had looped an arm around their waists.

All three of us were hauled behind the large pillars in the hall. I still wasn't at my full strength and it was getting harder to breathe. A quick jab to the solar plexus got my captor to loosen his grip enough for me to take a deep breath. None of the frantic crowd noticed as we were dragged into the coat-check room.

By the time I shook off my captor, the one who'd held Zemila had a bloody nose. Camile had elbowed the man restraining her in the stomach, then turned to knee him in the crotch.

I headbutted the guy behind me. He released me and I turned.

"Marco," I hissed, pushing him into Camile's attacker. The men fell into each other, into a coat rack, then down to the ground in a tangle of limbs.

I stepped toward them, flanked on either side by Cam and Zemila.

"Who are they?" Zemila asked, the alarm still blaring.

"I recognize him," I pointed at Marco. He glared at me as blood gushed from his nose. "He took our coats. He was there when I was—"

"He was—" Zemila cut off her words. "You helped hurt him?"

Marco bared his teeth and got slowly to his feet. "Do you know who you're running from?"

Before I could stop her, Zemila took two quick steps forward and sucker-punched Marco in the face. I grabbed her around the waist, hauling her back.

"We should go," I said in her ear, but she couldn't hear me. Marco was starting to stand, pulling on the sleeve of a hanging coat to help.

Zemila struggled in my hold and tried to get to him. Behind us, the sound of the crowd's steady footfalls slowed.

"And stay down!" Zemila said. Marco slipped on nothing, falling hard.

"Do you know running is useless?" he spat at us, trying to find his feet.

"Put me down, Lochlan," Zemila said. Her cold tone had me releasing her immediately.

When Zemila and Camile stepped in front of me, real fear showed in Marco's eyes.

"We're not running now," Camile said, stepping forward. "But you might want to."

"Cam," I said. "We have to leave."

"Are you safe with him?" Marco yelled after us as we backed away. "Do you know what he truly is?"

When we passed the last statue in the dark hall, the exit was in sight. We turned and walked as quickly as we could with the last few people filing out of the museum. The alarm had finally stopped blaring and a security guard was waving at us to get out of the building.

I jumped when Cam's phone started to ring.

"I guess phones are back," she said, tapping her watch to pick up as we walked down the stone museum steps. I could hear a faint siren and see red and blue flashing lights in the distance.

"Nemo," Cam said. "Well, we were a little busy. No, I didn't hear it ri—well, there was a rather loud alar . . .you were nowhere to be . . .yes, yes . . . okay. Two minutes. Have you heard from Jenner yet? Llowellyn? Dios . . . okay."

She disconnected.

"Nemo's outside," she said, looking at her watch. "Jenner messaged me. He's safe."

"Good," I said, scanning the crowd for the Proxy, but he was nowhere in sight. I reached for Magic again and couldn't touch it.

I knew Avery's abilities were blocking my Magic, and I knew would come back as soon as I was out of her reach. But even so, the strength of Avery's gift was cause to panic. If she could neutralize this many people, but—

"And stay down!" Zemila had said. Then Marco had slipped on nothing and fallen.

"Police are arriving now," Camile looked up from her watch, and I was snapped back to the present moment. "We should move."

"You know where Nemo is?" I asked Cam as the sirens turned off. She nodded. "Lead on."

Taxis and drivers alike were picking up frenzied people as they fled down the museum steps. An ambulance was parked to the left of the crowd, and the first two police cars were stopped not far from our path. We kept walking.

"The Proxy asked about you," Zemila told me as we walked. "About your mood, your abilities."

"My abilities?"

"If they had come back," she said. "And if I felt safe. He told me you were dangerous. That the people around you weren't safe."

A chill deep in my gut climbed my spine. I am dangerous. I am not safe. My worst fears. My darkest truth.

"Hey," Zemila squeezed my hand. "Did you hear what I said? Or did you start to spiral?"

"Spiral," I admitted.

"There's Nemo," Cam pointed at the black SUV parked up the block and across the street. He saw us and started the engine.

"I said," Zemila started, "I am telling you this so you know, I am not concerned about your control. I know I am safe with you. You are—"

A phone rang. I blinked. Cam turned. Zemila looked at her watch. It wasn't hers. Cam and I did the same.

A phone rang again.

"Is it you?" Cam asked, looking up from the dark screen of her watch.

"No," I said.

The phone rang a third time. Zemila looked down at my coat pocket.

"The coat-check guy," she reached into my pocket and pulled out an old-style flip phone. Zemila looked up and down the street. It was quiet, but for the taxis passing nearby and the last sirens turning off in the distance. She answered on speaker.

"I've missed you, Lochlan," said the cold bland voice of the Proxy.

"What do you want?" Zemila said.

"Oh, you're still there?" he said. "I thought you might have had second thoughts after learning Lochlan ate the soul of one of my men."

I looked up at her, panicked. I hadn't. I didn't.

"I know," she mouthed.

"Eat shit," Zemila said and was about to hang up when he spoke.

"You're not safe with him. No one is."

"And I'd be safe with you?" Zemila scoffed.

"Lochlan," the Proxy chided. "I called to speak to you. Come to us. We have the Spear. Bring us the sword. Do that and we won't hurt your little friends."

"Or I could stop you," I said.

"How can you stop us when you barely have your Magic back? When I can take it away from you whenever I like? Come to us, Lochlan, join us, and you will have the power to keep them safe."

"No," I said, thinking fast.

He didn't have Llowellyn. He would have gloated if he'd had Llowellyn.

"Then start saying goodbye to your friends," the Proxy said, and the line went dead.

A black SUV pulled up beside us. Cam looked between me and Zemila before striding over to the vehicle and opening the front passenger door. Nemo was drumming his fingers on the steering wheel, impatiently waiting while Zemila and I climbed into the back.

"Fill me in," Nemo said as he put his blinker on and turned down Thompson Drive. "Were you on the phone?"

"The Proxy," Zemila said. "Taunting us."

"We got what we came for?" Nemo met my eyes in the rear-view mirror.

"Aye," I answered.

You're back, my brother said in my mind and relief filled me. I feel you coming my way.

"Nemo, slow down," I said.

Where? I thought back to Llowellyn and I felt the buzz of my watch, looked down to see a location pin dropped three blocks from where we were.

"Nemo," I said, leaning forward and swiping two fingers across the top of my watch, sending the pin to the car's GPS. "Llowellyn's here."

Nemo muttered something under his breath, but after a quick mirror check, he turned left and headed towards Llowellyn's location.

"So, he has the Spear?" Nemo asked. "The real one?"

"He has the one on display," Zemila said. "I don't know if it was the right one, if the Proxy . . ."

Zemila trailed off as silence filled the car. A moment later, Nemo pulled over, and Llowellyn, no longer under the spell of camouflage, opened the door. The SUV had a tiny third row. I clambered into it as my brother got into the car.

"Is it the right one?" Zemila asked as she moved over. "The right spear?"

Llowellyn sat beside her, duffle bag in hand. I placed a hand on his shoulder, needing the contact. As soon as I did, I felt the buzz of power, the sense of Lugh, and I knew it was the right spear before Llowellyn opened his mouth.

"Yes," Llowellyn said. "It's Lugh's. I was sure as soon as I was in the same room as it. The stone reacted to it." Llowellyn placed his palm over his chest where Lugh's stone hung on a thin chain.

The roads were relatively clear as Nemo drove just above the speed limit back to my house. After a few minutes of silence, of feeling the pulse of the stone and spear in the same place after so long a time, I spoke.

"No trouble getting out?"

"I was lucky," Llowellyn said. "Virtue used a back exit with only a few others. I moved through the doors after him with little difficulty."

"Good," I said.

"The only tricky bit was when he almost heard me." Llowellyn looked over at Zemila.

"I felt your apology," Zemila said.

"You what?" Nemo asked sharply, speaking for the first time since Llowellyn had climbed into the car.

"I felt—" Zemila started, but Nemo cut her off.

"You let him mess around in your mind?"

"Nemo," Zemila chided. "He wasn't messing around, he was just—"

"Making you feel emotions that weren't yours," Nemo scoffed. "And you let him."

"What is wrong with you?" Zemila asked. "Why are you being like this?"

"What's wrong with me?" Nemo said, furious. "What's wrong with you? You would think after everything with Dad—"

"Dad?" Zemila blinked rapidly. "What the hell does this have to do with Dad?"

Nemo pulled up in front of my house and threw the SUV into park.

"Never mind," Nemo avoided her eyes. "I'm glad we got what we needed."

"This isn't over," Zemila said, pushing open her door. Everyone but Nemo got out, then, to my surprise, Cam got back in. She closed the door and I heard the engine turn off.

"I'll be inside," Llowellyn said, and he walked up my front steps. The home system detected motion and the porch light came on.

"Mila?" I asked, reaching out a hand as the cool night breeze lifted a few locks of hair that had fallen out of her bun. She took it and looked at me.

"You feeling okay?" she asked.

"Only bruised," I assured. "You?"

"Annoyed," she nodded towards her brother. "I'll tell you about my father sometime. Now, you want to show me this Magical basement you made?"

The sound of a car door opening had both of us turning around. Nemo walked around the front of the SUV, stopping where the porch light reached the sidewalk.

"I'm sorry I snapped," he said. "I just . . . there's some stuff I haven't told you."

"Okay," Zemila said, confused.

"About Dad," Nemo said.

"Okay," Zemila repeated.

"I saw him a while back and—"

"You what?"

"And he isn't Human," Nemo finished.

"Excuse me."

"He's an Empath."

CHAPTER TWENTY-THREE
Lochlan

I closed the front door behind me as Zemila and Nemo sat on my porch steps. As much as I was curious to learn about Zemila's parentage, it was not my business. I would be here when she wanted to tell me.

"Little One," my brother said, standing outside his bedroom door. "You made a basement?"

"I figured the Earth Magic protection spells were my best bet here." I stood beside him. "I felt . . ."

"The Anima?"

"Mayhap I did," I said, thinking back to the power I'd felt as I went deeper into the ground.

"How do we get in?" Llowellyn asked, opening his bedroom door and peaking inside. "It's still my room. It's a concealment spell."

"Portal cast with a door," I said, closing the door. I reached for my Magic and asked for the power I needed to open the door. After feeling the effects of Avery's gift, I was worried there would be no response, but Magic flowed into my body and powered the spell. "Aiteal-diamhair."

"Interesting," Llowellyn said as I opened the door to reveal a very narrow staircase. "Portal to where?"

I stepped onto the wood stairs and started to descend. "We're below your bedroom. I built this place as a training facility. A safe house, really."

"In case they came for you?" My brother's tone was dark as he followed me.

"And so they have," I said, turning on the light switch at the bottom of the stairs to reveal a simple but finished basement. It was the same width as the small bedroom above, but twice as long.

"Not bad, Little One," Llowellyn said, stepping off the wooden stairs and on to the vinyl floor. Fluorescent lights hummed in the basement that was more like a box than anything else. Llowellyn walked past the weapons cases, shelves, and racks lining the concrete walls, and over to the large chest on the floor. "I recognize this chest."

An ironwood chest wrapped in bands of a gold colored metal sat on the large Persian rug at the other end of the basement. I'd found the rug on the side of the road the year I'd moved in. The colors had been dulled and it was covered in dirt, but a simple spell had made the rug vibrant and plush. If only I could be healed so easily.

Llowellyn knelt down and ran his hand over the ancient chest. A ripple of Magic spread through the basement and dissipated.

"I went back for it," I said. "It took me a week to figure out how to break the rooting spell, but I wanted this piece of you."

Llowellyn opened the weapons chest he had made so many lifetimes ago. "The Spear will be safe here," he said, placing the cloth bundle inside. "I can feel its Magic held. The Spear will power the chest, and the chest will power the Spear."

"And they will both protect the house," I said.

"Brilliant Magic, Little Lochlan," Llowellyn said as he closed the chest and stood.

φ

"So," Mrs. Abernathy said, rocking back and forth on her chair. It was a new chair, one Llowellyn had made for her last month. She saw him out there one day finishing his shoe rack and, faster than she could say "yes, please," he'd started on a rocking chair for her porch.

"So . . ." I repeated, wondering what she was getting at. "How's church?"

"Mmm-hmm." She waved her floral-patterned fan through the air. "You're going to avoid talking about what I want to talk about then? Okay, church is church. We have our Fourth of July barbeque coming up. I don't suppose you'd like to come to that, would you?"

I smiled and drank some of her homemade sweet tea.

"I didn't think so," she said.

It was a warm afternoon and the sun was shining. Zemila was at work, and Mrs. Abernathy had come over to invite—or tell—me to have tea on her porch.

"I have a couple friends who would love to meet you, but I know with everything you don't want to talk about, you have a lot going on."

"Come now, Mrs. Abernathy," I said, putting down the glass. "I can't read minds. I don't know what you want to know."

"You can't read minds?" she asked, stopping her chair and leaning forward.

"I surely cannot," I said.

"Why don't you take a guess then?"

"The gala was nice," I said. "Zemila is doing well."

"Mmm-hmm." Mrs. Abernathy started rocking her chair. "And you are looking better, stronger. Not so skinny anymore."

"Thank you," I said. "I've been . . . I have . . ."

I couldn't tell her I'd been drinking vampire blood.

"Mmm," she said, before I could think of a lie. "I bet you have."

"Mmm-hmm," I said back to her.

"Don't you dare sass me." She tried to keep a stern expression, but I could see the sparkle in her eye. "Llowellyn brought his young lady over for dinner when she was here a couple months ago. Did you know that?"

"I did," I nodded.

"And do you know who has not been here for dinner with me?"

"Nemo?"

She snapped her fan shut and pointed it at me like a weapon. "Don't even get me started on that boy. Wasted potential, but he'll figure it out in time."

"Would you like Zemila and me to come to your church barbeque?" I asked.

She scoffed. "You think I want my first dinner with the two of you to be at church? Hoooo boy, you really can't read minds. I'm too selfish for that."

"It's not like you never see us," I said.

"I want to see you together," she said. "Next Sunday. At my dining room table. You can tell me about Camile's birthday party."

"Jenner told you about that?" I asked.

"He surely did," she smiled and fanned herself lazily. "What's your costume going to be?"

"I don't know," I said. "Zemila wants to do something together. I suggested Buttercup and the Man in Black—"

"The Man in Black?" Her eyes traveled over my black jeans and charcoal T-shirt. "Aren't you that already?"

"Haha," I deadpanned. "Anyway, Zemila vetoed it. She has something else in mind."

"Well, you can tell me all about it when you come for dinner." She smiled.

"That would be our first actual date," I said.

Mrs. Abernathy's eyes bugged out of her head. "Excuse me! You live together."

"Our relationship hasn't taken the usual trajectory, I admit."

"You haven't taken her out to dinner yet?" she asked, appalled.

"I was tied up for a while," I tried to joke.

"What did I say about sassing?" Her eyes went soft, sad, like maybe she knew more than I thought she did.

"I'm sorry," I said in earnest. "She moved in while I was away. She's been taking care of me. She's been . . ."

Everything. She has been everything to me.

"I think you should cook for her," Mrs. Abernathy proclaimed. "Jenner can stay with his sister. Llowellyn can stay here. He can bring that sweet dog."

"Sweet?" My eyebrows popped up.

"I like that dog," Mrs. Abernathy said. "She is a good girl."

"She is a pain in my—"

"I've heard," she laughed. "Llowellyn and Oriole can stay here for the night. I'll give her a nice brush before she comes inside, and you and Zemila can have a night alone."

I shifted in my seat, feeling exposed. Reaching for the sweet tea, I took a sip to have something to do.

"Mmm," she said smugly. "Why don't you cook for her tomorrow night? I'll let Llowellyn know when he's here for dinner. You can tell Jenner."

"Gods have mercy," I said as Mrs. Abernathy laughed.

CHAPTER TWENTY-FOUR
Zemila

"Ms. Alkevic." Diana popped her head into Zemila's office.

"What's up, Diana?" Zemila looked up from her article on arts funding in public schools.

"It's Friday. Go home," Diana said.

"Soon." Zemila was almost finished—so close to being done for the day she could taste it. "What are you still doing here?"

"I'm taking next Friday off for a friend's wedding," Diana said, putting on her coat. "I'll work late a few nights and take a half-day."

"Get home safe," Zemila said.

"Get home," Diana threw back.

Zemila left the office an hour later, her mind transitioning from her article to her father. For the last week he had dominated all the quiet moments in her mind. She hated it. She hated him. There was a part of her that was upset with Nemo for not telling her about him sooner, and a part of her that was upset with him for telling her at all.

"He's an Empath," she said as she maneuvered Llowellyn's big SUV through the late evening traffic.

Nemo had said their father had reached out to him a few years ago while he was traveling. He'd offered Nemo an online job, a steady source of income, and eventually asked Nemo to come visit him in Seoul. Nemo didn't go into detail about what had happened, only that it wasn't good.

She'd thought their father might be dead. Not only was he alive, but he was a Gifter. What did that mean for her? Nemo had called her again yesterday, but she didn't know if she wanted to talk about it. Not yet. Not with everything else going on.

Zemila parked the SUV up the street. The sun was low but wouldn't set for another thirty minutes or so. She looked at her watch as she approached the house.

7:50 p.m. Maybe we can go out for dinner, she thought. If he hasn't already eaten.

Zemila paused with her hand on the peeling white gate. The lights in the upstairs windows were off and the house seemed quiet. Too quiet. Fear gripped Zemila as tightly as she gripped the cool metal. She was about to turn around and call her brother, when a sound made her jump.

"Zemila," Llowellyn stood in Mrs. Abernathy's front doorway.

"Christ, Llow, you scared me," Zemila said. "What's going on? Where is everyone?" She gestured to the living room window. The lights were off, the blinds closed. Oriole poked her head out beside Llowellyn and yipped happily. "And why do you have my dog?"

"We thought we'd give you two some privacy for a night," Llowellyn said with a smirk, scratching Oriole behind the ear. "Louise has kindly offered me her second bedroom. Jenner is staying at Cam's."

Heat rushed to Zemila's cheeks and she looked down at what she was wearing. Black slacks and a white dress shirt. Not exactly what she would have picked to wear on her first date with Lochlan . . . if that's even what this was.

"Oh, I'm sure he doesn't care what you're wearing," Llowellyn said. "Don't worry. And have fun." He smiled and shut the door.

Zemila paused, staring at where Llowellyn had disappeared. Then she looked up at the old house she'd been calling home for almost a year.

My first date with Lochlan . . . she thought, butterflies coming alive in her stomach.

But this wasn't her first date with him. That would have been six years ago. He'd showed up at her dorm room just after the sun went down and asked if she wanted to go for a walk. He'd brought her to a small lake on a part of the school's property she'd never been to. The lake had glowed in the darkness. It was beautiful.

At the time, she didn't realize what was happening. She didn't understand what the little picnic basket he'd put together meant, or what the ache in her chest was. Because she couldn't then. She needed him to be there forever. And Zemila had learned all too well that, when men loved you, they left you.

So, Lochlan couldn't have loved her. Not then. Because if he had, he would have left . . . which he did anyway. That's when something had snapped inside her. Something had broken. It still wasn't fixed.

Will tonight help fix it? she wondered. Will tonight help me unlearn what life has taught me about men, about love?

Maybe not all of it, she thought. But it could be a start.

Heat welled up in her chest. She tried to steady her breathing and climbed the few steps to the front door. She hesitated for a moment before scanning her palm and walking inside. The smell of tomatoes and dough and cheese wafted down the hall towards her.

"Lochlan?" she called down the hallway.

"Mila," a surprised voice said. Then there was a loud clang and a curse. "Oh, Danu. Mila, one second—ouch!"

Zemila hid a laugh behind her hand, and the bubble of tension around her popped. She flicked on the hall light.

Still just Lochlan, she mused.

"I didn't hear the home system," Lochlan said, walking out of the kitchen and towards her.

He looked good. Healthy. Zemila let her eyes roam over his face, still wearing glasses for some unknown reason.

Comfort, maybe?

She looked down to his chest. His black T-shirt had more than a little flour on it. His shoulders had filled out further than she'd thought possible in the two weeks since Sahrias's visit.

Her eyes lingered on the intricate knots of black starting at his left wrist, moving up his arm, over his bicep. His body was no longer gaunt and thin, but full—as it used to be. She looked back up to his bright green eyes, sparing only a moment's thought to the tomato sauce on his cheek.

"I thought I would make you dinner," Lochlan said. "Pizza."

"You made me pizza?"

"Aye," he nodded.

"Jenner told me about this pizza."

"Aye," he said again and smiled. Then he reached up and scratched the back of his head. His T-shirt pulled up and exposed a sliver of skin. Zemila bit her lip and managed to school her expression before Lochlan looked back at her.

"But Jenner isn't here tonight," she breathed, reminding herself it was impolite to jump people when they've made you dinner.

"No." Lochlan looked at her with heat in his eyes. "Jenner isn't here tonight."

Anticipation filled the silence between them.

"I know I said I would take you out, but I planned a little evening in . . . if that's all right with you."

She grinned like an idiot, hot helium filling up her insides.

"That's all right with me." She took a step towards him. Then another. "You have sauce on your cheek."

"What?" He lifted his hand to wipe it away, but she caught his wrist before he could. Electricity zinged between them at the contact and Lochlan's breathing picked up.

She leaned closer to him.

"Jenner said it was the best pizza sauce he'd ever had," she whispered.

Moving slowly, giving Lochlan every opportunity to pull away, she parted her lips then closed them around the spot on his cheek. She let her tongue touch his skin, and Lochlan let out a low sound, gripping her hip with a hand.

"Holy shit," Zemila whispered in shock, pulling away. Lochlan let her go, but the look on his face told her he didn't want to. "That's actually really good."

"For me too," he said, heat burning in his eyes.

Zemila stepped backwards, smiling wide. "I'll going to—I'm—" She shook her head and covered her mouth. "Change out of my work clothes."

She turned and started up the stairs, taking them two at a time in her haste.

"I'll be here," Lochlan said. "Covered in sauce."

She laughed openly and headed for the washroom.

After a quick shower, Zemila stood in front of her overflowing suitcase, wondering what to wear. Lochlan had told her countless times over the past months to use his closet, but she hadn't done it yet. She didn't know why.

It had been almost seven months of living out of a suitcase and barely sleeping in her own bed. Not that she'd been sleeping much. Since Lochlan was back, she'd slept better, but still would sometimes wake up scared he wasn't there. That he wasn't beside her.

Get it together, Mila, she told herself. You've been sleeping next to this guy for two months. A date isn't a big deal.

But it felt like a big deal.

Even though it wasn't out at a restaurant. Even if it was nothing fancy. It felt like a big deal. She had no idea what to wear.

Finally, she decided on a loose pair of light-wash jeans, and a thin long-sleeve knit shirt.

"It's just Lochlan," she told her reflection, pulling at the U-neck of the shirt. "You don't have to be fancy for pizza with Lochlan."

Her hair had been half-up for most of the day. She'd run damp fingers through it when she'd gotten out of the shower and made a conscious effort not to care. Running her fingers through it again, Zemila let the dark waves fall over her shoulders.

Giving herself one last look, one last pep talk, she walked downstairs.

When Zemila entered the kitchen, she couldn't help her smile. Lochlan had pulled the small table out from the wall and had a chair on either side. The table was set with a few candles in the center.

An empty bottle of Cabernet Sauvignon was on the counter and a beautiful glass decanter sat on the table, full. Beside the decanter was . . .

"Jenga?" Zemila said, pausing at the door. Lochlan was elbow-deep in sudsy water, washing dishes.

"Jenga," he echoed. "I had an idea for a game after dinner."

He pulled his hands out of the water, and reached for the tea towel hanging on the stove. Looking over his shoulder at her, he did a double-take and stared open-mouthed for a moment. Heat rose off her skin everywhere Lochlan's eyes touched. He seemed to realize what he was doing because he blinked furiously and continued to dry his hands.

"Sorry," he said. "You look . . . you are so beautiful. You're always so beautiful."

The sincerity in his words made Zemila squirm. She was used to men finding her attractive. In fact, she hated when they told her so. She hated it because she was more than her face, a thing she had done zero work to achieve. But somehow, when it came from Lochlan, when he looked at her like that and said she was stunning, she knew he meant more than her physical appearance. She knew he saw all of her.

And she didn't know how to handle it.

"We're playing Jenga?" Zemila said, pulling out a chair and sitting down.

"In a manner of speaking." Lochlan took a step over to the table and picked up the decanter. "Cam told me this wine was your favorite."

He nodded to the bottle on the counter.

"You did your research," Zemila grinned, then took the glass he'd poured for her. "Thank you."

"I know you have a lot of questions for me, Zemila," Lochlan started.

"I don't—No, I . . . Oh, all right, fine." She gave in when he hit her with a look.

"I have questions for you too, you know?" He poured his own glass and sat down across from her.

She raised her glass and he touched it lightly with his. They drank, and Lochlan kept talking.

"I thought this might be a lower pressure, fun way of getting to ask them."

"By playing Jenga?" Zemila asked. "I don't think I'm following."

Lochlan stood and took the box over to the counter. He poured out half the Jenga blocks, counted them quickly, put a few back in the box, and handed it to her. Then he went to the kitchen counter and pulled open a drawer.

When he sat down again, he had two black markers in hand. He handed one to Zemila.

"You write your questions on the blocks," he said. "And every block you pull, you have to answer that question."

"What if the block is too small for the question?" she asked.

"Find a shorter way to ask," he said.

"What if you pull a block with your own question?"

Lochlan smiled over the wine he brought to his lips, and Zemila so badly wanted to occupy his mouth with other things.

"You have to answer," he said simply.

That makes things easier and harder, Zemila thought as questions raced through her mind.

"How long do I have to think of the questions?" she asked as the stove dinged. Lochlan stood to put on oven mitts.

"Dinner, and . . ." He paused. "I won't ask about your father."

Zemila hadn't realized she was tense until she relaxed at his words. How had he known?

"I have had a lot of time to think about my parents and my past, so please, ask me anything," he said and his smile was soft. "But I want you to know, I won't ask about that."

"Thank you," she said, falling in love with him a little more. "And you're not allowed to ask about our costumes for Cam's birthday either," she added quickly.

"No fair," he said, but she saw him smile.

The pizza was as good as Jenner had said it was. The dough was soft and the sauce was like nothing Zemila had ever tasted.

"What did you put in here?" She looked from her third slice of pizza to the man sitting across from her. He was carefully writing something on a Jenga block she couldn't see.

"Magic," he said without looking up.

"Oh my god, really!" she exclaimed.

"No!" he laughed, and her heart felt warm at the sound. "Herbs and spices, and a very long life to perfect the recipe."

"Oh." She was simultaneously happy and disappointed. "Well, what's in it?" she asked again. "And how long a life?"

"The recipe is a secret." His eyes flicked up at her. "You can use blocks for it, though."

Zemila looked down at the box of Jenga blocks.

"I've already written on all of mine." She pouted when he looked up at her and his eyes went to her lips. A zing of heat shot through Zemila.

"This," he breathed. Blinked and looked away. "This was my last block," he said. "No more of your Magic. It's not fair."

She flushed as his eyes met hers.

"Shall we start?" he said slowly, and she could have skipped the Jenga for something more fulfilling, but no. She liked Lochlan's idea for this game. It was almost like playing catch-up and getting to know each other at the same time.

Her questions were all over the place and she was hungry for answers. Sure, she knew him. Or she had. They had gone to school together for the better part of ten years, but that was a long time ago.

It seemed like a long time ago.

Now she could know him. Really know him. Not like before when she was scared and he was guarded. When she felt if she loved him he would leave, and he felt if anyone knew him they wouldn't be safe. Now that the secrets didn't hold them apart, an eagerness filled her.

This was a whole new chapter, a whole new life. And they could start it together.

"Yes," she said, bouncing a little in her seat. "Let's start."

She hopped up from the table, took the second bottle of wine from the counter and hurried into the living room. "Bring your blocks!" she called over her shoulder.

"A little excited, are we?" he asked.

"You have no idea," she muttered, sitting down on the living room floor. She moved the small coffee table off to the side and laid all her blocks questions face down in front of her.

A moment later, Lochlan walked into the room holding two glasses of water in one hand, and the Jenga blocks in the hem of his shirt. Zemila watched as he struggled to place the water down without spilling.

"You enjoyed that didn't you?" he said, dumping the blocks on the ground in front of him.

"Maybe I enjoy watching you," she said, letting her voice drop.

He froze in his actions of arranging his blocks questions-down.

"Don't start." His green eyes met her brown ones. "Or you won't get any of your questions answered."

"I have no idea what you're talking about," she said coyly, biting her bottom lip.

"Keep looking at me like that and you're going to find out." His words were promising.

Heat rushed to her core and she was tempted to push, to see what he would do. But she had questions she wanted answered. She looked down at the blocks and started to mix them up.

It didn't take long to set up the Jenga tower, and then they were playing and laughing and answering questions. Some were easy. Zemila told Lochlan that her favorite color was blue. Lochlan told Zemila about the time Lugh had accidently burned off half his hair while lighting an arrow in training.

Some had long answers. Zemila pulled a block saying, "What is your favorite memory?" and she told Lochlan about a carnival she went to with Nemo and their mother. It was near a home they had in the country. Zemila had won them each a large stuffed animal at a ring toss game.

Sometimes the answers were complicated. Lochlan pulled a block Zemila wrote asking "Have you ever had children?" And though the simple answer was "no," Lochlan told her more. He told her why he didn't, and why it was okay.

"Do you want children?" Lochlan asked her.

"A question outside the game?" Zemila said, taking a sip of her wine. "That's cheating." But since he had shared so much with her, she did the same for him.

The truth was, she didn't know.

On and on it went, and they talked and laughed and learned of each other. Lochlan asked, "What is your favorite smell?" Zemila asked, "What is your favorite flavor?" Lochlan pulled one of his own blocks. He handed it to her as he answered his own question. "I do miss my homeland, but this question was for you."

They had a similar exchange when Zemila pulled her own block saying, "Did you ever meet your mother?"

Lochlan talked about his father, Zemila shared stories of her mother. They talked and listened and slowly inched closer together on the floor until Lochlan's hand rested on her calf and her leg pressed against his.

"How many times have you been in love?" Lochlan read, his face falling. "Oh, Mila, why did you ask me this?"

"Because I want to know," she said. "I want to know how many women you've loved."

"Only the women?" he raised a playful eyebrow and Zemila's mouth popped open.

"I . . . Oh, I didn't. I'm sorry, I shouldn't have assu—"

"It's okay, Mila," Lochlan said gently. "I know you didn't mean anything by it."

"You've loved men?"

"When you've lived as long as I have, the importance of things like that shifts."

Zemila felt small at his words, insignificant. Like she could never understand the world the way he did. Like she could never be at his level, be someone he could find interesting.

Why did you even ask that question? She silently berated herself. Why, why, why?

"Zemila," Lochlan said, squeezing her leg. His voice was soft—but firm. "I have loved many people in my life. I have loved them fiercely and with all my heart. But none of them are you. And here, now, I am hopelessly, embarrassingly, drowning in my love for you. I love you. Not because of how beautiful you are, or how smart you are. Not because we happened to be in the same place at the same time. Not because we were both pulled here by some Dark Magic, or forgotten prophecy. But because I feel as though you were made for me, and I for you. Because you are not perfect in the most perfect ways and because I feel my truest self when I can sit and be with you."

Where was the shy boy who could barely look at her? The teenager who had been her brother's best friend? The man who would have shied away from the mere thought of such a confession?

Now the roles seemed to be reversed. Zemila was the speechless one. The one who shied away from such statements.

"That's how I feel." He lifted a shoulder and let it drop. "That's how I love you. Because you are all of those things, and because you are, I hope . . . I hope you're mine."

There was that helium feeling again, pumping her up from the little insignificant person, back to someone who was worthy, not just of his love but of loving herself in a way she had been losing.

Zemila almost toppled the tower on her next turn. She was so shaken by his words and shamed by her lack of response. But he smiled at her and said, "We're all right."

And the crazy thing was, she believed him.

A few turns later, Zemila pulled a block and raised her eyebrows. "Is this a demand?" She turned the block toward Lochlan.

"A request," he said, waving his hand through the air. "There is a question mark."

She looked at the block that used to read, "Kiss me." But now said "Kiss me?" Then she turned back to him. "It didn't say that a second ago."

"It does now," he said, heat lighting his eyes.

Zemila carefully placed the block on the top of the teetering tower. Then even more carefully, she started to crawl towards him.

"What if you had pulled this block?" she asked, moving slowly to where he leaned against the couch. One of his legs was long on the floor, while the other was bent. His arm rested lazily on his bent knee and his eyes burned into her.

Watching him watch her like this was an aphrodisiac. She slowed her movements to prolong the moment, and as he watched her, she watched him. The rise and fall of his chest, the new stiffness of his shoulders, his arm, as she was sure he was forcing himself not to move. To let her be in control of this moment.

"What if you had pulled this block?" Zemila asked again, her face, now only inches away from him.

"I wouldn't have." He started to lean forward, but Zemila moved back. A soft sound of disappointment and yearning escaped him. The sound made her smile.

"How do you know?" she asked, moving close again, brushing her nose along his.

"Magic," he said and closed the distance between them.

CHAPTER TWENTY-FIVE
Lochlan

I felt her smile as I pressed my mouth to hers. She was soft, and gentle, and moaned into my touch. At first the kiss was chaste. Just a slow press of lips, then she opened to me, capturing my bottom lip between hers. She deepened the kiss, and when her hand on my cheek moved to tangle in my hair, to pull me towards her, it was my turn to moan.

I breathed her in, memorizing the softness of her mouth and every curve of her body. I moved Zemila back, keeping my lips on hers, readjusting until we were kneeling. I pressed her closer to me. The tower of Jenga blocks fell beside us and she broke our kiss and pulled away.

I didn't let her go far.

"Does that mean I won?" she asked, her breathing heavier than it had been a moment ago. I ran my lips down the line of her jaw, and bit lightly at her neck. She groaned at the pressure of my teeth and I almost lost control on that sound alone.

"If this is losing," I said as she pulled my lips to hers, "I never want to win again."

I felt the smile in her kiss before she parted my lips with her tongue.

Kneeling on the floor surrounded by fallen Jenga blocks, we moved slowly. With intention. I pulled her shirt free from where it was tucked at her waist. I didn't want to rush. I didn't want to miss a single inch of her. I let my hands explore the soft skin of her back, I stroked my fingers up and down her spine, I pulled the shirt over her head and tossed it aside.

Our mouths moved lazy and languid. Zemila took me over. She tasted like the wine we drank, and the chocolate I'd bought, and something akin to that specific way she smelled. She was ambrosial, and when she took my bottom lip between her teeth, biting down softly, it took everything I had to not take her there on the living room floor.

I moved my hands under her and pulled her hips to mine. Her moan of pleasure had me pushing a few blocks out of the way before laying her down. She laughed as I dragged my mouth down her neck, over the center of her black bra, kissing a trail down the middle of her stomach. I nipped lightly at her ribs and she squirmed and laughed again.

"Oh my god!" she exclaimed. "You dirty cheater!" I didn't look up from where I was moving my lips back up her body. "I thought it was only one."

"I have no idea what you mean," I said, cupping her breast over her bra and sucking lightly on her collar bone.

She moaned and rolled her hips beneath me. Her hand found bare skin under my shirt.

"You can't distract me with your—" I moved my hips and her words ended in a moan.

"What was that?" I asked, repeating the motion.

I was holding most of my weight on an elbow and knee as I slowly moved a hand down her body, to her inner thigh. "You were calling me a cheater because . . ."

I let the word hang in the air as I lightly circled my fingertips over the seam of her jeans.

Her hips moved up, begging for pressure. I didn't give it to her.

"Oh no," I said, moving back to her inner thigh. She groaned in frustration. "What did I do that upset you?"

"You stopped touching me," she ground out.

"Before that." I smiled and moved my hand between her legs.

Her head fell back with a sigh. "You changed the blocks."

"I changed them?"

"You, ahh, changed what they said."

I looked over at the jumble of blocks, all of them reading "Kiss me," but for one that had a question mark.

"So I did," I said, my fingers teasing. "Are you complaining?"

I shifted. She gasped.

"No, nope, not— uhh, not complaining."

She reached up, grabbed a fistful of my shirt, and pulled my mouth down to hers.

Her hands were on my stomach, my chest, my back. But it wasn't enough. I wanted to feel more of her skin on mine. She must have been thinking the same thing because she pulled her mouth away and dragged my shirt off my body.

"This can go," she said.

"Yes, ma'am." I pulled back to my hands and knees above her. I looked down at the goddess as her hands undid the buttons at my waist. She moved under me, trying to regain the contact we'd lost. And somehow the action eased me.

Somehow seeing she wanted me as much as I wanted her soothed an ache I didn't know I carried. It made me feel less rushed, less afraid of losing her. She moved under me again, pulling at my belt loops.

"Patience," I said, tossing my T-shirt aside.

"I've been patient," Zemila said, sliding out from between my thighs and kneeling. We faced each other and she traced my tattoo with light fingers. "I have been so, so patient."

Heat radiated from everywhere she touched. First her fingertips were at my wrist where the tattoo started, then her palm followed the knotted design up my forearm and over my biceps. Her mouth replaced her hand when she reached my shoulder where the pattern splayed over my chest before it finished over my heart.

"Do you know," she said, kissing my neck while her hands explored my body, "how hard it has been to sleep beside you every night? To be so . . ." She kissed my neck. ". . . very . . ." She unzipped my jeans. ". . . patient?"

I groaned as she held me and rocked her body to the rhythm of her hand.

"Oh." She smirked and bit my earlobe. The mix of pleasure and pain made me hiss out my desire and I thrust my hips forward to meet her pressure. "Maybe you do know how hard it was."

She stood in front of me. I looked up at her from my knees. Taking my face in her hands, she bent down and kissed me.

"Come now," she said, straightening, taking my hand in hers. Pulling me to my feet. "We have been patient enough."

She led me upstairs and took off my clothes, then hers. She pulled me down onto the bed, and aligned our bodies. Her skin was hot and smooth, I wanted to taste every part of her, and I did.

Sometime later, once we'd explored each other over and over, once I had lost control, and so had she, I looked at her long body, and snaked an arm under her waist. I pulled her to me again and watched as her head fell back and her body arched. I paused and blew softly. I kissed her inner thigh. I licked and backed away. I touched, but it was light. Then I waited. I waited to hear her ask me in that sweet way she did. The way that drove me to such distraction.

"Please, Lochlan," she said, and I smiled at the sound of my name on her lips. "Please."

"Please what?" I asked. She made a frustrated sound and shifted her hips.

"Ah ah ah," I scolded, nipping her inner thigh with my teeth.

"Lochlan," she said again. "Please, I need to feel you. Loch—"

Her taste, her sound, her hands in my hair, it was all too much. It was ecstasy. It was electricity. And we were lost.

The next morning, I woke up slowly. Slower than I had in centuries. I woke up with the memory of Zemila's hand in my hair, my name on her lips. I'd fallen asleep sometime in the early morning, after Zemila had snaked an arm around my waist and slung a leg over my hips.

But that wasn't what I was feeling now. I rolled over to find the space next to me empty but still warm.

I breathed in her scent, pressed my hips into the mattress, and groaned at the friction, at the thought of her, at the fragrance she left in my bed.

Where was she?

A clang from downstairs and a muttered curse answered that question.

"Airéist," I said. The small spell enhanced my hearing and I revelled in the ability to do casual Magic again.

"Damnit," I heard Zemila say from the kitchen. "Okay. Coffee, coffee, he likes the French pre—shit, no, not the flour!"

"Cagair," I said, returning my hearing to normal. I smiled into the pillow that smelled like her. Heat and lust and want rushed through my body and I rolled onto my back. Pointedly ignoring the ever-growing water damage.

I might have to redo the roof, I thought then looked down at myself. The stained ceiling did nothing to sate my desire.

I shouldn't go downstairs like this.

"Zipper, yak, Xerox, waffle," I said to my ceiling. "Vestibule, university, teeth, sabbath, retrograde amnesia."

I'd started using this trick when I'd gone to Erroin Peritia. Though I looked twenty-three when I'd arrived, I was much older. The founder of the school, Niloc Erroin, gave me a choice. Enroll in the university, stay for a couple years—or longer if I wished to reveal who I was—or he could cast a spell that would return me to the gangly fourteen-year-old I had been many millennia ago and age with my classmates.

I chose the latter and was happy I did . . . for the most part.

Going through puberty again, having so little dominion over my body after lifetimes of control, was frustrating to say the least. That's when I had come up with this focus trick.

By the time I got to "cottage cheese, bumble bee, aardvark" I had my body under control. I pulled on a T-shirt and a pair of sweat pants before brushing my teeth and heading downstairs.

The old house creaked, but Zemila didn't hear me. She sang and moved around the kitchen in one of my shirts. Although I was now very familiar with her long legs and smooth skin, I leaned against the doorway a little stunned she was mine.

She checked a bowl on the counter. It was covered with a tea towel.

Was she making bread?

Chopped vegetables filled separate bowls on the counter and a carton of eggs sat waiting to be used. The kettle started to whistle and she moved it to a different burner, then looked up at a high cupboard.

"Come here, you," she said, standing on tip-toe to reach the French press. Even though she was nearly as tall as I was, the French press was still too high. My shirt rode up as she reached, exposing more olive skin and a flash of purple lace.

"Zodiac, Yahtzee, xylene," I muttered before moving behind her and saying, "Can I help?"

She jumped a little at my voice and at the contact.

"You're awake," she said, at the exact same time I realized I really hadn't thought this through.

I really, really, hadn't thought this through.

When I'd reached for the French press, I'd pinned Zemila's body between mine and the counter.

Zodiac, Yahtzee, xylene, I mentally repeated.

But now she was pushing her hips back and arching as she slowly turned to face me.

"Wales, Velcro, ulcer," I said aloud.

"Oh," she looked down and laughed. "You are awake."

"Tasmania, safari, retraction," I muttered.

"What are you doing?" she asked, a smile curving her lips. Lips I would soon possess.

"Quantum, platypus, ostentatious— I'm trying to make it go away," I said, which was immediately made more difficult by Zemila sliding her hand between us.

"Why?" she breathed.

I groaned and the French press clattered from my hand to the counter. I braced myself against the countertop with my hands on either side of her. She moved slowly, torturously, and I let my head fall into the crook of her neck. I inhaled deeply.

I loved her smell, her hair, her taste.

"Good morning," she said, her lips brushing my ear. "Did you sleep well?"

"Gods, yes," I groaned.

"Did you miss me when you woke up alone?" Her words were followed by the sinful feel of her lips and tongue. First on my earlobe, then down my neck.

"Yes," I groaned again, as she quickened her pace. My voice was rough and harsh and I could barely stay standing she felt so good.

"Would you like to take me back upstairs?" she asked.

"I'd like to take you right here," I growled. "Fuck," I bit out before grabbing her by the hips and sitting her on the edge of the counter.

It took only a moment for me to rid her of the purple lace and drop to my knees.

We eventually made it back up to my bedroom. We even made it back downstairs for breakfast.

"Perfect timing," she said when she slid the pizza stone into the oven with the rolled dough. "It needed more time to rise anyway."

She took two steps across the room and kissed me quickly before starting to make a frittata. I watched her move, so at home in my space, and it made something ache inside me. She brought me a coffee but straddled me the second I put the mug down.

She kissed me lazily until the timer went off. We ate. The eggs were good. The bread was amazing. When we were done, I took her back to my room.

For the rest of the day, I watched her body, her expression, her everything as I touched her. I wanted to learn everything she liked, everything she loved. I wanted to take her apart with my lips and fingers then bring us both to that electric ecstasy.

Later, when the sun was passing its zenith, we lay tangled in my bed and Zemila asked.

"Did that thing happen? That light thing?" She twined her fingers in mine and brushed my knuckles with her lips. "It happened when we found you but . . ."

"I don't know," I said, thoughtful. "I don't remember it happening, but I don't think we realized we were doing it before. Right?"

"Right," Zemila agreed, looking off at something I couldn't see. "You have said that Magic needs intention."

I nodded when she paused and looked at me.

"When you weren't healing, I tried and nothing happened."

"Inanna said this new Magic was hard to control. Unreliable," I said. "But I would really like to not ask her for help on this one."

Zemila laughed.

"I wouldn't make you do that," she said.

"I don't want you to do it either." I turned my face into my pillow. I knew it was childish because if we needed to, we would ask. We would be foolish not to.

"Oh my god! You're embarrassed to talk about sex!"

I grumbled into my pillow and squeezed my eyes shut. "With the Goddess of sexual desire? Aren't you?"

"I didn't think of it that way." Zemila ran her fingers through my hair, pushing my head out of the pillow.

I opened my eyes to look at her.

"So, if we were to be intentional, what would that mean?" She blinked up at me coyly, but there was mischief behind her eyes.

"You're not tired?" I asked. I felt like I needed an energy drink.

"You're too tired?" she retorted. Then she reached down and dragged her nails up my inner thigh.

"Ha, that's not fair," I huffed.

"How would we be intentional?" she said. "I want to practice."

She dragged her nails up my inner thigh again and I pushed towards her. She immediately backed off.

"But you're too tired," she said.

"You temptress." I rolled over and trapped her body beneath mine. She laughed her pleasure at winning this game, but the laugh turned into a moan as I rolled my hips into hers.

"All right," I said. "Let's practice."

CHAPTER TWENTY-SIX
Zemila

"Stop having sex!" Jenner yelled from the front door. "I am coming in and your heteronormativity is revolting to me. Please stop!"

"We're watching a movie, you loser," Zemila yelled, and Lochlan flinched. "Oh, sorry," she said realizing that had been directly in Lochlan's ear.

"Who needs eardrums," he said, and she lightly punched him in the arm.

It was after seven o'clock and it had been a perfect day. Though most of it was spent in bed, they did manage to take a shower, go for a walk, and pick up dinner from a local Thai place. Llowellyn was out back in the shed, and Oriole sat begging for food next to Zemila's feet.

"I am coming in to the living room—ouch!—now," Jenner said, stubbing his toe.

"Gods Below, Jenner," Lochlan took a handful of popcorn and threw it at him. The popcorn hit the back of Jenner's hands where they were covering his eyes. Immediately, the dog got up to devour the popcorn.

"You're so dramatic," Lochlan said.

"Boooooo!" Zemila took a handful of popcorn and threw it at Jenner. "Hiss!"

Oriole was in heaven and Zemila let her eat for a moment before pulling her back.

"You know you are going to have to clean that up, right?" Jenner said, peaking through his fingers after the second handful of popcorn hit him.

"The dog got most of it," Lochlan shrugged a shoulder, "but, Tórramh." He waved a hand in the air. The fallen popcorn flew from the ground, landing in a neat pile in the garbage can by the door, and if possible, Zemila fell in love with him a little more.

"Well, that hardly seems fair," Jenner said.

Zemila snorted and Oriole whined in protest.

"Don't you snort at me, She-Devil. Or you, dog of She-Devil."

"She has a name," Zemila said.

"I come bearing gifts," Jenner went on. "Shilton Morningham."

"Who?" Zemila and Lochlan said at the same time.

"Shilton Morningham," Jenner repeated. He placed his watch on the stand and connected to the home system. Then he placed an old-school cell phone on the coffee table and sat on the floor with his back to them. "I found him. Applaud my greatness."

"As soon as you tell me who 'him' is," Zemila said. "I will see if it's worthy of my applause."

"Get those hands ready because—oh god, I don't know what those hands have been doing. Keep your hands away from me! Clap on the other side of the room. Maybe sanitize first."

Oriole slunk under the coffee table, over to Jenner, and plopped her head on his knee.

"Are you here to applaud my greatness, puppy? Or get away from their hands?"

"Jenner," Lochlan's tone was warning. Zemila wasn't sure if it was annoyance at Jenner or at the dog who seemed to love everyone but him. "Who is Shilton Morningham?"

"He was—keyword 'was'—a professor of Theology and Experimental Physics at Northwestern University," Jenner said over his shoulder before turning back to his watch. An illuminated keyboard appeared in front of him and he connected to the home system.

"That's an odd pairing," Zemila said. She noticed Lochlan was rubbing that spot on his chest. She took his hand and linked her fingers through his. Their eyes met for a moment, and Zemila turned back to Jenner.

"And why do we care about Shilton Morning-whatever?" she asked. "Morningham."

"Because, before this morning, we called him the Proxy," Jenner said.

Silence filled the room. Zemila looked from Lochlan's mirrored expression of shock to the old flip phone on the table.

"Yes, yes, I know," Jenner said. "My greatness is shocking, but I will share this honor with Stacey Burbank who uploaded photos to an event for the Northwestern Experimental Theology Club's thirtieth anniversary party."

"Thank you, Stacey," Lochlan said. "Why am I thanking Stacey?"

"Well, mostly you should be thanking me," Jenner said. "Because I wrote the facial recognition software that found the image, and since it is still up, I don't think it's been noticed. But! It was Stacey who uploaded the picture."

Jenner moved his hand over the keyboard and an image expanded on the wall that had been showing a rom-com. Zemila had wanted to watch a drama, but Lochlan thought they'd had enough drama in their lives. When he'd put it like that, she was all for a comedy.

The image Jenner displayed showed a class of mostly women, sitting in three rows. They all wore the same white-collared shirt and dark slacks or skirts.

"School uniform in university," Zemila observed, trying to identify the Proxy.

"That seems a little dated," Lochlan said.

"You're dated," Jenner said, then dodged a handful of popcorn. Lochlan threw a few more pieces at him and he tried to catch a piece out of the air with his mouth, but missed. Oriole hoovered the popcorn, then returned her head to Jenner's knee.

"Experimental Theology," Zemila said. As nice as it was seeing Lochlan and Jenner in their natural habitat, she wanted answers. "What does that mean?"

"Well, that is the question of the day," Jenner said. "I have no idea what it means. The post says, 'Celebrating thirty years of curiosity, magic, and the mysteries of the universe.' " Jenner turned to Lochlan, who shrugged. "That kind of confuses me more."

"Northwestern is in Chicago," Zemila's eyes went back to the picture, finally identifying the Proxy. It was the blankness of his eyes that gave him away.

That blankness was all the more terrifying up close. After the gala, there was a bruise on Zemila's arm where he'd grabbed her. That night she'd scrubbed her body in the hottest shower she could stand trying to rid herself of his touch.

"Correct." Jenner looked back to the image. "The members are a little scattered now. I am a genius, so of course I have found someone of use to us."

"Oh?" Lochlan raised his eyebrows.

"A couple of the club members live on the East Coast. Four live right here in DC. Two of them are involved in the arts, and of those two—" An image of a woman with kind eyes and dark hair appeared on the projection. "One works in community outreach. Meet Martha Ramos."

"You want me to make up a story to meet with her and get her talking about the Proxy," Zemila stated.

"Yes. That is exactly what I want you to do." Jenner nodded vigorously. "I want more details of who he was. That said, this image did allow me to find a few other yearbooks, articles, and journals he was in."

Lochlan leaned forward. "Tell us who he is."

"Sir, yes, sir." Jenner gave him a curt nod and turned back to the projection. "Shilton Morningham seems to have grown up in Pleasant Hill, outside of Des Moines, Iowa. Little to no interaction with the law, stays relatively off the grid until he attends Iowa State. Here I was able to track down a complaint written by a professor about Morningham's views in his Physics, Philosophy, and Theology class."

"Cool class," Zemila muttered and reached down to scratch Oriole's bum. Oriole wagged her tail a little before resettling on Jenner's lap.

"'Mr. Morningham,'" Jenner read, " 'has a lack of empathy for those who do not share his opinion on the balance of power in society.

He has an over-active imagination when it comes to the bounds of science.' It looks like he focused on experimental physics with a minor in biology and then—" He paused.

"And then what?" Lochlan asked.

"He found God." Jenner turned to look at them for a moment, hands raised to the heavens for dramatic effect.

"He found God?" Zemila repeated.

"Well, that. And maybe something else happened too," Jenner shrugged. "Either way, he had a change in motivation."

"What do you mean?" Lochlan said.

"He wanted to become a pastor. He joined a Pentecostal church and was successful for a while. He went through divinity school but was never able to get a preacher's job."

"Do we know why?" Zemila asked.

"That will be a great question for you to discover while you're talking to Martha Ramos."

"That means you don't know why?" she said.

"It happens sometimes." Jenner had a note of disgust in his voice. "He went to Northwestern for their PhD program in Theology, I think, to help him get a position."

"That's a lot of money to become a pastor," Zemila said.

"You found all this off of one photo?" Lochlan asked.

"I may have had some help from a few online people."

"You told people?" Zemila was surprised. She looked at Lochlan for his response. His face gave nothing away.

"I told hackers." Jenner sounded annoyed. "That is hardly the same thing. And I told my tiny little corner of the internet I was looking for this guy. None of us knows each other IRL." He turned away from the projection. "I know you like to think I am this all-knowing super human, which I am. But a guy still needs a hand here and there."

"Aye," Lochlan rolled his eyes. "How foolish of me not to consider."

"He started publishing papers, but I haven't been able to find any yet. Zemila, I hope you will have more luck with Martha, if you are able to contact her."

"Give me something for her," Zemila asked. "Is she involved in any youth causes, anything art-related, any charities?"

"I have the perfect in," Jenner said, and an image filled the screen.

φ

"Hello, Ms. Ramos." Zemila stood from the small round table, in the busy French-style café, and offered a hand. The coffee bar had a long line for take-away and servers moved quickly around tables and customers to deliver sandwiches and drinks.

"You can call me Martha." She shook Zemila's hand and took a seat. Martha was short with shoulder-length hair, thick-rimmed purple cat-eye glasses, and a warm smile. "I was surprised to hear from you. I didn't know JACE Co. was interested in community art centers."

It had taken over a week to arrange a time to meet and Zemila was antsy at the chance for new information about the Proxy.

"We at JACE Co are active supporters of the Day Dream Ball," Zemila explained, raising her voice a little as the noise in the café grew. "We often look for smaller groups to highlight. Your community art group came up."

"Oh, how wonderful," Martha nodded, her big curls bouncing around her head. "Thank you. I read the gala was a success this year, despite the last-minute change."

"It was," Zemila said. "That's where I learned about your organization, actually."

"Virtue has a wonderful collection. I hope you were able to view it?"

"I was," Zemila asked. "Have you seen it?"

"Oh, yes," Martha nodded vigorously and smiled wide. "I took a birthday trip to Europe and was able to see several pieces. I have followed his career for some time."

"Really? Why him?" Zemila asked.

"It is a bit of an open secret that there are collectors trying to find mythological items. He's one of them."

A server with a red apron brought Zemila a coffee. Martha ordered a London Fog.

"Secret?" Zemila said, when the server left.

"Oh, yes," Martha went on. "There are several very wealthy and well-known collectors who believe that certain artifacts have magical properties."

"You're kidding." Zemila looked at Martha in disbelief. "Like, actual magic?"

"Oh, yes!" Martha nodded, excitement lighting her eyes. "Actual magic."

"I can see why that part might be secret."

"Oh, yes," Martha said again, her purple glasses slipping down her nose. "In fact, some of them fund labs to try and test these artifacts for evidence of magic."

"Okay," Zemila smiled. "Now you're pulling my leg."

"No, no." Martha shook her head and pushed the purple frames back into place. "Some help put together whole institutions dedicated to the study of mysticism in ancient mythological artifacts."

"How much money are we talking about here?" Zemila asked.

"Millions," Martha leaned forward, her bright pink chunky necklace swinging at her neck. "Millions and millions of dollars towards extracting magic from ancient artifacts."

Zemila gasped. Hot coffee spilled over her hand. Her eyes stung with instant tears. "Damnit," she muttered. Extracting Magic? Was that what had happened to Lochlan?

"Oh my goodness." Martha hurried to get some napkins. A server came over with a rag and Martha's London Fog.

"Are you okay?" Martha asked.

"Yeah," Zemila sighed, annoyed with herself. "I'm okay. You were saying? Extracting?"

Martha didn't miss a beat and it was five minutes before Zemila could get a word in. Zemila thought she must not get much opportunity to talk about this.

"Wait a second," Zemila interrupted Martha's story of a necklace rumored to carry the gift of prophecy. "Was anyone successful?"

There was a beat of silence. Then Martha let out a burst of laughter. The restaurant went quiet as everyone looked over at their table. Martha snorted and waved her hand in the air.

"I'm sorry. I'm sorry," she said, still laughing as the noise volume returned to normal. "But the look on your face. Oh, it just goes to show everyone—even a journalist—can be taken in by a good story."

"Ah," Zemila said, a little sheepishly. "I see."

"No," Martha went on, composing herself. "No one was ever successful. But that light in your eyes, that moment of wanting to believe, that's what keeps the money rolling in."

"When did you first get exposed to this?" Zemila asked.

"It was my boyfriend in college, actually," Martha said after taking a sip of her London Fog. Unlike the tea and coffee cups, Martha's mug was the size of a soup bowl. Martha didn't seem to mind. "I was studying art history. He was studying physics."

Martha took another sip slowly, as if considering her words.

"I met some of my best friends through him, even though he and I didn't last. He ended up transferring to another program after something—" She shrugged. "I am not exactly sure what happened but, one day, he was just gone."

"What was his name?" Zemila asked as casually as she could, hoping against hope Martha was going to say Shilton Morningham.

"Diego," she said. "Diego Pelton. He was in this club. Experimental Theology."

Better than nothing, Zemila thought.

"What exactly does that mean?" she asked.

"It was different for everyone," Martha explained. "For some, like me, it was fun. Researching where science and religion bumped up against each other. Apollo pulling the sun across the sky in a carriage, that sort of thing."

"But wasn't it that for everyone?" Zemila prompted, and a dark shadow fell over Martha's face.

"No," she said. "No, some people took it too far."

"How so?" Zemila asked.

"You know—" Martha looked out the window. The patio was full of people sitting under big red umbrellas enjoying the summer sun. "I always thought that was part of the reason Diego left. Because of something that happened in that club. There was a night where . . . no . . . I don't think . . ."

"What happened?" Zemlila reached across the table taking Martha's hand.

"There was this boy, man, who was—was—" Martha searched for her words. "Very interested in the origins of Greek mythology and how certain gods could control certain elements. How gods could share or pass on their power. How blood, faith, magic, and science all wrapped up together. He started doing experiments. It was . . . It was hard to see."

"What kind of experiments did he do?" Zemila said, not releasing the woman's hand.

"He—he thought the soul was something that could be captured. Held. Used. He thought it could be a battery of sorts. He thought prayer and intention were powered by the soul." Martha looked up into Zemila's eyes and gripped her hand tight. Zemila hid her wince and didn't let go.

"I don't know the extent of it," Martha went on, her voice darker than it had been before. "He left the club after a while, since none of us were buying in—but the way he talked sometimes. Especially after Diego left. He thought there were people who prayed, who believed hard enough to use magic, real magic. He thought their magic was transferable."

Zemila fought to compose her face, fought to keep everything in check. Zemila released Martha's hand and sat back in her chair.

"What was his name?" Zemila asked.

"I never liked him," Martha said, not hearing Zemila's question. "Diego did, though. Diego thought he was a revolutionary. A genius. Oh, how he would rave about the experiments they had planned and how they were going to prove the existence of magic."

"What was his name?" Zemila repeated.

"Hmm?" Martha turned back to Zemila, looking dazed.

"Diego's friend," Zemila pushed, but she already knew the answer.

"Oh," Martha breathed. "His name was Shilton. Shilton Morningham."

CHAPTER TWENTY-SEVEN
Lochlan

I brought the kitchen table into the living room and set up my computer. Jenner sat cross-legged at the coffee table on the floor. Zemila was projected on the wall, telling us what she'd learned.

"A 'secret' group of wealthy collectors who use their ancient artifacts to get out of paying taxes—shocker!" Jenner said.

"And search for proof of Magic," she said.

"Mayhap this is what has Inanna worried," I said, sitting down and connecting to Jenner's projection.

"Why?" Jenner asked. His fingers paused over his glowing keys.

"This group is trying to extract Magic from ancient mythological artifacts," I said. "And Inanna lost a very powerful and unique Gifter when Heaven fell."

Jenner blinked slowly at me. "I am sorry . . . extract?" He pointed at my chest. "But—"

I grimaced.

"Yeah, I thought that too," Zemila said. "A possible connection between the collectors and the Proxy."

"Are we thinking of you as an ancient mythological artifact now?" Jenner asked.

"Something like that," I said. "The Magical brownout at the gala proves Avery's abilities are stronger than we thought. I can only imagine what's going on at Heaven."

"Qillian is worried about her, stressed. Add to that, he says Candle is making people stronger, more aggravated. Making everything harder. I am a little worried about him," Jenner said.

I exchanged a look with Zemila on screen.

"What?" Jenner said. "What?"

I grinned and Zemila hid a laugh.

"What is this hetero-Magic talking?" Jenner said.

"You're worried, huh?" Zemila asked. "That's . . . new."

"Moving right along, She-Devil," Jenner said.

"Wait a minute." Zemila's expression changed. "Candle gives you wings," she muttered.

"What?" Jenner asked.

"I had a source who said . . . and you just said . . . and if the Proxy is connected—and the Ruiz cartel—"

I was trying to follow Zemila's thought pattern, working to keep up.

"And if Candle makes you stronger—" she said.

"Then maybe the Proxy manufactured this drug," I said.

"Jesus," Zemila whispered.

"And is using it to amplify Avery's abilities," I finished.

"Is that possible?" Jenner asked.

"I don't know," I said. "We'll have to look into it." I turned back to the screen. "We'll tell you anything we find, of course."

"I'll see what I can find here," she said. "I have to get back to work. I'll pass on what I dig up."

"Also, I got the thing you need for Saturday," Jenner said with a sideways glance at me.

"What thing?" I asked. "You know what my costume is?"

"I surely do," he smiled. "But not everything is about you, Lochlan. What I have is for her, the She-Devil." He turned back to Zemila. "And it is glorious. I got mine too."

"Excellent," she said. "I cannot wait to see it." Zemila ended the call.

I looked back and forth between Jenner's projected screen and the man himself. "You're really not going to tell me?"

"Really not going to tell you," he said, as his fingers started to move. "Avery's gift is being weaponized."

"And amplified," I said, putting my costume for Camile's birthday party out of my mind.

"Okay," Jenner swiped his hand over the keys, and a second projection expanded on my living room wall. I sat behind the table I'd brought from the kitchen and put my watch on a stand. "You see what I am doing here? This algorithm?" he asked.

"Aye." I nodded and hit a button on the side of my watch. A blue glowing keyboard appeared on the table in front of me and I got ready to work.

"Here is where I want you to start to implement that program." He sent me to the Virtue Arts Foundation. "There is a site behind this one. See how it is on the Smits Co. Research."

I flicked my eyes over to his projection. "Yes."

"I think we go through these sites, see what we find, see how many collectors we can identify—"

"Then trace the Proxy or the cartel back to them," I finished.

"Sí," he said, fingers fast at work.

The tricky thing about hacking, research, and Magic, was that you needed a specific spell. If you knew exactly what you were looking for, it was easy, but if you only had a general idea, you got general results.

"Here," Jenner said, swiping his hand in front of him. The document on his projection moved over to mine. "Follow that and see where it takes you."

"Sir, yes, sir," I muttered as I scanned the document.

It was a receipt for museum-grade glass, and a generator along with a delivery notice to Hubert Smiths. He was one of our guys. One of the collectors.

"Why this?" I asked. "It's a—"

"But if you look at the—" Jenner started before I answered my own question.

"Battery."

"Exactly," he nodded.

"Nice find," I said. The power storage in the generator was exactly the thread we needed to follow.

"Here," I sent a file to Jenner's projection. A few receipts of a similar shopping list to Smiths' but with a different delivery address.

"Ahh, you think this is the Proxy?" Jenner asked, looking over the delivery order.

"Possible," I shrugged.

"Yes, possible," Jenner echoed. "Can we put that to the side for a moment? I think we can get through this security system faster if you help. I've been seeing this code a lot recently." He looped me into his hack. "And multiple attack points will get us through."

It took us thirty minutes of back-door attempts and password scrambles to get into the server Jenner had located. There were thousands of files on everything from home renovations to taxes, but only one was encrypted enough to stand out.

"Got something," Jenner said, opening the file and playing the first video he saw.

"Attempt five-three-eight," a voice said from the video before a man in a white coat walked into the frame.

A cold sweat broke over my skin when the man pushed a button and an all-too-familiar whirring sound filled the lab. The video showed a large upright rectangle on the floor with cords attaching it to a glass box on a metal table. Inside the glass box was a crystal. An array of cables connected the box to what looked like a small sphere.

"Dios," Jenner said. Light shone brightly in the box. "What are they doing?"

I tried to answer, but my mouth was dry.

"Five-three-eight, failure," the man in the video said. "Five-three-nine. I will attempt a newly acquired artifact. Still unsure what happened in three-six-three, but all attempts to replicate it have been—"

Jenner exited the video and searched for three-six-three.

"Top." I coughed to clear my throat. "Top left."

"Gracias," Jenner located the file labeled "Three Series."

The setup of this video was the same. All but for the contents of the glass box. Instead of a crystal, there was a short sword.

"Attempt three-six-two," the man in the lab coat said. His voice was tired and dull. "A satyr sword, labeled Sword 32 in the collection." He pressed a button and the whirring sound still echoing in my dreams started to fill the room.

"Oh my god," said the man in the video. "Oh my god!"

Light seemed to emanate from the sword, sparks flew from where the glass box was connected to the machine holding the smooth black ball. Quickly, the man turned off the machine.

"We, we—" he stammered, looking into the lens of the camera, all sense of tiredness gone from his voice. "More, balance, more . . ." He took a breath and adjusted a dial before typing rapidly on a nearby keyboard.

"Here," he said pointing to the monitor. "Here we see the reading of three-six-two. We can see the balance was off between the artifact extraction and the containment device." He gestured to the small sphere. "We need to feed more power to the storage transfer and allow the artifact to balance the extractor."

He typed furiously for a few moments before circling the device. He changed the configuration of something out of view and came back to the camera.

"I have changed the S-5 and the 8R-2 power output points. This is so exciting. Three-six-three, here we go."

He pushed a button and the soft whir grew louder and louder. As the sound grew, so did the light in the box. It took a moment for me to realize it was the sword itself that was glowing. It was almost too bright to look at before it started to fade.

But the light wasn't fading. It was moving.

It traveled through the cords attached to the machine holding the small black ball. The ball began to hover above the metal claws holding it. Hover and glow.

As the sword grew dim, the ball seemed to fill with light. Black became a bright glowing silver. The man in the lab coat whooped in celebration before an alarm started. A loud beeping overtook the whirring sound, which slowly died away.

"No, no, no, no, no," the man said, rushing forward. Then there was an explosion of light and the video fizzled out.

"What happened?" Jenner asked.

"Power surge shorted out the camera, maybe?" I guessed.

The video started again. The man was kneeling, picking up the camera from the ground. The lens looked like it had been cracked, but the man's expression was elated.

"Our first successful extraction," he gasped. "Readings on the satyr sword now show it has only a 3.6 power output, where it used to sit around 7.9. Not full extraction, but a start. Our containment device, formerly reading at 0 now reads 2.1. There is a discrepancy. Much was lost in the transfer process. But success." He nodded, smiling wide. "Success."

The video ended.

"Can we see what happened with the containment device?" I asked.

"Looking for that now," Jenner said, searching for particular phrases in the file. "Here," Jenner said. "I am sure there is video of it, but this is what I found."

"Report dated September 26, 2043," I read. "Though we were unable to replicate the results of three-six-three, the containment device still reads 2.1, seven weeks after the transfer. This is when we attempted to move that transfer into a living host.

"This proved fatal for all rodent subjects. The larger rodents seemed to have more resistance to the toxic nature of the extraction device. Subject 12 and 43 tested at 0.85 each before expiring three days later. Most interestingly, Subject 43 tested at a 1.1 as it expired. I theorize it is in those final moments of struggle the animal is able to connect to its new ability.

"Autopsy shows Subjects 12 and 43 had recovered from previous ailments before their hearts gave out under the increased pressure of their new ability. The containment device is still reading at a level we can utilize for further tests. We will begin human trials tomorrow."

Jenner looked at me.

"That was a few years ago," I said, itching the spot on my chest. "I guess they've made progress."

"So . . . they are connected," Jenner said. "But how did the Proxy get involved?"

"I have no idea," I said, realizing what I was doing and dropping my arm.

CHAPTER TWENTY-EIGHT
Lochlan

"No punching this time, Lochlan," Jenner said walking down the street toward his favorite karaoke bar.

"Promise," I yelled ahead to him, shaking my head at the memory. There had been little progress made on the Proxy or his connection to the art collectors' extraction project. Jenner had asked his "corner of the internet" to send him anything relevant, and now it was a waiting game.

"You remind me of the babe," Jenner called over his shoulder to Camile and Zemila.

"What babe?" Cam asked, tossing her short curls over her shoulder with a white-lace-covered hand.

Jenner turned so sharply, his wig almost fell off. He righted it and pointed a finger at her. "The babe with the power."

It was Camile's birthday party, the theme was the 80s, and we were all dressed for it. All except Llowellyn who had elected to stay home tonight.

"I'll be in the basement," he'd said. "I've been meaning to spend some time examining the Spear, seeing how it may interact with the stone."

"Maybe the Shannon will visit you," I'd said.

"Not likely," he'd responded, and I'd left my brother with two of the three Tools of Lugh.

Once More with Feeling was busy as usual.

"Themed party?" the bartender said when I went to get a couple pitchers.

I looked back at my friends. Jenner went all out with high-waisted gray pants, a vest, a puffy white shirt and the most ridiculous wig. Cam looked gorgeous in white lace and promised to sing "Like A Virgin" if I sang "Johnny B. Goode."

"It's a birthday party," I said.

Zemila had been ridiculously happy when she'd revealed our costumes to me. Her wig, though smaller than Jenner's, matched her white jumpsuit and a stop watch was slung around her neck. Though the night had cooled off, I was sweating in blue jeans and a red puffy vest.

"Barely a costume." Jenner shook his head in disgust at Nemo when he arrived an hour after us. Jenner had text Nemo to confirm Cam hadn't invited the guy she was maybe dating before Nemo showed up.

"I think it's pretty accurate." Nemo looked down at his red flannel under a jean jacket.

"You're wearing sunglasses inside," Zemila said.

"For better hallway vision," Nemo answered, pushing them up onto his head

"The bandana around the boot is what does it," Camile said. Nemo smiled at her, and for a moment, they got lost in each other's eyes.

I managed to dust off my guitar skills enough to embarrass myself with a rendition of "Johnny B. Goode." When handing back the instrument to the middle-aged guitarist, he said, "Not bad. Keep working at it and you'll get there."

"Your kids are gonna love it," I told him, and he laughed.

Camile put a fingerless lace-gloved hand up for a high-five, as she walked past me to the stage. I slid in next to Zemila.

"That wasn't nearly as bad as you said it was going to be," she said.

"That's because I stopped playing halfway through and one of the other guys took over." I smiled and reached for my beer.

Cam sang "Like a Virgin," and to everyone's surprise, Nemo got up for a rendition of "Don't You" by Simple Minds.

"A wild success," Jenner said when the lights came on and we were shuffled out the front door.

"I can't believe you didn't sing," Nemo said to Jenner. "Even I sang."

"It was great," Cam said, smiling up at him and taking his hand. I grabbed Jenner in a headlock before he could say anything and hailed a cab.

"We're going the other way," Cam told us when Jenner, Zemila and I got into the same cab.

Jenner was in the middle and crawled over my lap to yell, "I bet you are!" I shoved him back.

"Happy Birthday, Cam," I said.

"Get my brother out of here, please." She smiled pulling Nemo away from us in the direction of her apartment.

"You're ridiculous," I told Jenner.

"I can't help myself," he said.

"I really think you can," Zemila shook a finger at him. "You just don't want to."

"You know me so well, Doc," Jenner smiled. "So, so well."

"I am exhausted," I said.

"Me too," Zemila added.

"A successful night all around!" Jenner practically yelled. We quickly both shushed him. I leaned my head back and closed my eyes.

φ

"Lochlan!" I felt a hand shove my shoulder.

"I'm going to drop you guys off here, okay?" I heard. "I don't want to . . ."

"No problem," Zemila said to the cab driver. The stress in her voice, more than anything else had me rubbing the sleep out of my eyes.

The flashing red and white lights. I got out of the cab and blinked in confusion.

We stood a block away from my house as the cab drove off. Up the street, I saw an ambulance, a pair of police cars, and a fire truck.

Llowellyn was home. Alone.

Llowellyn, I thought to my brother, walking quickly up the block.

Silence.

Llowellyn! I tried again.

Silence.

They wouldn't have been able to get into my house. It wasn't just the home system but my protection spells. They couldn't have gotten in. They shouldn't have been able to even find it. Besides, he was in the basement. Nothing could happen to him there. Right?

I cursed myself for not updating the spells, but they were made to last. They shouldn't have needed updating unless . . .

The only way a spell like that broke is if the caster died. Is a division from Magic the same as death? Did Avery's gift nullify my spells? Was my home protected?

"Excuse me," Zemila said, stepping up to the police tape and getting one of the officers' attention. "Can we pass, we live a few houses up."

The fire truck blocked our view. We couldn't see where they were parked.

"Can I see some ID please?" the officer put out her hand.

"Oh," Zemila said. "Yes, but I actually haven't had my license changed yet."

"I own the house." I pulled out my driver's license. It was a fake Llowellyn had insisted I get when he bought a car. Jenner had put it into the state system. "I have a few roommates."

"All three of you live there?" the officer said as she looked at Jenner's ID, then Zemila's.

"Yes, and we have another roommate," Jenner said, voice tight and anxious.

"My brother has been staying with us. Can you please tell us what's going on?" My nerves were reaching their boiling point as the officer turned away from us and spoke into her radio.

"I have the residence of 34A here. What would you like me to tell them?"

I couldn't hear the response coming through her earpiece.

"What's going on?" Jenner said, more forcefully than I had.

The officer held up a hand but didn't turn back.

"Enough of this." I ducked under the police tape and ran around the fire truck.

My heart picked up and blood rushed in my ears as I saw the police tape strewn across the gates of my house.

"Llowellyn," I whispered as rage and pain threatened to overtake me.

Llowellyn, I thought to him. There was no response. Slowing my run, I looked up at my front door.

No tape.

I looked back to the gate at the same time as a hand gripped my shoulder.

"Sir," said a gruff male voice. "You can't be here."

"Lochlan," I heard from behind me. I turned.

Llowellyn was sitting in the back of an ambulance. His face was tear-stained and his hand shaky. I looked at my house, confused.

Then I realized what I'd overlooked. It wasn't my door. It was . . .

"Louise," I breathed as a stretcher with a zipped-up black body bag was being pushed through my neighbor's front door. "Gods Below."

My knees felt weak as I pushed the officer off and started towards my neighbor's house.

"Lochlan," Llowellyn said again. But closer this time. "I couldn't hear her." Llowellyn turned me around and gripped the red vest in his fists. "I couldn't feel her, nothing. I was in the basement—I couldn't—" He threw his arms around me.

"Louise," I said again.

I don't know how long Llowellyn and I stood there. It was only then I could feel him in my mind again.

What happened? I asked him.

Brownout, he responded. That's the only thing I could think of.

But why? I thought. Why her?

I don't know, Llowellyn answered.

I felt a hand on my shoulder. It was Zemila. There was a police officer who wanted to speak with me.

"How do you know the victim?" asked a man with brown skin and a faded though well-fitting suit.

"Louise Abernathy," I said. Jenner stood beside me. Llowellyn was speaking to another officer.

"Huh?" the detective looked up from his watch where he was typing notes.

"Her name was Louise Abernathy," Jenner said, then he said only to me, "Le dije su nombre tres veces a ese pendejo."

"You know," the detective ran his hand through his short black hair. "I can understand you."

"Bueno, entonces su nombre era Louise Abernathy. Lo voy a decir en español porque obviamente usted no entiende el inglés."

"Jenner," I chided. I wanted to get the police out of here quickly. I wanted to find out what had happened and—

"Listen, we can do this at the station if you prefer."

"No," I said. "I'm sorry, Detective . . ."

"Martin," he said, still staring at Jenner. "Do you have some ID, Mr . . .?" Detective Martin checked his notes. "Hernandez," he said, butchering the pronunciation.

"My ID has already been checked, but," Jenner dug around in his pocket, "here you go, Detective Martinez." Jenner rolled the r longer than he needed to.

"I'm warning you." The man stepped forward.

"I apologize, Detective Martin," I said. "As you can imagine, this is a very large shock. Please, my roommate and I will fully cooperate."

"Roommate, huh?" Martin said, looking at Jenner's driver's license, then back and forth between the two of us. "For how long?"

"About a year and a half," I said.

"And is that how long you knew the vic—Louise Abernathy?"

"No, I've known her longer. I moved here in '44. We are," I stopped, swallowed. "We were good, good friends."

"How often were you in contact with her?" the detective asked.

"I would see her almost every day," I said. "In her garden or getting her mail."

Gods. We were supposed to have dinner tomorrow night. I would never have dinner with her again. I would never sit on her porch drinking sweet tea with her again. She'd never slap my cheek after giving me advice. I'd never joke with her about her mail, or hear about her Harvey, or—

"Mr. Ellyll, hello," the detective said, trying to get my attention.

"I'm sorry," I said. "What?"

"Do you know anyone who would want to harm her? Have you noticed anything unusual?"

"No." I shook my head. It was hard to focus. Hard to remain calm. But I needed to make sure they had no reason to enter my house. No reason to look for Llowellyn. No reason to look into Llowellyn. Or me, for that matter.

"Do you know why anyone might be trying to get into your home?" he asked.

"My home?" I repeated.

"There was some damage done to a connecting wall," Detective Martin said. "There is a chance whoever did this was trying to get access to your residence. Why they wanted to do it through the kitchen wall is beyond me."

"Aye," I said, my mind racing. "Beyond me."

"I'm sorry for your loss," he said, handing me his card. "We may contact you again." Then he looked at Jenner. "Don't go anywhere."

He started to turn away.

"Excuse me," I said. "She lived alone. I don't think she has—had—much family. What happens to her house?"

"Someone will have to hire a cleaner." He scratched the stubble on his chin. "There's blood everywhere. It's not pretty."

Jenner made a pained noise beside me.

"Yeah," Martin shrugged. "Sorry." Then he turned away, not seeming sorry at all.

"They came for me," I said when Martin was out of earshot. "They tried to go through her house. Why else would this have happened?"

"Don't do that, Lochlan," Jenner said, pulling me over to sit on the sidewalk while Martin spoke with Llowellyn and Zemila.

"Do what?"

"You are not responsible for this," he said.

I didn't believe him.

Ten minutes later, Zemila joined us on the sidewalk. She sat down next to me, put an arm through mine and laid her head on my shoulder. Ten minutes later, Llowellyn extended a hand and pulled me to my feet.

The ambulance was gone. So was the fire truck. The police cars might be here for a while.

"I'm so sorry, Lochlan," Zemila said, standing too. "We will—God. There is no way to make this right but, Lochlan—" She lifted her head and looked at me. I stared at Mrs. Abernathy's house. She put her hand on my cheek and forced me to meet her gaze. Her brown eyes were filled with angry tears. "We will make them pay for this. They will regret this."

Somehow, her anger, her rage, seeing my emotions reflected in her eyes, helped. Ruthless though my intentions were, I knew I had a partner in them. I knew I would not be alone.

A light flicked on behind us and my front door opened.

"Lochlan," Llowellyn whispered into the night. "Something's wrong."

Jenner turned quickly and opened his mouth.

"Something else," Llowellyn said through gritted teeth. He sounded tense. "Can we get inside, please?"

"What could possibly be more wrong?" Jenner asked as we all headed to the front door. I cursed myself for not extending my protection spells to Louise's house.

Selfish, selfish, dangerous, I mentally chided.

"Little One." Llowellyn tapped his temple when we were all back inside. Zemila had kicked off her shoes and sat on the stairs while Llowellyn and I stood facing each other in the narrow hallway. Jenner went into the living room and I heard him connect to the home system.

"What?" I said.

"You're gone." His green eyes, a mirror to mine, were panicked and confused.

"What?" I repeated.

"Try to speak to me," he said.

"I am speaking to you," I replied.

"Up here," he softly touched my temple.

We hadn't tried to mentally communicate for the last half-hour or so, but it had come back. Hadn't it? It was only gone for a moment, a brownout. It had come back.

I am speaking to you, I sent to my brother.

My brows pulled together and my lips parted. My thoughts met nothing.

I am speaking to you, I sent to him again, but again there was nothing.

"No," I said aloud. "No, no, not now."

"What's going on?" Zemila asked and Jenner reappeared in the living room doorway.

"Ignis," I said, calling Magic and heat to the palm of my upturned hand.

Nothing.

"Gada," I threw the spell at the front door with the intention of blasting a hole through to the front vestibule.

Nothing.

"What?" Zemila stood, her tone impatient.

"Use your gift," Llowellyn said to her.

"Use my gift?" Zemila said, raising a hand. When nothing happened, she blinked rapidly and repeated the action. "What the—?"

"I'm calling Nemo," I said, tapping my watch and pushing past Jenner into the living room.

"He's with Cam," Jenner said, flicking his fingers over his watch. "I doubt he'll pick up. I'll call Qillian."

After only a few rings, Qillian's face filled the screen of Jenner's watch.

"I was about to call you," Qillian said. Jenner moved two fingers over the screen, sending the call to my home system.

"Are you all right?" I asked, hoping against hope I was wrong.

"The Queen is freaking out," Qillian said. "Everyone is freaking out. No one can do anything."

"What do you mean no one can do anything?" I asked again.

"Magic is down, Lochlan," Qillian said. "None of them can do anything. Across the entire city, Magic is down."

CHAPTER TWENTY-NINE
Lochlan

"What do you mean, Magic is down?" Zemila put a hand on my shoulder. I turned to meet her eyes and saw a reflection of my fear.

"It's not only us then," I said, mentally reaching for my power, refusing to believe the connection was gone.

"Queen Anne is in a panic, she's never been so vulnerable," Qillian said, from the home system screen. "We were hoping it wasn't down for you too. We think—"

"Avery," I said, scratching at the scar on my chest. Zemila laced her fingers through mine and pulled my hand down to my side.

The gala was one thing, but the whole city? No.

"They must have found a way to amplify her abilities," I said.

"Candle," Zemila said.

"The drug?" Qillian asked.

"It's been making people stronger, right?" She released my hand and sat on the couch. "And we're talking about powering down a city."

"Is it the whole city or a targeted attack?" Llowellyn asked. He frowned and I didn't have to read his mind to know his thoughts.

This kind of over-draw would kill Avery.

"We don't know how far-reaching it is," Qillian said. "Would Candle have to have Magical properties to enhance an ability?"

"Not necessarily," I started.

"Though it might," Llowellyn finished.

"Okay," Qillian swallowed. "The Queen, she told me, if you all didn't have access to Magic, that Zemila, you should still have your gift."

There was silence in the room as all eyes turned to her.

"What?" she asked, a quaver in her voice. "Why would I have something none of you have?"

"I don't know," Qillian said. "But she said you should. I'll check in soon."

"Wait," Jenner called out before Qillian hung up. "Do you know where they are? Where this is coming from?"

"I tracked the brownouts to around Wesley Heights," Qillian said.

"Wesley Heights, that sounds familiar," Jenner muttered, flicking his fingers over his own watch and starting to type. "Be safe, Qillian." Jenner looked from his watch to the projection. "I mean it."

"I will," Qillian said, then hung up.

I sat next to Zemila on the couch. Llowellyn stood, waiting for her to accept Inanna's words.

"This is crazy." Zemila looked between me and Llowellyn. "You saw me try. Nothing happened."

"The wall," Llowellyn said.

"Screw the wall." Zemila stood. "I don't have access, just like you. Why would I have access when you don't?"

"Because you are stronger than all of us," Llowellyn said.

"I'm not," she nearly shouted.

"You are, Mila." I looked up at her and reached for her hand. "Try again."

"I—"

"Try again," I gave her hand a squeeze and she hissed out a frustrated breath.

The room stilled as we waited for Zemila to close her eyes. I released her and she opened her right palm.

Her face went blank, serene, then she frowned.

"There's nothing." She opened her eyes and looked at me. "I can't reach it."

"Hmm," Llowellyn said.

"Lochlan." Jenner sat cross-legged on the floor; I looked down. His watch was projected on the wall. "Wesley Heights is not far from Ravenscraig." He flicked his fingers and an image appeared.

It was a map. A neighborhood. A house I recognized from an image Jenner had shown me last week.

"This is the surveillance camera from Ravenscraig, the gated community. Guess who lives there." Jenner didn't wait for an answer. "One Aaron Cartwrytte and his son. This is what it registered twenty minutes ago."

Jenner tapped his watch.

"What am I looking at?" Llowellyn asked, moving toward the door to better see the projection.

"Wait for it." Jenner held up a finger. "There."

"Hmm," I said. "Can we see that again?"

"See what again?" Zemila asked.

"There was a pulse," I said.

"Good eye." Jenner nodded to me at the same time as Llowellyn slipped out of the room. "Here it is again."

Jenner skipped back fifteen seconds and we waited, staring at the image of the quiet neighborhood. And there it was. It started small—and moved quickly. The bubble of light shimmered and expanded out from the Cartwrytte house, covering the surrounding houses, then out of frame.

"Do we know how far it went?" I asked.

"I'll try and find out," Jenner said.

"Do we know how it originated?" Zemila asked.

"We need to talk to Inanna," I said.

"I hate to bring another problem." Llowellyn stepped into the doorway and leaned on the frame. He crossed his arms and my heart sank.

"The Spear is in the basement," I said.

"Right in one." Llowellyn pointed at me, and Jenner groaned. "And I just checked—the door is my bedroom again."

Llowellyn turned and led us to his bedroom.

"The moment is finally here," Jenner whispered as he reached for the handle of his bedroom door. "Not my preferred method of gaining entry to your bedroom, babe, but I'll take it."

Llowellyn opened the door wide enough to throw in a spell.

"I doubt it will work," Llowellyn said, before closing the door with a snap. He opened it again. His well-kept bedroom was all we saw.

"Danu," I said, and reached for my brother's hand. "Mayhap together."

"We can try it," he said taking my hand.

"Aiteal-diamhair," we said in unison.

Nothing.

"Might Magic being down, like . . . erase the basement?" Zemila asked after we'd tried and failed a third time. "Because it's a spell, right?"

"No, it's still there because it's . . . because." I released my brother's hand and looked at Zemila.

"More than likely, yes," Llowellyn said, not needing to read my mind to know my thoughts.

"Zemila," I said, reaching for her. "I need to use you as a bond, a tether to Magic."

"Lochlan," she said, crossing her arms. "None of us has a connection to Magic right now."

"Inanna—" I started.

"I don't care what she said," Zemila raised her voice. "I tried. I can't do it."

"You did it before," I said.

"When?" Zemila asked.

"At the gala. You got through to your Magic when we all had nothing. To Marco," I reminded her. "You made him fall."

"I did not," she said.

"You said to him, 'get down' and he fell," I retorted. "None of us had access and you did."

"He just fell!" Zemila said. "Coincidence!"

"It was not a coinci—"

"It was!"

"Please!" I begged. "Let's try again. Together. Please."

Zemila huffed.

"The spell didn't break because it is deep within the foundation of the house. It didn't break because it is Earth Magic, Elemental Magic. Please. Please try." I held out my hand.

Zemila uncrossed her arms and reluctantly stepped forward. "Fine, but it's not going to work."

She linked her fingers into mine.

"Thank you," I breathed. "Llow, talk us through."

"Zemila," he said, and even though his empathic abilities were gone, is voice was soothing. "Think about how you normally access your abilities."

"I am," she snapped. "There's nothing."

"Slow your mind," Llowellyn said, and I could hear the smile in his voice. "Don't try and force your way to your gift. You are an Earth Driver. The Earth does not need to be pushed. Give into it. Breathe it in."

Zemila took in a deep breath and let it out slow.

"Just be," Llowellyn said. "Think about how you normally access your abilities and just be. The Earth doesn't move for us. We move for the Earth. Even Elementals."

Suddenly, Magic surged through my hand where it clutched Zemila's, as if my tattoos were alive. A dark glow illuminated a path up my arm, through the weaving knots, up to my chest.

"Aiteal-diamhair," I said, opening Llowellyn's bedroom door before closing it again.

"Let's hope th–that, wo–worked—" Zemila was falling.

I lunged forwards to catch her. So did Jenner and Llowellyn. Together, we kept her head from connecting with the old radiator on the wall behind her.

"Zemila," I said, feeling her forehead, the side of her neck.

"Dios," Jenner said. "What happened to her?"

"Zemila, open your eyes," I said, placing a hand on her cheek. "I need you," I whispered. "I need you to open your eyes."

"She's breathing," Llowellyn said. "But I'm not sure . . . Inanna thought maybe—" He paused.

"What aren't you telling me?" I glared at him.

"Ninja Turtles," Jenner said, and I looked up at him from where I held Zemila on the floor. "I hate to be that bitch but you two need to go down your magical staircase into your freak basement and get the super weapons you need."

"I'll get what we need," my brother said, knowing I wasn't going to leave Zemila. "You two get her into the car. We need Inanna."

φ

"What do you mean there is nothing to be done?" I said, outraged at Inanna's flippant response. We were at Heaven's service entrance and I was holding Zemila in my arms.

"I mean . . ." Inanna said, rolling her eyes. She gestured for us to follow her, then walked away. "She will wake up when she is ready, and we have more pressing concerns."

"When she is ready?" I felt like an idiot repeating back to Inanna what she said, but I was scared and confused. "Inanna!"

"You didn't tell him," she said to Llowellyn as we filed into her office. Inanna gestured for me to put Zemila down in one of the armchairs.

"What didn't you tell me?" I placed Zemila's limp body down.

"There wasn't really a moment," Llowellyn said to Inanna.

"What are you two talking about?" I asked, annoyed.

"We will do that later, Balorson," Inanna said, to me. "Right now, we need to figure out what has happened to our Magic. But trust me—"

"I do not."

"She will be all right."

I scoffed at the same time as there was a soft knock at the door.

"Lochlan," Inanna said.

I ignored her.

"Lochlan," she said again using my name as a command, with even more power in one used rarely. "I give you my word, she will be all right."

Even without her Magic, she had power. The word of a God is no small thing. I took in a deep breath and let it out. Slowly.

"This," I gestured at the three of us, "is your null. Avery."

"Not of her own will." Inanna pushed a button on her desk and Qillian stepped into the room. "I am sure," Inanna went on. "Avery is powerful, but nothing like this. Qillian told me your theory. I have not examined Candle in that way."

Qillian held up a bag of pills. The office seemed small with all of us in here, even without the regular hum of power.

"Perfect timing." Inanna held out her hand. Qillian stepped forward and gave her the drugs. "Without my Magic, I will learn nothing from these. It wasn't until I spoke to you, Ethinnson, I truly feared what was happening. Your Jenner was kind enough to share what information he found of the Proxy, and we did a bit of digging on our end. We didn't come up with anything new."

"But why?" Llowellyn asked.

"What is worth this?" I asked, still kneeling next to Zemila. "They think they have the authentic Spear. What could they do now that they couldn't do before?"

"The Spear has several functions," Llowellyn explained. "It is of course a weapon, but because of its age and its long connection to the three of us, it is extremely magically charged."

"So?" Qillian asked from the back corner of the office. "What does that mean?"

"Danu." I sat back on my heels next to Zemila and rubbed a hand over my face. I knew what they were attempting tonight.

"It can be used for a big spell," Inanna answered. "It can be used in place of an old God."

"It can be used to give Balor corporeal form," Llowellyn said.

"But Magic is down." Qillian looked between the Gods. "How can they do a spell if Magic is down?"

"Not all Magic is down," Inanna said, staring at Zemila. "Her gift does not erase Magic. Her gift pulls it."

"Pulls it where?" I asked, standing and thinking of the small black ball in Hubert Smiths' experiments. His containment device. The concentrated power of all the Magic in a city near a door to the Anima Mundi . . .

"I would imagine the Magic is being pulled into your grandfather," Inanna said.

The thought sent a chill down my spine.

"They will have her guarded," I said, thinking out loud. "And they will have their spell room guarded. The corporeal spell is an easy one with an Old God, but challenging for a mortal."

"But they don't have the real Spear," Qillian said. "We have that."

"Right," I said. "The only problem is—"

"Gods," Llowellyn swore. "With all that extra power—"

"—it might not matter," I finished.

"I should have known better," Llowellyn muttered to himself.

"What?" asked Qillian. "Why?"

"Yes, Ethinnson, you should have known better," Inanna said.

"What choice did I have, Inanna?" Llowellyn asked. "I needed it to be believable. To pass any authentication checks Virtue might have done in the future."

The Goddess of Love and War inclined her head and Llowellyn turned to Qillian. "The replacement spear will still work, just more slowly."

"Foolish," Inanna muttered.

"They won't be able to complete the spell. They shouldn't be able to," I said, looking at Zemila. "Unless . . ."

"Unless," Inanna nodded. "And I am sure they will use a complementary amplifying power source."

I already knew the answer. I feared it.

"Souls," Llowellyn said.

"How do you know this?" Qillian asked.

"It's what I would do," Inanna and I said in unison.

Her eyes, sharp and dark, cut to mine.

"Don't look at me like that, Inanna," I said, and a darkness tinged my words.

"Like what, Balorson?" she purred.

"Like we are the same," I said. "We are not the same."

"No," she said. "Not the same. But so close."

There was a sharp intake of breath, and I turned to see Zemila blink awake and look around.

"Zemila," I knelt beside her.

"I know that name already," she mumbled. "I know them all."

"Are you all right?" I asked, looking between her and Inanna. I ignored Inanna's knowing smile.

"Lochlan?" she said. "I'm okay. I'm fine, I'm . . . We have to go." Her brown eyes were sharp and alert. "We have little time."

"How do you—"

"Don't question the Gods, Balorson," Inanna said.

"The Gods?" I looked quickly at Inanna, then back to Zemila. I nodded and offered her my hand. She took it and stood.

CHAPTER THIRTY

Zemila

"The Earth doesn't move for us. We move for the Earth. Even Elementals."

The Earth doesn't move for you, Zemila thought. But it moves for me.

Magic surged and a spray of water hit her face. Zemila opened her eyes.

"You're learning," said the Shannon. Zemila knew it was the Shannon despite being alone in a vast white void.

"Where am I?" Zemila asked the emptiness. Before she could get an answer, she mentally scanned her surroundings.

For a moment, she felt the echo of Lochlan's hand in hers, but then it was gone. Replaced by the feel of his arms. She took in a breath and tasted sea air. She inhaled through her nose and smelt the faint smoke of fire before a gust of wind blew it away.

"Where would you like to be?" said a different but familiar voice.

"Somewhere I can see who I'm talking to," she said, and in a moment, she was in a green field, lush and sweet-smelling. Sun shone through the figure before her. A figure shaped like a woman, but made of water. "Shannon," Zemila stated.

"Yes," the water said in many voices. "That is one of our many names."

"What other names do you have?" Zemila asked.

Water splashed up against the sides of the figure before moving beyond its female shape. One woman became two, then three, then solidified.

"We have been called Abzu," said the woman with terracotta skin.

"Boдa," said the one with narrow, upturned eyes.

"Engur," said the third, whose form kept shifting.

"Ah, Aw, Anuket—"

"Néro, Mazu, Wai—"

"Ceto, Nineve, Ganga—"

The names flowed over each other, mixing into a rhythmic chant. The rhythm moved Zemila back and forth until it slowed and stopped.

"You too have many names," they said in eerie unison. "Shall we tell—"

"No." Zemila held up a hand. "I don't think I am ready for that yet."

"You are," said one.

"You have but to believe you are," said another.

"You will be," said the third.

"Do you have individual names?" Zemila asked.

The three women looked back and forth between each other, in apparent confusion.

"Do you have a preference to the form you hold right now?" Zemila asked, hoping they would understand.

"I like this hair," said the alabaster-skinned woman, holding up her jet-black braid.

"I liked it too, but I wanted more," said the one with a wide, stern face.

"I have no preference for this form," said the third, whose hair had been red and was now black coils.

"I would like to call you Abzu," Zemila said to the third. "Can I think of you that way?"

"I am Abzu," she said. "We all are."

"Okay," Zemila smiled. "Wai?" she asked of the second. After receiving a nod, she shifted her gaze to the last. "Mazu?"

"You always give us these names," Mazu said. "Every time."

"Every time?" Zemila echoed.

"Never Shannon," Abzu said, turning to Wai. "Is that odd?"

"We are all Shannon?" Wai said.

"We are all all," Abzu said. Then she turned to Zemila and asked, "Are you ready for your names now?"

"I'm ready," she said, somehow already knowing them.

φ

"Zemila," she heard from somewhere above her.

"I know that name already," Zemila said. "I know them all."

"Are you all right?" Lochlan asked.

"Lochlan?" she said.

I'm back, she thought. The Shannon sent me back.

"I'm okay. I'm fine, I'm . . . We have to go." She looked at Lochlan urging him to not ask questions. "We have little time."

"How do you—"

"Don't question the Gods, Balorson," Queen Anne said.

Lochlan looked quickly at the Goddess of Love and War. He nodded and offered Zemila his hand. She took it and he pulled her to her feet.

CHAPTER THIRTY-ONE
Lochlan

Inanna gave us clothes. My bright red puffer vest and Zemila's white jumpsuit were exchanged for black pants and long-sleeve shirts. After changing, we headed back to the service entrance with Llowellyn and Qillian. Nemo arrived as we were climbing into a black SUV.

"I'll fill you in on the way," Zemila said, closing the passenger door.

With Jenner's help, getting into Ravenscraig was easy enough. The five of us stood in the shadows of pine trees in the large backyard. The water in the uncovered pool was full of leaves and sticks. The lawn furniture looked distinctly unused. A light breeze moved the fallen umbrella back and forth.

White pillars framed the back door under a curved second-floor balcony. We looked up at the three-story mansion. All the lights were off. All the curtains were drawn. We stood in silence.

No movement. No sound. No Magic.

"This is strange," Nemo said. "Right? This feels strange?"

"Jen, you got anything for us?" Qillian asked.

"When that bubble went up, I lost all external cameras," Jenner said in my ear. He connected us all on the call as soon as we started driving. "I was never able to get a view inside."

"Is the home system still active?" I asked.

"I'm not sure." Jenner sounded frustrated. "I can't get access and there is no working generator attached to this residence. They're offline entirely. Anyone know how to pick a lock?"

"Yes," all five of us answered in unison.

"Degenerates," Jenner chuckled. "Hey, ahh, demigods . . ." Jenner's voice was shy, cautious. "I wasn't sure if I wanted to ask this, and I am asking more so you all know or at least so you all have this in mind and you can think about it and be safe and—"

"Jenner," I prompted.

"Right, right," he sighed. "Without Magic, does this mean your gift-curse thing is gone too?"

There was a moment of silence. I looked at my brother.

"Like," Jenner continued, "the only way you can die is water, but that was Magic, right? So—so can you, are you . . ."

"I've been wondering that myself," Llowellyn said, stealing the words from my lips.

"And I know you have had this creepy vampire blood helping you, but are you back to full strength?" Jenner asked.

I gritted my teeth. "I'll have to be," I said.

"Lochlan." Zemila took my hand in hers.

"This doesn't change anything," I said.

Qillian opened his mouth to speak but Llowellyn cut him off.

"He's right," Llowellyn said. "This is bigger than the two of us."

"No hero stuff," Jenner said. "Okay?"

"Okay," Llowellyn said, and I could hear the lie without reading his thoughts.

"Yes," I lied as well.

"I hate you guys," Jenner breathed. "Just try to stay alive. Everyone will be on the same line for this one, yeah?"

"Yeah," Nemo said. "Good call."

Qillian took a step away and muttered quietly. I could only assume he and Jenner were having a private conversation.

"I'd be furious with you if I thought it would make any difference," Zemila said.

"Zemi." Nemo took a step closer to us and nodded across the lawn to the back entryway. "Go show off."

My eyes widened as I looked from Nemo to Zemila.

"I haven't done it in years," she said. "I'm rusty and, besides, I don't have a—"

Nemo held up a small leather bundle and she scoffed.

"Of course," she said, taking it. She planted a kiss on my cheek and took off around the edge of the tree-lined yard to the back veranda before I had a chance to speak.

I looked to Llowellyn who shrugged, then over to Nemo.

"Yeah," Nemo said. "She looks all sweet and innocent, right? But then she can pick a lock in seconds with her eyes closed and you wonder who the hell you're dealing with."

"But," Llowellyn said. "How—"

"Does she know how to do that?" Nemo smiled. The smile said more than we could get into here and now. The smile was sad, but proud. "Let's just say there were a lot of locked doors in our house growing up."

For a moment, the shadow of memory crossed Nemo's face. He blinked and it was gone. "She got good at being—"

There was a short whistle. My head snapped to the back door.

"Fast," he finished, then he whistled back and snapped his fingers twice.

Qillian took two quick steps towards us and Nemo spoke. "It's open, but I told her to wait."

"Who are you?" Qillian asked as we moved in shadow. Nemo gave a small dark laugh.

"I'll tell you about it sometime," he said.

We crossed the lawn as quickly as we could. Zemila waited, kneeling at the door. Qillian pulled out a Smith & Wesson and stepped in front of us. I wanted to protest but knew it would do no good. With a look from Qillian, and a nod from each of us, Zemila turned the knob and pushed the door open.

Qillian took a few quick steps, followed by Nemo, then the rest of us. We were in a great room with vaulted ceilings and a view straight through to the grand foyer. Two large staircases framed the walkway to the front door. To my left were a fireplace and couches. A pool table and a bookshelf-lined wall were on my right. The moon cast long shadows through the large windows behind us.

"There," Qillian whispered, nodding to one of the two doorways. Then he nodded to the other. "And there. Meet in the foyer after a sweep?"

"Two groups," Nemo said.

Qillian nodded to Llowellyn, who had one of my daggers in his hand. The pair exited to the left, while Zemila, Nemo, and I moved right. I spared only a moment's thought for the lack of connection with my brother, for how much more vulnerable we were than normal. Then he turned the corner and was swallowed by the darkness of the room beyond.

Nemo and I had a short and silent battle of who would take the lead before Zemila settled it by pulling Nemo's second gun from his shoulder harness and pushing past us.

I followed her in to a large dining room and through a butler's pantry. The kitchen on the other side was the size of my entire first floor. We moved around the island, through the breakfast nook, and into an office.

"Nothing," Nemo said.

"We can come back and look through if we need to." Zemila moved some papers aside on the old-school wooden desk.

We went back through the kitchen. There was an exterior door.

"Garage," I speculated, and I was right. "Nothing. Where are they?"

"Let's head to the foyer," Zemila said.

"Jen, you still got everyone?" Nemo asked.

"Sí," he said. "All's quiet on the—" A chocking sound came through our comms. The sound of flesh hitting flesh and a grunt. "Llowellyn?"

I was running before I could think. Back through the garage door and through the kitchen.

"Here," Nemo said, pushing through a swinging door. I was right behind him, but the grand foyer was empty.

"Where are they, Jenner?" I asked, hearing the sounds of my brother fighting in my comm, but not in the house.

"I don't have eyes in there," Jenner shot back. "I can only hear what you hear."

"Llowellyn," I said, as we sprinted through a study, a bedroom, a bathroom, past a home gym, and back in to the grand foyer. "Qillian?"

"Garage," I heard my brother say through the comms, and there was an audible thud. This time I did hear it in the house.

"We just came from the garage," Nemo said.

"It has two," Jenner told us. "I pulled up the floor plan. You're in the foyer?"

"Yes," Zemila almost shouted. I understood her frustration. We had no direction, no means of helping, no way of knowing what to do. The feeling of helplessness was maddening.

"Go through the gym," he said, and we were sprinting.

"Hold on, Llow," I muttered.

"Back of the gym, there's a door to the second garage," Jenner said.

I wrenched open the door and Nemo launched himself into the fray, closely followed by Zemila. I stepped in behind her in time to see Nemo jump from the stairs and knock over a Famorian who was about to deliver a death blow to Qillian.

Zemila hurried down and over to Qillian and dragged him out of the action. His face was a bloody mess, and he was holding his arm at an odd angle, but he was still conscious. I followed close behind.

"Duck," I yelled as a stone fist whizzed through the air above her head. She dropped to the ground, and I planted my left foot as firmly as I could before kicking the Famorian squarely in the chest with my right.

The creature stumbled back far enough for Zemila to pull Qillian away. I advanced on the thing that used to be a man. His stone leg was visible through his torn jeans. The Famorian regained his balance quickly and stepped forward.

"I cannot understand why we would need this," Lugh had said all those lifetimes ago. Only thirteen, he had already been tall and broad as the full-grown men we'd trained with.

"There is value in developing skills away from Magic," Llowellyn had said.

I'd scoffed, thin and weak compared to my brothers. My Magic was different than theirs, but without it, what could I do? I was quicker than them, I knew that. I would rely on that.

It had been centuries since I'd fought without Magic. I hated it then as I hated it now, but I had a new appreciation for our old teacher. Lugh, Llowellyn, and I would be routinely stripped of our abilities.

I had relied on my speed then, against men in armor and in later sessions against my brothers. I would rely on it again now against this Famorian.

I slipped the first hit, his stone hand narrowly avoiding my face, and parried the second. Catching the Famorian's human wrist, I pulled it while striking him in the back of his shoulder, forcing him to the ground.

The Famorian fell. I quickly knelt, a knee in the middle of his back.

I spared a moment of regret. He was a man once. But I had little choice, and no time.

"Forgive me," I said. The Famorian bucked and nearly dislodged me before I pulled out my dagger and plunged it into the base of his neck. He twitched, then went still.

Looking up, I saw Nemo shoot a Famorian in the chest. The bullet hit stone and ricocheted off.

"Shit," Nemo cursed at the same time as Llowellyn, who had a Famoiran in a choke hold, snapped the man's neck.

Nemo aimed for the advancing Famorian's head, but missed. I pulled the dagger out from the neck of the man beneath me and threw it across the room. It sank to the hilt into the Famorian's temple. The demon slowed, stumbled, and fell at Nemo's feet.

"Holy shit," Nemo looked from the dagger to where I knelt. "Thanks."

"Don't mention it," I said, standing and looking around.

"Update?" Jenner asked in my ear.

"All still alive." I looked around the two-car garage. It had a wall of storage units on one side, and paint-splattered garden tools hanging on the other. Four Famorians lay dead on the ground. Two I'd put down with my dagger, one Llowellyn had taken care of, and a fourth was crumpled against the far wall, a dented can leaking white paint on the ground beside him.

Heavy breathing broke the silence. I looked to my brother. His sharp nod told me he was fine.

"Qillian?" Jenner asked.

"Fine," Qillian responded. Zemila helped him to stand. "It looks worse than it is."

"He's got a cut over his eye that won't stop bleeding and a dislocated shoulder." Zemila held a bloody cloth to his forehead. "There must be some Crazy Glue in here or something. Hold this," she said to Qillian who slowly raised his good arm to hold the cloth.

"I'll go look for some disinfectant," Nemo said. "I saw a liquor cabinet."

Before I could tell him to wait for someone to go with him, he was out of the garage.

"The house is empty, Little One." Llowellyn stepped over the bodies and came to stand beside me. Zemila was opening drawers and cabinets looking for glue.

"You can't know that," I said.

"They were guarding something in here." Llowellyn looked around the garage. "Waiting for us. That's how I know. Jenner?"

"Talk to me," Jenner responded.

"Is there anything on the floor plans for this place, maybe indicating a basement, an additional room, something coming off this garage?" Llowellyn asked.

"Give me a moment," Jenner said.

"I got the best of both worlds." Nemo re-entered the garage with a bottle in either hand. "For the cut." He held up some rubbing alcohol. "And for the pain." He held up a bottle of whiskey.

"Glue!" Zemila said triumphantly. She straightened from her crouched position, closed the bottom drawer with a foot, and walked over.

"Eye first, then shoulder," Llowellyn instructed. Qillian nodded.

I looked around for a table.

"Nothing on the floor plans," Jenner said. "I'm looking through Cartwrytte's purchase history to see if that gives us anything."

I listened to Jenner rattle off different purchases and deliveries in the neighborhood, as Zemila and I cleared off the stainless-steel work table. Llowellyn and Nemo moved a body and some scattered debris out of the way, clearing a path to Qillian.

"Sit," Llowellyn said. "We also need a—oh, thank you." He took the offered towel and rubbing alcohol from Nemo who didn't meet his eyes. "Lochlan, would you—"

"Aye." I came around the table and helped Qillian to lie back. While Llowellyn examined Qillian's shoulder, I cleaned the wound on his forehead.

"Where's the Proxy?" Nemo asked, handing me the rubbing alcohol. "Where's Cartwrytte?"

"Where's the kid— OW!" Qillian flinched.

"I haven't even touched you yet." I looked down at him.

"Shoulder," he grumbled

"Sorry," Llowellyn said. "Basic dislocation."

"This will be a second," I said. I took off the bloody cloth and cleaned Qillian's forehead. Zemila applied the glue to his cut.

"Done," Zemila said, when the glue was dry enough for her to let go. "Not the perfect solution but it will work for now." She wiped the cut with rubbing alcohol again and stepped away.

"Thanks," Qillian tried to smile. "Now the shoulder?"

"Now the shoulder," Llowellyn echoed.

Nemo offered Qillian the bottle of whiskey, but Qillian shook his head. "I'm trying to be good." His eyes flicked heavenward.

"Right," Nemo nodded. "Sorry. I forgot."

"No worries, brother."

We looped the bloody towel under Qillian's dislocated shoulder, and he lay back down.

"Traction with the towel, Little One," Llowellyn started. "Do you—"

"I know how," I said. "Qillian, you're going to need to relax."

"Easier said than done," Qillian said.

"Jenner, what's our next move here?" I asked. "Try to take Qillian's mind off the pain. Talk to us, talk to Qillian. Zemila." I nodded to her and she came over and held Qillian's hand on his good side.

"I've got you," she said, and Qillian took in a deep breath. "Right here, just you and me and the scrawny geek who thinks he's prettier than us."

"She-Devil," Jenner hissed, and Qillian smiled. "Okay, amigo, I found a few noise complaints from neighbors about three weeks ago. Looked into building permits leading to that time. Nothing."

I looked at Llowellyn. He bent Qillian's arm at the elbow and braced it against his own shoulder.

"Then I found the Right Waters Party had a campaign office for Cartwrytte." Jenner continued. Llowellyn was watching Qillian, watching the muscles of his shoulder, waiting for him to relax.

"And they ordered a jack hammer, a table saw, and dry wall, and other renovate-a-basement stuff," Jenner said.

Llowellyn saw what he wanted to see and gave me a nod. I pulled on the towel and he pulled on Qillian's arm at the elbow.

"Ahh!" Qillian cried out. "God, that was—that—"

"You okay, big guy?" Zemila asked.

"Yeah, I mean no, but I'll manage."

"All right," Zemila said. "Let's get you up."

"It'll hurt to move," Llowellyn told Qillian. "It will come out easier right now and could cause significant damage. I'd say you need a sling but—"

"We're trying to stop a Demon King," Qillian finished.

"Yeah," Llowellyn nodded. "If you can keep it still, not use it . . ."

"I'll do what I can," he said. "So, what now?"

"Well, there was definitely some construction happening in that house, or nearby," Jenner said.

"And they were guarding this room," I added.

"We didn't check the whole house," Nemo said.

"The noise would have brought anyone else here," Zemila countered. "If there's nothing here, we look elsewhere."

"There's nothing here." Nemo took a step back and held his arms open. "It's just a garage."

He was right. It was a garage. I turned on the spot, taking everything in. The work table was now in the middle of the space big enough for two cars. There was a wall of cabinets and tools, a rack on the ceiling holding skis and poles. Stairs to the main house. The back wall of the garage was blank and white, unused space but for the two garbage bins against the wall. To my left were shelves, winter tires, rubber boxes, folding chairs.

What was I missing?

As I scanned the room, everyone else fanned out. Zemila started looking through the boxes, Nemo was scouring the tools. I saw him pick up a long screw driver. He held it like an ice pick and moved it quickly through the air before putting it in his belt. Qillian, cradling his arm when he could, was going over the bodies of the Famorians, and Llowellyn—

"Llowellyn," I said, stepping over to him.

He was along the back wall of the garage, beside the stairs. The wall was painted the same white that was now leaking out of a garbage bag and across the floor.

"Jenner," I said. "The paint—was that a recent purchase?"

"Yesterday," Jenner said. "How did you know?"

I rubbed my hand along the wall and it came away white. Llowellyn turned and opened one of the black garbage bags beside him.

"Paint rollers and a drop cloth," Llowellyn said.

"Llowellyn," Zemila said, and we turned. Zemila, Qillian, and Nemo were all staring open-mouthed at us. At Llowellyn's bag. Llowellyn looked down too and saw the tip of the Spear peeking out.

"Is that glowing?" Qillian asked. "I thought—I thought Magic was down."

I reached for my power. Still nothing.

"It is down," I said, looking from the glowing tip of the Spear up to my brother. "For me."

"Me too," Nemo said.

"I still have nothing," Llowellyn prompted.

We all stopped and turned to Zemila.

"I—" she started. "I don't want to pass out again."

"We need to know," Nemo said.

"Focus," Llowellyn said. "Don't try to use it. Just try to feel it."

She nodded and closed her eyes. With a sharp inhale, her bright brown eyes flew open.

"I didn't notice before, but I feel . . . more." She stepped towards us, towards the Spear, towards the wall. "More than I did trying to get into your basement. Even more than I did from across the garage." She reached out a hand toward the wall but I grabbed her wrist. A zing of heat ran through me as it always did at her touch.

"The paint is still wet," I said.

"I don't know how we didn't smell it before," she said. The smell was faint, but it was there. "Is this the same as your basement?"

"No," I said. "I don't think so. I think they've boarded up the entrance to another room."

"A wine cellar," Jenner added. "The previous owners redid a lot of the house and submitted new plans to the city. I had to dig to find the original. There used to be a wine cellar."

"That's where Avery is," Qillian stated. "It must be."

"Likely," Llowellyn said. "The null—and the other spear."

"Of course," I said. "It's reacting to the nearness of the other spear. You've outdone yourself," I said to Llowellyn. "A brother weapon is no small task."

"To our detriment," he grumbled.

Creating linked weapons was a challenge at the best of times. How Llowellyn managed it by accident was impressive.

"I didn't know I was back to my former strength," Llowellyn said, "or I would have been more careful."

"Could crafting the second spear have brought back your strength?" Zemila asked.

"Hmm," he said. "No, that wouldn't be enough. It doesn't make sense."

No, it didn't make sense. Not when I thought about it. The replica is overpowered. That meant Llowellyn has been overpowered.

"Can I hold it?" Zemila stepped closer to us. "The Spear. I feel . . . I want to hold it."

"Okay." Llowellyn pulled out the Spear and unwrapped it.

Avery must have been overpowered. Mayhap more than what could be done with a drug. Mayhap the drug made her human body strong enough to withstand the amplification of her ability.

"Did you use any Earth Magic when you were crafting this?" Zemila said. "Anything I would respond to?"

"It was a long time ago," he said.

She took the Spear. The moment it touched her skin, Llowellyn and I both inhaled sharply. The weapon glowed brighter, and I understood why Aaron Cartwrytte had been targeted.

"What was that?" Nemo asked.

"I felt—" I started.

"Me too—" Llowellyn said.

"We're basically in Sunnydale," Inanna had explained last summer when I'd asked her why she'd settled in DC.

"The capital is a door," I said to myself, remembering her words. "There are only a few doors like this one."

Maggie Cartwrytte had been murdered in her home, in this home. But she wasn't supposed to be home when it happened. What must they have found that was worth drawing that kind of attention? What power source was worth that level of risk? Exposure?

I thought I knew.

"Step back," Zemila told us. "Step away from the wall."

CHAPTER THIRTY-TWO
Zemila

Zemila's skin touched the ancient Spear. A surge of connection ran through her and echoed in the Immortals beside her. For a moment, the wall in her mind fell and the haze lifted.

As if watching from outside herself, Zemila heard her own voice and saw herself move.

"Step back," she said to the demigods. "Step away from the wall."

They moved back and she stepped forward. She watched herself raise a hand, palm up, then she and her other self breathed together. She closed her eyes. She closed her fist. The newly painted wall disintegrated.

Zemila was propelled back into herself and she opened her eyes. Thick powder that used to be fresh paint and plywood was piled on the floor where the wall used to be. Without warning, her fingers loosened and she dropped the Spear.

Llowellyn lunged to catch it before it hit the ground. Lochlan reached out a hand to steady Zemila as she swayed on the spot.

"Are you okay?" he asked.

"Zemi," Nemo said from behind her. "What the hell was that? You were flying."

"I was what?" Zemila turned to her brother's stunned face.

"Not the time," Qillian said and nodded at the new doorway in the garage wall.

"Not the time," Llowellyn echoed, pointing the ancient fragmented Spear like a blade to the other side of the new door. "Stairs."

"Do you know what that was?" she asked Lochlan.

"I think Llowellyn is connected to the Spear as its crafter. He and I, of course, have a common bloodline. And this," Lochlan nodded to his tattooed arm. The tattoo was made of an ancient spell, of death and love and blood. Solidifying Zemila's connection to Lochlan or creating it, they did not know, only that they were bonded. "This connects me to you."

That didn't explain everything. It didn't tell her why this Magic could work when nothing else in the city did. It didn't tell her how she was outside herself, or how—in the moment—she felt the power of her other names. But Qillian was right, this wasn't the time. That explanation would have to be enough for now.

"What do we think is down there?" Nemo asked.

"The old foundation is made of pretty thick stone," Jenner said. "I think the call will disconnect. Not sure what good I would be anyway."

"You okay?" Qillian asked him.

"You guys come back safe and I'll be okay," he said.

Zemila turned her attention to Llowellyn. "Plan?"

"We need to find Avery," Llowellyn said, "then shut down whatever is powering the spell that is knocking out Magic, and hope we can stop the Proxy in the process. There is no doubt in my mind they know we're here."

"So, no real plan," Nemo said.

"No plan," the voice of the Proxy flowed up from the basement. It bounced off the garage walls and sunk beneath their skin. "No plan can stop the inevitable. But you, Lochlan."

Zemila felt Lochlan's body go rigid. "Have you come to take your rightful place?"

Llowellyn placed a hand on his right shoulder and he relaxed despite their lack of Magical ability.

"Come, Lochlan," the Proxy taunted. "Your grandfather will be so pleased. Pleased you've brought sacrifices."

Qillian stepped towards Lochlan as well, as did Nemo.

"Come watch your grandfather's rebirth," the Proxy went on. "Lochlan, come."

Zemila stepped in front of him and put a hand on his chest. Nemo stood to his left, Qillian behind him.

"You are so much more than your past," Zemila said. "Or some prophecy."

Lochlan took in a shaky breath and let it out slowly.

"You belong to yourself." Zemila forced his chin up with a hand when he tried to look down. "You belong to us." She let her gaze flick to the men around them. "You belong to me, not him, and we have a job to do here."

She grabbed his chin, angrier than she thought she'd be. Almost too angry to control. She felt fire behind her eyes at everything they had been through and everything they still had to face. But she had waited too long for Lochlan. She would not lose him now.

"Do you understand me?" she asked slowly.

When Lochlan truly met her eyes, she felt a surge of connection. His eyes widened and she knew he felt it too. It wasn't Magic, not the way they knew it. The connection seemed deeper, stronger, more primal. Something the Proxy couldn't touch.

She released him.

He sniffed. Nodded. Pulled his shoulders back.

"Good," she said, turning and heading into the dark hole she had created. "Let's go kill a God."

The wine cellar glowed a pale celadon green. Zemila stepped off the stone stairs and walked forward. The stone floor changed to packed earth under her feet. Empty wine racks lined the cellar and a shimmering wall of light cut the cellar in half.

Lochlan picked up a stone from the ground and threw it at the barrier. It bounced off. He stepped forward to lay a hand on it, testing it. Ripples of greens moved away from where he'd touched.

Zemila followed Llowellyn's eyes. He was watching the movement of several figures on the other side of the shimmering wall. Famorians. Five of them. They paced back and forth, waiting for their next fight. Behind them, a figure knelt next to a covered form.

The Proxy, she thought. And Cartwrytte, she realized when the form moved.

"How do we get through?" Qillian asked.

"How is it even working?" Nemo said.

"Technology and Magic." Lochlan pointed to where several small black boxes were dug into the wall behind the barrier. "It's smart. Ingenious, really. They project the barrier forward so we can't get at the mechanism powering it. They are charged crystals, maybe, from before the spell went up. There is Magic inside the barrier."

"We'll have our Magic inside the barrier?" Nemo asked.

"I don't know," Llowellyn said. "But—"

"Avery?" Zemila's heart clenched.

Through the green-yellow barrier she could see a large metal contraption trapping someone against the wall. Cords ran from the thick metal belt over Avery's waist to a computer on the table next to her. From the computer, the wires ran to boxes projecting the barrier.

"Avery!" Qillian said. "We gotta get her out of there. How can we get through this?"

"You submit!" called a voice over the soft crackling light and Magic. The Proxy stood and turned. Aaron Cartwrytte was visible, barely conscious on the ground. "That's how. You bend to Balor's will. He is ready to welcome you."

Lochlan scratched the spot on his chest and the Proxy laughed.

"Llowellyn," Zemila said, grabbing Lochlan's hand and linking her fingers through his. "Give me the Spear."

He did, and when her fingers touched the wood, she felt that same force try to eject her from her body.

No, she told it. Not yet.

"How cute," the Proxy said, looking from Zemila and Lochlan's held hands to the glowing weapon. "Did you make yourself a spear, Ethinnson? I'm sure your grandfather will be thrilled you have another weapon for him."

The corners of Zemila's mouth lifted as a power deep, deep in the earth flowed up through the muddy ground and into her body.

"The three of us are connected, right?" she asked Lochlan, then looked past him to Llowellyn. "Right?"

"I—" Llowellyn started. "I don't know."

"Worth a try," Lochlan said, holding his hand out to his brother.

When Llowellyn took it, Zemila felt a zing rush through her. She felt the echo of the sensation in Lochlan at the same time as that force tried to push her out of her body.

She pushed back.

Zemila drove the glowing Spear into the first barrier and watched as the smile slid off the Proxy's face. He turned quickly and knelt. The Spear interacted with the Magic and burned through her. She clenched her teeth against the pain, willing it not to move from her and into Lochlan. Pulling the Spear up and around, she seemed to cut an opening in the barrier. Through the hole, she could see two Famorians waiting for her. They growled and screamed and as soon as the hole was large enough, one reached through.

No sooner had the stone arm extended through the hole, then it was gone.

"Qillian!" Lochlan yelled as Qillian dove through the hole, tackling the Famorian.

"Do not let go!" she yelled back when she felt Lochlan's hold slacken. He re-gripped her hand. Nemo followed Qillian through the gap in the barrier. Zemila saw the Proxy produce a red fist-sized crystal. He tossed it between himself and the Famorians. A wall of fire shimmered to life and faded from her view.

Zemila continued to pull the Spear up and down, keeping the barrier open. Llowellyn went through next. When he had to release Lochlan's hand, Zemila felt a drop in power. The barrier began to close.

"No," Zemila whispered. She and Lochlan were trapped on the outside, watching Llowellyn, Nemo, and Qillian fight. And they were outnumbered.

Panic started to rise in Zemila's chest. Her brother was trapped with five Famorians trying to kill him and she couldn't help.

Nothing, nothing, nothing, her mind whispered to her.

A light squeeze of her hand. A soft touch to her cheek.

"You can do it," Lochlan said. She met his bright green eyes. They burned with a kind of belief she had in him, and never in herself.

"You have to believe you are ready," the Shannon had said.

If the Shannon saw this in her, if Lochlan saw it, if he could know so fiercely she was capable of this, she would decide to believe him.

"Okay," she said. Zemila took a breath and focused her mind. "Okay."

This time, when the unseen force tried to push her out of her body, she let it.

Watching from above, and through her own eyes, Zemila saw herself take a breath, and step through the barrier. Without breaking stride, she kept walking, spear gripped in one hand and Lochlan in the other.

"Zemila," Lochlan said, panic lacing his words. "There's a second barrier. He created a—" But she didn't care. She didn't need to.

Zemila saw herself step forward through the second barrier, pulling Lochlan with her. Lochlan grabbed Llowellyn's arm at the last minute and brought him through as well.

"Avery," Zemila whispered to her other self, knowing the girl needed saving, knowing her other self would forget.

Zemila saw herself step back. She released Lochlan's hand, dropped the Spear, stepped through the second barrier again, and returned to herself.

"Jesus, Zemi," Nemo said. She blinked up at him, disoriented. "We've got a lot to talk about after this."

"Let's make sure there is an 'after this.' " She looked to Llowellyn and Lochlan. They stood, shoulder to shoulder, facing the Proxy.

That was their battle, she thought. Freeing Avery is mine.

Five Famorians had been guarding Avery. Two had been shot in the chest and head. Two lay crumpled in a heap on the floor. The last was twitching with a screw driver sticking out of his neck.

Zemila tried to speak when she looked up at Avery, but the words died in her throat. She tried to swallow, to breathe. The thing hooked up to the large metal machine looked barely Human.

Qillian went to a control panel beside the machine. He typed with one hand, his other tucked close to his chest.

"Avery," Zemila said softly. "Avery? Can you hear me?"

"I can't figure out how to shut down the barrier," Qillian said.

"Can't we turn the whole thing off?" Nemo asked.

"It's keeping her alive," Qillian answered and Nemo went to look at the screen. "We need Jenner."

"I already tried," Nemo said. "I think the barrier is doing something to the comms."

"Avery," Zemila said again, and a soft whisper answered her. "Nemo, help me!"

Zemila rushed forward. Avery's feet were strapped to the wall, a platform under each one. Her thin, atrophied thighs were held so tightly to the wall that the leather straps cut through skin. The wounds were festering. Zemila couldn't think about that now.

Her hands were on the thick metal belt covering Avery's stomach. Zemila's fingers fumbled over the smooth metal, trying to find a weakness in the hinges, or a space where the metal met skin. There was nothing.

Avery whimpered.

"I'm trying," Zemila said. "I'm trying. But I don't know how."

Panic was getting the better of her.

"Zemila," Qillian said calmly.

"No!" Zemila shouted, looking at the metal belt and seeing several long needles piercing Avery's belly. "She deserves to live after all this. She deserves a life."

"She deserves to be free," Qillian said, his voice too calm, too serene. Zemila knew what that meant and she rejected it.

"She will be free, when I free her." Zemila moved up to what looked like a heart rate monitor, but placed too low on her body. It pressed against the base of her ribcage.

Zemila looked up to meet Avery's eyes.

"No," Zemila said, when she saw the hope there, hope of release, hope of an ending. "No, Avery, I can save you, I can get you out."

"Zemila," Nemo said.

But Zemila ignored him. She needed to do this, she needed to save this girl whose life had been stolen from her by forces she had no control over.

"I can open it here," Zemila said. "I think."

She reached for her gift. She could open this if she had her gift.

Damnit, Zemila cursed herself. I can feel it. I can feel it.

No, said the voice of her other self.

"Why?!" she screamed, tears filling her eyes and blurring her vision.

"We can't turn it off without turning everything off," Nemo said. "And this thing is breathing for her."

Zemila stepped away from the iron contraption holding Avery and closed her eyes. She reached for her Magic, the gift, the power she felt deep inside herself but could never touch. She dug deep, opened her eyes, and raised a hand.

She pushed and pushed and pushed at her gift but nothing happened. She screamed in frustration. She dug her fingernails under the grooves in a metal panel she hoped would reveal a latch.

"Zemila," Qillian said again.

"No!" she screamed.

"Allah, forgive me," Qillian said, and two quick blasts echoed through the room.

Zemila whipped around. Qillian stood, his feet set and gun in his hand. Zemila looked in horror from the weapon, to the girl, and back to Qillian. But he wasn't aiming at her. He was aiming at the panel beside her.

"What are you—" Zemila lunged at Qillian, but Nemo held her back.

Moving quickly to the panel, Qillian pulled open the now-swinging door. The whirring sound slowly stopped. Avery gasped for air. There were several small snapping sounds. Zemila saw the belt around Avery's waist click open.

Shaking Nemo off her, Zemila went over to Avery and started to free her from the metal contraption. When she tried to open the belt, Avery screamed in pain.

"I'm sorry," Zemila said as Nemo came over to help. "I am so sorry. I don't know how to take it off without hurting you."

"Look here," Qillian said, gently moving Zemila aside and pointing to a small circular disc protruding slightly from what looked like a heart rate monitor. "Something here is going through the belt."

"Ka–Kareem?" Avery's voice was horse.

"Hey, Avy," he said. "It's almost over. I'm going to get you out of this but it's gonna hurt."

Avery blinked and nodded. Zemila saw a tear run down her cheek.

With his good hand, Qillian dug his nails under the small circle. Zemila was sure she would never forget the scream when Qillian pulled. The disc was attached to a long thin rod stabbed up and under Avery's ribs.

Once the rod was out, the belt opened easily. Nemo, Zemila, and Qillian helped Avery down. Her legs were too weak to hold her. Her breathing was labored. Qillian held her in his arms like a child.

"Thank you," Avery whispered.

"I'm sorry I didn't find you sooner, in time," Qillian said. "I'm sorry I—"

She shook her head. "No," she gasped, trying to breathe. "Freed . . . me . . . you have . . . freed . . ."

Avery went still.

Zemila looked away as Qillian raised his good arm to close her eyes. Nemo reached for Zemila and pulled her into a hug. Clutching him to her, she looked over his shoulder to where Lochlan and Llowellyn stood. Their voices were muffled, and Zemila could see the soft glint of a second barrier.

"Nemo." Her tone was worried. "Do you have access to your gift?"

Nemo raised a hand, trying to use his telekinesis.

"Nothing," he said. "You?"

Lochlan's back was to her, but she could see Llowellyn. His eyes were full of pain, of fear. He was frozen in space with the Spear pressed to his own chest.

Balor approached Lochlan, hand outstretched in invitation.

"Zemi," Nemo repeated. "Do you have access to your Magic?"

Yes, said the voice of her other self.

Zemila released her brother and brought her hands to her sides. Pulling from deeper than she thought she could, Zemila breathed deep, knelt, and drove her fingers deep into the earth.

CHAPTER THIRTY-THREE
Lochlan

Llowellyn caught the Spear before it touched the ground. Zemila turned away from me and stepped easily through the barrier that should have incinerated us on contact.

"You're too late," the Proxy said, drawing my attention to him. A surge of power rippled through the Magic-less air. Power I couldn't reach. "Far too late."

Llowellyn and I stood shoulder to shoulder as the Proxy stepped aside and revealed Aaron Cartwrytte crouched in the center of a runic chalk circle. The false spear clutched in his left hand. His right hand deep in the ground.

But it wasn't dirt and mud that Aaron Cartwrytte had sunk his fingers into. It was a stream of glowing celadon-green energy.

"The Anima," Llowellyn whispered at my side.

"The Anima," I repeated, my fears confirmed.

The Proxy had found a place where the wall between world and soul was shallow enough to directly access the Anima Mundi. This was why they were able to nullify the Magic of a city. This was why the false spear was working the way the true Spear should. This was why the Cartwrytte family had been targeted.

The All, the Cosmic Spirit, the Connector, the World Soul, the Anima Mundi—was here.

A metal band around the false spear connected it to thin wires snaking across the ground. The wires were attached to a computer and a control panel holding a glowing smooth black ball. A breeze from nowhere and everywhere lifted the dark brown waves off Cartwrytte's bowed forehead. The spear pulsed and another power surge washed over me.

Cartwrytte stood slowly, looking at his hands, the spear, the space around him.

"Dad," said a quiet voice. My eyes snapped to the far corner of the room.

Cartwrytte's son sat with his back to the wall, as far away from his father as possible. His arms wrapped around his legs and his tear-stained eyes peeked over his knees. He shouldn't be here. He shouldn't have had his life stolen, ravaged by a Magical world he didn't even know existed.

"Quiet," the Proxy said kicking dirt at the boy. The child ducked his head and didn't speak again.

My eyes moved back to Cartwrytte. The slow pressure in the air was building. As I looked into his eyes, I saw Aaron Cartwrytte was gone.

"Balor," Llowellyn whispered as his hand tightened around the true Spear.

"It has been an age."

The King of Famorians cool gray eyes looked between us. He reached his right hand toward me and I felt a dark warmth crawl over my skin. "And you have come to serve. As you know you should."

I rolled my neck as the intoxicating freedom hugged me. It was almost like having my Magic back. I felt strong and capable and warm underneath my skin.

"No," Llowellyn said, deep and calm. The single word pushed against the hold Balor held over me.

"Are you sure?" Balor asked my brother. He flicked the fingers of his right hand and Llowellyn dropped to a knee.

I tried to turn, to see Llowellyn, but Balor had my gaze locked to his. The gray eyes promised strength. They promised ease.

"Do you miss the taste of true power, my son?" Balor asked, somehow standing taller than Cartwrytte had.

I licked my lips, trying to resist. The shameful truth was, I did miss it. I missed it every day. Darkness was simplicity. It was bliss. It was power and control and dominance.

Balor's knowing leer chilled me. When his eyes left me, the hunger building in my gut lessened. His cold gaze settled on my brother. Llowellyn fought to stand—and collapsed again under whatever spell Balor used.

I tried to stay in the room. To be aware of the boy cowering back as the Proxy neared him. I tried to fight the way Llowellyn fought.

"He is my true heir," Balor said to Llowellyn. "And he will serve again. It is destined. You—" he pointed the false spear at me, the wires swaying softly with the movement. "You are churlish. You should be so lucky to have had Birog gift you so."

At his words, I felt grateful. I felt blessed. Leadership and strength? What would I have done with Lugh's gifts? Leadership was a true curse. It was a life without rest. A life of service. No. Not a life for me.

Llowellyn's gifts, empathy and compassion, the poor soul. I could think of no greater anguish than the constant emotions of those around. To feel everything and change nothing is true torture.

But my gifts—oh, how Birog had favored me. Wit, defiance—what more could one need but the desire to claim and the keen eye to see how? I had but to—

"No," Llowellyn said, fighting harder than I was able to.

Was I so susceptible? So weak?

"Llowellyn?" I asked, my mind clearing. I tried to step forward, to stand tall. It took everything I had to fight the urge to kneel, to offer myself to him, to give in to that dark warmth. I felt my head slowly bowing and my shoulders rounding. I fought to stand tall.

"Llowellyn," I said again, hearing the fear in my voice.

That is not me anymore, I told myself over and over, like a mantra. He puts thoughts in my mind, but that's not me. Not who I am. Stronger together. Be as strong as Llowellyn, as Lugh, as the boy in the corner who still whispers to his father.

"Did you bring me an offering?" The Demon King spoke through the mouth of a man. Balor nodded at the other side of the shimmering barrier. "Souls, how kind."

"We also have the boy once the ritual is complete." The Proxy took a knee before the God.

"We may not need hi— help my son, please, please." Balor hunched forward, arms outstretched, eyes terrified and pleading. Then he straightened. Cleared his throat. Looked to the boy who quickly hid his face.

"Not quite finished yet." Balor looked down at the spear. "I guess your craftsmanship wasn't what we thought."

Balor lifted stone-cold eyes to meet Llowellyn at the same time as Llowellyn lunged. I tried to kick forward, to throw Balor back, onto the Spear my brother thrust at Balor's chest, to end this madness and deliver the second death long prophesized.

But Balor smiled. He easily evaded my blow. Raising a hand, he froze Llowellyn in mid-air, spear raised like a dagger.

"Tut, tut, tut." Balor shook a finger in Llowellyn's face. "Ill-advised."

His eyes went from the Spear in Llowellyn's hand to the spear in his own.

"A replica?" his eyes lit. "Oh dear boy, did you try to outsmart me with a replica?" He looked back and forth between the two. He held a hand up, closer to the Spear Llowellyn held. His eyes went wide as comprehension dawned. Then he threw his head back and laughed.

"You poor stupid child," he said, wiping tears of mirth from his eyes. "You created a replica, tricked my man—" He glared at the Proxy who shrank back. "And thought it would not have— help me—have power?" Balor looked down at the false spear. "Did you learn nothing of value with the Tuatha Dé?"

Balor's eyes met Llowellyn's as he waited for an answer. Sweat dripped into Llowellyn's eyes from the effort of fighting the spell holding him.

"Did you, a demigod, craft a spear with Magic using fire on this metal and wood? Did you use water to cool it and not think of the air as you worked? Did you do this in a city you knew to be a door?" He gestured at the small break in reality, the hole in the wall between planes to the World Soul. "Did you not know the Anima was here? You are not that foolish."

Llowellyn looked toward me, behind me, and back to Balor.

"Did you think the Shannon in your life—oh, yes," Balor said at the widening of Llowellyn's eyes. Balor's mouth twisted in disgust. "I know how much she sees you. All of you. Did you think her visiting you over and over again wouldn't make a difference in the Magic?

"A valiant effort," he said, turning back to Llowellyn. "An abysmal failure. Your spear may be more powerful. But mine will do what is needed. You keep this one."

Balor brought his hand up, and rage turned to panic in Llowellyn's eyes. With a slow closing of his fist, Balor watched as Llowellyn turned the Spear toward himself.

"No," I said. "Stop, please."

"You can make this stop, Lochlan," Balor soothed. The Spear tip drew closer to Llowellyn's chest. "You can make it all stop."

"Please, please," I said, helpless to do anything but beg. The Proxy made a sound of approval at my plea.

"I value those I work with, Lochlan. I listen to them. Isn't that right, Shilton?"

"Oh, yes," said the Proxy, his smile widening as the Spear broke skin.

Llowellyn was panting hard, fighting the compulsion to stab himself in the chest.

"Join me, Lochlan," he said.

"Don't," my brother demanded through sharp breaths. "Do not listen to him."

The Spear sunk an inch into Llowellyn's chest when Balor said, "We'll leave it there for now. Can't have you dying too quickly. I am sure Shilton will have a use for you."

"Thank you." The Proxy bowed his head. "Thank you."

Balor's eyes slid from Llowellyn to Zemila, Nemo, and Qillian. "I'll kill them," he said to me. "I will eat their Spark and banish their souls."

A soul banished was never at rest. An eternity of hanging in the balance. Forever waiting for nothing. Few things were worse than such a fate.

"Calm yourself, Balorson," Balor said, waving the false yet powerful spear in my direction. Calm washed over me. "Your friends will be spared when you submit."

He wore the dark slacks, pale blue shirt, and smile of a politician. "You believe you're—help him, please!!— here to complete the prophecy?" Balor said. "I see no sword, and I have the Spear here in your brother's chest." Balor pressed the Spear deeper and Llowellyn groaned.

"Have you the—my son, save my son!— stone?"

My brows drew together in confusion. The Proxy recoiled. Llowellyn's eyes moved from the Spear lodged in his chest to the boy huddled in the corner. The boy looked up at the puppet his father had become.

Could Balor not hear, not feel how hard Aaron Cartwrytte was fighting to reclaim his body? He couldn't feel the proximity of the stone. Llowellyn wore it under his shirt. Mayhap it was why he was able to resist, able to fight back.

"You will be better off, Lochlan." Balor pointed the false spear at me again. "Better off accepting your nature. That's all I want. Acceptance. We are the power that should rule this plane of existence." He stepped toward me and placed a hand on my cheek.

"I would allow you your pets, of course. I would allow you so much. But this plane needs the chaos of the Old World. Does it not? You cannot tell me it is better now than it was?"

Balor turned away. He stepped over the long wires attaching the false spear to the Anima Mundi. It fed power into him. It allowed him to inhabit Cartwrytte's body.

"We can save this world. Restore it." Balor stood tall, righteous. He looked over his shoulder and hissed, "It is not easy to bear the weight of difficult decisions for the greater good."

His gray eyes were earnest.

"When was this world at its best? Where was there the most unity, the most compassion?" His eyes flicked to Llowellyn and back to me. "The most faith. It was when order and chaos ruled equally, openly. Now even the chaos of this world is ordered," he said in disgust.

"Salvation requires someone to bear the weight of destiny no matter the cost. This world needs saving. The belief in one's own redemption requires one to carry the burdens of fate, undeterred by its price. Can you bear the burden of your own redemption, Lochlan?"

Could I? I wasn't sure. I didn't know if I would ever reach what I sought. That promised land seemed so far away. Is Balor's version of redemption the only peace I will receive? The only quiet I'm worthy of?

"Will you seek that redemption with me? Will you help me right the world? Bring back the balance of chaos and order." He reached out his hand, offering it to me. "It is a haven for us, for everyone."

Out of the corner of my eye, Llowellyn spoke, yelled maybe, but I heard nothing. The Proxy watched with a look of fascination and malice.

I doubted myself, my strength, my ability to stay strong as the waves of power washed over me again and again.

My hand moved of its own accord, reaching towards my grandfather. My salvation was there, just there, in the hand Balor offered.

And I wanted it. I wanted the quiet of confident power. The peace of knowing those around me were untouchable.

No, whispered a small voice, a familiar voice, a voice that felt like home.

No, it said so softly I could barely hear it.

Balor's eyes snapped to mine. I didn't think I'd spoken aloud.

"No," I heard again as the ground shook. The smell of sweet earth and something else filled my senses as power radiated up my left arm, and over my chest. It filled the dry well of my body and exploded out of me.

"No," I told Balor Famorian King, his hold over me again broken. "I will not help you throw this world into your chaos, your order, your new world.

"Nartha," I said, feeling stronger than I had in months. The spell moved from my chest, down the knots on my arm and out, toward my brother, still fighting to stand.

Stronger together, I heard in my mind the moment the Magic touched him.

"Not alone," I said aloud.

I called Magic. "Ag mo ag mo breatha, aire cagair-gada, beannachd nartha, beannachd nartha."

I didn't know where the power surge had come from. All I hoped was I had enough to give to Llowellyn as well.

Not alone, Llowellyn said in my mind.

Llowellyn roared aloud and pulled the splintered wood out from inside his chest.

"Stop!" the Proxy yelled, as Llowellyn lunged at our grandfather, Spear in hand. "NO!"

"Forgive me," Llowellyn said, meeting eyes with Aaron Cartwrytte and plunging the spear into his heart.

Cartwrytte turned away from Llowellyn and stumbled toward me. He clutched my shoulder and collapsed forward.

"My son," he said, and pushed weakly on my chest to look me in the eye. I looked down and saw the Magical Spear deep in his chest.

"Aaron?" I asked.

"Protect—" Blood coated his lips. "My son."

"Aaron, oh gods, I am so sorry," I said, guiding him to the ground. We knelt facing each other.

"My," he gasped, "s–s–son."

"Aaron," I asked again, but the light behind his eyes went out.

A crash sounded in the dank basement and the machine the false spear had been attached to started to smoke, then catch fire. The ground shook and the hole exposing the Anima Mundi closed.

"We must leave, Little One," my brother said.

"Aaron." I shook his limp form, knowing it was useless.

"Lochlan." My brother pulled me to my feet, shaking me.

"Lochlan," Zemila said to my right. I felt her hand on my shoulder. I turned to meet her eyes. "Lochl—"

"The boy," I said, guiding the body of Aaron Cartwrytte to the ground. I looked to the place the child had been huddled, watching us fail to save his father. "Where is—"

"Gone," Llowellyn said.

The fire grew.

"Gelum," I flicked my fingers at the flame and the spell turned it to a block of ice.

"Lochlan," my brother said, and I heard caution in his voice.

"The boy," I grit through my teeth, "Where is the boy?"

My eyes searched the basement.

"He's gone."

I turned to see the speaker. Qillian stood, cradling his arm. Nemo was beside him carrying the limp body of Avery.

"Gone where?" I asked, fury laced in every word.

"There was another exit. The Proxy took him. He's gone."

CHAPTER THIRTY-FOUR
Lochlan

No black. That's what the invitation said. I wasn't sure who sent it to us, which of Mrs. Abernathy's friends knew who I was, but the invitation said Louise Abernathy requested a day of laughter and light.

So much of what I wore was black and gray. Jenner eagerly took up the task of dressing me. We were close to the same height but I was wider than him.

"These are a little big on me," he had said, throwing light gray slacks at my face. "You can wear it with your white dress shirt."

Mrs. Abernathy's funeral was held at the Mount Zion Church. It was standing room only.

"For her." Llowellyn leaned over to me from where we stood at the back with Nemo. Zemila, Jenner, and Qillian were able to find seats. "Are you surprised?"

"Not at all," I said, the bittersweet tang of a life well-lived clutching at my chest.

Nemo smiled and blinked rapidly. "Mrs. A was a real one."

Mrs. Abernathy's friends and past co-workers told stories and I learned things she'd never shared. A man stood and spoke of his relationship with Mrs. Abernathy and her son, who'd been a social worker before he died. "The family I never knew I needed," the man said.

A woman stood and shared how she had first met Mrs. Abernathy. "She held my hand in the waiting room," the woman said. "I didn't know she'd helped open the clinic."

When the service was done and it was time for her to be laid next to her husband and son, Llowellyn, Nemo, and I waited under a few trees outside the church. The mass of brightly colored hats and dresses spilled out into the late October air.

Zemila didn't see us as she walked past, but I saw her. This morning, before we left the house, Zemila had looped a yellow tie she'd bought for me around my neck.

"You work so hard to be unremarkable," she'd said. I'd looked away. "You know Mrs. Abernathy is getting a kick out of me forcing us to match."

I'd let out a half chuckle, half sob and I'd wiped my eyes.

"I'm sure she is," I'd said.

Zemila's yellow sundress next to Jenner's mint and pink floral-print suit was hard to miss. Qillian was a bit more subdued in maroon. I only watched Zemila for a moment before she stopped and turned. Bright brown eyes met mine and I couldn't keep the smile from my lips.

I saw her say something to Jenner. They extricated themselves from the crowd and headed toward us.

"You guys okay?" she asked. She hugged her brother, who'd barely spoken all day.

"I feel her presence so strongly," Llowellyn said. "Like she's still here—"

"Oww," said Jenner, turning to Qillian who'd poked him in the shoulder. Nemo and Zemila broke apart. "Why did you do that?"

"Get over yourself," Qillian smiled.

"Why did you aggressively poke me?" Jenner asked.

"Because didn't I say that too, and you made fun of me?"

Jenner looked sheepishly from Qillian to Llowellyn, then to the ground.

"Yes," he admitted. "Yes, I did."

"Fascinating," Llowellyn said, looking at Qillian. "And you are completely Human."

"Hey." Jenner looked from Llowellyn to Qillian and back. "Hey, don't look at him like that, don't look at him like that. He's mine, you're both mine, but separately. I am allowed to look at you like that, you may look at me like that, but not each other. Mine!" he said, linking his fingers in Qillian's and pulling him away after the precession.

"We'll talk," Qillian said over his shoulder to Llowellyn before gesturing to Nemo. "Let's go, Kev."

"You won't!" Jenner yelled. "Sister-stealing—" Qillian clapped a hand over Jenner's mouth and Nemo chuckled before following them.

Zemila shook her head, smiling. We stood in silence for a moment, the sun high and the breeze cool.

Perhaps I could feel Mrs. Abernathy here, in a way.

Zemila walked over and stood between Llowellyn and me.

"Shall we?" she said, offering me her hand and nodding after Jenner and Qillian. I took in a deep breath and let my shoulders drop.

"Yeah," I said.

"You too." Zemila offered her other hand to Llowellyn who took it.

We walked, hand in hand in hand. Despite the sorrow, the guilt, the shame, I felt a sense of wholeness too.

The burial didn't take long. Only a few more words were spoken. The five of us stood slightly away from the other mourners. Separate from their world, but still in it. A song carried across the cool breeze as Louise Abernathy was laid to rest with her kin. Zemila squeezed my hand and I tried to blink away my tears.

Before long, the large group began to disperse. No doubt making their way back to their cars and on to the celebration of life in the basement of Mrs. Abernathy's church.

Nemo sat at the base of a tree; I leaned against it. We watched the bright colors move toward the parking lot. Zemila and Jenner sat on a bench in the sun, not far off. Llowellyn and Qillian were deep in conversation beside us about the real and theoretical links between Faith and Magic.

I noticed a pair of women break off from the group and head in our direction. I looked behind me, unsure if there were cars over here. Were they headed to us?

"Lochlan," I heard Mrs. Abernathy say and Nemo's head snapped up. He tossed away the small stick he'd been digging into the ground and I closed my eyes against the bittersweet memory of my friend.

"Lochlan?" I heard again.

I opened my eyes. A tall dark-skinned woman with a bright pink cane and laugh lines looked at me with a question in her eyes. "You must be Lochlan. Louise said you'd be hiding in the back somewhere."

"That's what she said," said the second woman. She had a medium build, pale skin, and a large floppy hat protecting her face from the sun.

"Hello." I pushed off the tree and stepped towards them.

"Just as she described," said the first woman. "I'm Wanda, this is Suzie. We played cribbage or some such with Louise every week."

"Every week," Suzie echoed. "Mahjong, dominoes too, 'til it would get too heated."

"Oh." I extended my hand to Wanda, then Suzie. Llowellyn and Qillian stopped their conversation to listen. "Very nice to meet you."

"You too, hon," Wanda nodded. "Finally. Listen here, Lou-Lou wanted us to make sure you came today, and that you got a couple other things from her."

"Things from her to you," Suzie clarified. "You and some others."

"She told us you might not come unless you got an invitation, old-school," Wanda smiled.

"We like old-school," Suzie nodded.

"You sent me the invitation," I said. "But how did she—how . . ."

"She knew a lot of things, but she didn't know her time," Wanda answered my unasked question.

"Didn't know her time." Suzie shook her head. "Who does?"

"Who does, indeed," Wanda agreed. "But when you're old like us—"

"Like us," Suzie said as though she was singing back up at the church of Wanda.

"You prepare," Wanda nodded solemnly. "You make sure those who love you and who you leave behind have what they need, and do what you want." Wanda pointed a finger at me to emphasize her words.

"Mmm-hmm," Suzie nodded.

"And Mrs. Abernathy wanted . . ." I trailed off, waiting.

"We have a letter here, for one Zemila Alkevic," Suzie said. Zemila stood from the bench and walked over to us. "She gave this one to us just a couple months ago. We have a box, see, where we all put the letters we want goin' out after we go." Suzie handed Zemila the letter. "This was the most recent addition."

"Jensilvadonner Hernandez," Wanda said holding out a bright pink envelope. Jenner burst into tears from his seat on the bench.

"I'll give it to him," Zemila offered and Wanda handed it over.

"Nemanja Alkevic," Suzie held up a small box. "That'll be you then? There is a note inside." She tossed the box to Nemo who was still sitting at the base of the tree.

"Llowellyn MacEthan," Suzie said. She held up a recipe card.

"No way," Llowellyn said.

"Way," Suzie nodded, handing him the card. "Glad to see you'll treat that like the gift it is. You keep it to yourself, you hear?"

"Yes, ma'am," Llowellyn said.

There was a stretch of silence as the two women looked at me. And I looked back. I wanted something too, I wanted to know I was important to her, as important as she was to me.

But did I deserve it? She wasn't here anymore because of me. Because I couldn't . . . no . . . because I didn't protect her. I deserved nothing but atonement for this sin and all my others.

I looked away from Wanda and Suzie, no longer able to meet their eyes.

"I called the city after it happened," Wanda said. I could feel her eyes examining me. "I called and asked what to do about—about her house, about cleaning her house."

I swallowed, nodded. I'd called too.

"They gave me a number," Wanda said, a hint of annoyance creeping into her voice. "Which I called, and they gave me another number, which I called. It went on like that for a little while until finally I got in touch with an organization that took care of that kind of thing. Young man, do you know what they told me?" She paused.

I didn't speak.

"Of course you do. They said, 'Ma'am, we went by the home to do the consult, to give you a quote.' I said, 'Yes.' Then they told me, 'Ma'am, there was a young man there. He was already cleaning. He was mostly done. Must have been cleaning through the night, looked exhausted.' "

It had taken me a day and a half to get all the blood out. I'd torn out the carpet in the front hall. I'd scrubbed the grout in the kitchen. The white living room loveseat was covered in plastic, so that was spared, but the paisley patterned couch was a lost cause. It had to be fully reupholstered.

The walls were the hardest part. After the upholstery and stuffing were gone, after the carpet had been taken out, after the kitchen was mopped, there were the walls.

I'd scrubbed them for hours, refusing to accept help. The only Magic I'd used was to bar Llowellyn's entry. I'd cleaned it alone. I'd washed away Louise's blood in hopes the act would leave my soul feeling cleaner too.

It didn't.

Wanda waited for me to meet her eyes. "Did she ever tell you about her son?"

"Very little," I said, still staring at my shoes. "I didn't ask. I could see it hurt her to think of him."

"It did," Suzie nodded.

"She always had this dark cloud over her since Antoine passed," Wanda said. "I'd grown up with Lou-Lou, you see. Some people are born to be mothers, caregivers—that's their gift, and that was hers."

"That was hers," Suzie nodded.

"We moved up here. She was so protective of Antoine. Still, she let him live at the same time." Wanda said it with reverence. "A balancing act I'd never achieved with my children."

"Nor I with mine," Suzie shook her head.

"He wanted to be a social worker with the police. Went to school to be an officer and everything. He was already a social worker see, but thought he could do more. He was shot on the job in his first year. She was never the same."

"Nope," Suzie shook her head sadly. "Never the same. Not 'til 'bout some four years ago."

I looked up, finally meeting their eyes.

"That's right," Wanda said. "Four years ago, something changed. She didn't tell us what at first."

"Played it close to the chest, you see," Suzie said.

"She showed up to Mahjong one day and seemed . . ." Wanda trailed off and smiled.

"Lighter," said Suzie.

"Happier," said Wanda. "Took some three, four months for her to tell us—"

"That she'd been bullying her new neighbor to have tea with her near every single day," Suzie finished.

I blinked rapidly. I tried not to let the full weight of what I'd lost land on me.

"She said it was like she had her son back." Wanda reached out and patted my cheek, just as Mrs. Abernathy had done. "She was so proud of you."

I laughed in disbelief. What could she have been so proud of? What did she even know?

"Don't believe us?" Suzie said.

"Lochlan has finally got a job, Lochlan has finally joined the community center," Wanda said in an impressive impersonation of Mrs. Abernathy. "Lochlan is starting to accept his brother's death was not his fault."

"Lochlan has finally got a friend, Lochlan has got himself a girl," Suzie said. "Lochlan's girl has a boyfriend but I don't think it will last too long."

I laughed in earnest.

"I got to meet Lochlan's friend, I got to meet Lochlan's girlfriend, and on and on she went." Wanda smiled. It was a sad, knowing smile. " 'Lochlan takes everything on his shoulders,' she would say to us. 'I wish he would let me help.' "

"She did," I said through the tears. "She helped."

"Before I tell you one last thing she'd always say, let me give you what's yours now." Wanda handed me a large manila envelope and a set of keys. "She left you her house."

"What?" I said, looking from the keys in my hand to Wanda to Suzie.

"That there," Suzie pointed to the envelope, "are instructions on what to do with the financial side of things, what to donate and where to donate it. She left you . . . everything."

"I don't— I—" I couldn't accept and didn't know how to give it back. I knew she had little to no family, but I was not deserving of this. I opened my mouth to protest. Wanda cut me off.

"The last thing she would always tell us, about you," she said.

"Tell him the last thing before he tries to give this all back," Suzie said.

"The thing she'd tell us about you more than anything else, more than your kindness, more than your bravery, more than your compassion, was with you she felt whole again. She felt like she could go on living a little while longer. She said she wasn't sad anymore.

"She would tell us over and over and over again." Wanda sighed, smiled, patted me on the cheek one more time. "She would tell us you saved her life."

CHAPTER THIRTY-FIVE
Zemila

Zemila didn't know why she lied to Lochlan, to everyone, about where she was going. All she knew was after reading the letter from Mrs. Abernathy, she needed time to think. She needed answers.

Zemila took a cab from the cemetery across town. On the way, she read the letter again and again. There was one paragraph, one spot that had spurred her into action. One part of this beautiful letter that made Zemila act on what she'd known she'd have to do for a long time.

"Welcome," said an androgynous voice. "Welcome to Heaven."

Five minutes later, letter still in hand, Zemila sat in an uncomfortable chair across from the only person who might know what was happening to her.

"Little Luman girl," Queen Anne said, drumming her gold-painted fingernails on the oak desktop. "What do you have for me?"

"A story," Zemila said. "In exchange for some answers."

"Answers to what?" the Queen asked. Zemila was sure she already knew.

"What I am," Zemila said.

"You keep telling me you are an Earth Driver."

"I don't believe that anymore." Zemila lifted her chin. "Llowellyn has suggested I am an Earth Elemental."

"Earth, yes, Elemental, no," the Queen said. "No, I do not think that is the case."

"What do you think?" Zemila clutched the letter tight in her hand.

"Tell me first why you no longer believe yourself to be an Earth Driver," Queen Anne leaned back in her chair.

"Okay," Zemila swallowed. "Okay," she repeated, organizing her thoughts. "This thing has been happening . . . all my life. But I thought it was in my head, you know?"

Zemila looked up at Queen Anne who gestured for her to continue.

"It started when I was a kid, and my dad did something really horrible to Nemo or my mom. He would turn to me. Nemo and my mother would cower before him. Not me. This little voice in my head would say 'no' and I would stand tall. 'My strong girl,' he would say.

"As I got older it happened less or maybe I noticed it less. I tried to talk to Nemo about it once, about the voice, but he didn't understand, or I didn't explain it properly. I thought it was me. This voice was in my head, so it's me. Right?"

Queen Anne's eyes were bright with interest. She leaned forward.

"That's all the voice would ever say. Just 'no' and then I would be okay." Zemila drifted off into thought.

"And then," Queen Anne said. Zemila snapped back.

"After Lochlan was taken, it came back. Back like when I was a girl."

"And when Magic was down," Queen Anne prompted.

"Yes," Zemila said. "When Magic was down, I still had power. Not the same, not as easy to access, but I had it. Sometimes stronger than ever.

I had to focus, had to dig, but when I dug in my mind, I think I—I think I—"

"Yes?"

"I think I woke something up," Zemila said. "There was this wall, a Magical wall that we couldn't get through at the Cartwrytte house. The voice asked, I said yes, and then we were through. And then Balor was there, and I was so scared, Lochlan and Llowellyn were trapped with him and I had no idea what to do. I kept thinking, they're going to die because they don't have their Magic.

"And then something happened. In my head, in my—" She flattened Mrs. Abernathy's letter to her chest. "I thought 'no' and I dug my fingers into the ground. I pulled on a Magic deeper than I knew existed. I pushed that Magic through my bond with Lochlan, a bond I didn't know I had. I pushed it into him, and then . . ."

"You restored his connection."

Zemila nodded and asked, "What does it mean?"

"What do you think it means?" Queen Anne sat a little straighter.

"I think it means I am an Elemental." Zemila thought back to Ember's words months ago.

"I feel you pull on my fire," Ember had said. "My element, when we train."

"That I have a connection to all the Elements," Zemila went on. "But my strongest connection is to the earth."

"Earth Magic is incredibly powerful," Queen Anne said.

"I think as an Elemental, I was able to access Magic deeper than the spell blocking it. And that is why I still had my abilities."

"Not a bad theory," Queen Anne said. "But I think you could aim a little higher."

"Higher?" Zemila asked.

"Higher on the proverbial food chain. As I said before, Earth, yes. Elemental, no."

"But what does that mean?" Zemila asked, still confused.

"I do not think you are an Elemental," Queen Anne said. "I think you're an Element. One of the four Elements. I think you are Earth."

Remember child, we are everything the women before us hoped we'd be and more. They carved us space, clawed it by their fingernails, and we carry that strength and their determination with us every day. We carry in our bones the knowledge of that ruthless power, the knowledge that we can prosper against all odds. I said to you before, and it's still true—we are resilient beyond our wildest imaginings. We may lose our way. We may feel lost and alone. Maybe even helpless and worried. Always remember, we control the ride. We have but to grab the wheel and steer.

Louise Abernathy, in a letter to

her friend, Zemila Alkevic

This novel is over, but Sahrias's story continues in:

BLOOD, KIN, AND CURSES

Enjoy a free preview now.

Dyson hated that her hands were covered in blood. Again. She hated the scent of fear in the air and how it mixed with the sour tang of Magic gone wrong. She hated the ache in her swollen knuckles when she loosened her clenched fists.

She'd known she'd end up here, in this room.

Eventually.

This room, or one just like it. As soon as she'd learned how the Magical protections worked, Dyson had known it was inevitable. Only she could get through the barrier. Only she could end the war.

And she hated that too.

Her eyes traveled over a broken settee and the remnants of a table. They fell on the door to the en suite bathroom. She looked down at her hands. Some of the dark red liquid was hers. Most wasn't. Some of it had dried and crusted, looking like it would flake right off. Most of it was fresh and gleaming.

Using one hand to gather the light, flowing fabric of her black dress, and the other for balance, she walked through the vestiges of what was once a lavish bedroom. It was harder than it should have been. She stumbled twice, fell once, but finally managed to crawl to the sink in the bathroom.

"Almost like the first time I died," Dyson said, leaving a trail of deep red hand prints on the white and gold tile beneath her palms.

The first time she'd been covered in blood, about to fall into the waiting arms of death, the tile beneath her had been dirty. Too dirty to see what color it was. The first time she'd died, her blood had pooled in the fissures of the cracked subway floor.

"But I can't die again. Not yet, anyway."

With two hands on the edge of the white marble sink, Dyson steadied herself. She didn't look up at the mirror in front of her because she knew what she'd see there. Jaded hazel eyes that were once so full of hope. Blood splattered over her freckled caramel skin.

She'd stopped looking in the mirror a long time ago. She'd stopped looking because it made her sad to think of the hopeful girl she'd used to be and how everything had gone wrong.

Swollen knuckles protested when she gripped, then twisted the silver faucet. The cool water hit her cuts and they stung as she scrubbed away the blood. Then she washed her face as best she could.

The blood I can get rid of, she thought.

"But that feeling," she said, knowing and not caring that her voice wouldn't carry to the bedroom. "The feeling of bone breaking under my grip. I don't think I'll ever be rid of that."

She shook her head. The small movement made her lose her balance and she swayed. Grabbing the sink for support, Dyson flinched, as pain radiated through her body.

I need to focus on something else, she thought. I need to keep talking.

CHAPTER ONE
2014

Today, my life starts again.

Four years ago, when Dad died, everything fell apart. I inherited my childhood home. I couldn't afford it, so I dropped out of school to work full time.

My life, my goals, my dreams, were all put on hold. But today was my last day of work, of full-time work, at least. And on Monday, I would be a student again. I'd be picking up right where I left off.

"You're going back to school, you nerd!" My best friend Tina bear-hugged me, rocking me back and forth.

"I'm going back to school," I said, my eyes stinging with tears. Tina pulled back, and tucked my brown curls behind my ears.

"Oh, Dyson don't cry." She held my face in her hands. "Your parents would be so proud of you. So proud of how you handled everything. How you made it through."

I nodded and wiped away tears I'd tried not to shed.

My parents would be happy for me. I knew they would.

"Where's Roan?" I asked of Tina's partner.

"Oh, they're meeting us at the Fish and Fox," she said, starting up the stairs to my bedroom. "And they said they'll do that stupid song with you."

" 'Fairytale of New York' is not a stupid song," I said, aghast.

"It is when it's July!" Tina yelled over her shoulder.

Debatably, it's a Christmas song.

"Roan also requests 'Take on Me' as a duet," she went on. "I will not attempt the high note, so it's gotta be you." Tina walked into my bedroom and pulled a bottle of champagne out of her bag.

I smiled. I'd liked Roan a lot when I'd first met them a few weeks ago. I liked them more now. Someone who not only accepted my and Tina's obsession with karaoke, but who also wanted to join in was A-OK by me.

"Are Thomas and Kai coming?" Tina asked. I rolled my eyes in response.

I'd hoped that my brothers would get over themselves and celebrate with me today, but no. Losing Dad two years after Mom had broken something in their relationship.

"Never mind," Tina waved a hand through the air, before surveying my outfit.

As usual, I waited patiently for her to pass judgement. I wore light washed jeans and a burgundy top that looked good against my pale caramel skin.

"I love it." She popped the champagne. I gestured at the glasses I'd brought up stairs before she'd arrived. "I just think you should—"

"I am not wearing heels," I said.

Tina scoffed, then poured.

The next hour was spent drinking, laughing, and doing make-up.

"It really is art," I said as I watched her smoothly move the dark liquid liner over her cream-colored skin.

When the champagne bottle was empty, and we were thoroughly giggly, I slid my small copy of *Carmilla* into the back pocket of my jeans, and headed for the front door.

"You are not bringing a book," Tina said.

"I always bring a book on the subway," I shrugged.

"I know but . . . I just thought that . . ."

I blinked slowly at her, and she trailed off. This was an argument we'd had many times, and one she always lost.

"You're too tipsy to read!" she shouted as we walked out the front door.

"Shhhhhh," I said through a laugh.

"Sorry," she whispered. "Sorry," she said again, this time in the direction of my elderly neighbor's dark windows.

We walked arm in arm down the street, heading to the nearest streetcar stop and destination number one. Karaoke.

Roan met us there. They had a fantastic voice that got everyone in the Fish and Fox clapping and singing to their rendition of "Come Together."

"Go do that stupid song," Tina said dismissively when my name was called for the third time. Roan and I were joined by an enthusiastic Irish couple on vacation halfway through the opening of "Fairytale of New York."

"Let us buy you a round," the couple said after. We gladly accepted.

Next was Church Street and a drag show at Troops and Trollies. Tina had several friends performing. When the show was over, we danced like it was our last night on earth.

At last call, I started saying my goodbyes. With the price of metro passes, I refused to take any means of transport other than the TTC. Roan stayed behind with plans to meet us for breakfast the next morning. I told Tina to stay too, but she flat out refused to not finish the night with pizza on my couch.

She ordered just as we walked into Wellesley subway station and I smiled at my best friend.

At 1:48am, when I flopped down on one of the last trains of the night, I felt happy, tired, and still a little drunk. Tina let her head fall on my shoulder. I pulled out my book.

"You're such a nerd," Tina said.

"I love you too," I told her.

I heard the three-tone bell of the subway at the same time as I found my page in *Carmilla*. The sliding car doors started to close, but right before they did, someone stuck their foot out, triggering the motion sensor.

One of the subway platform lights flickered and died. Or was that me? Was I flickering, and dying? Everything hurt. I tried to breathe. There was a gurgling sound and I coughed.

Good that Tina got away. Better if she comes back with help. Better still if this one time, I'd taken a cab.

My vision flickered. Or was that another light?

I hadn't thought anything of the group of men that had hopped onto the train as the doors were closing. I could tell they were drunk and thought they were just being assholes by sitting so near us. When they got off at our stop, I'd thought, or maybe I'd hoped, they lived in the same neighborhood.

When one of them grabbed me, my hopes died.

I pushed away from the one who'd snaked an arm around my waist, then landed a solid punch to the guy who held Tina.

"Run!" I'd screamed at her.

I was about to do the same when the guy I'd punched returned the favor with interest. I'd never been hit like that in my life.

God, this sucks. God, this hurts. God, I should have taken that trip to

Jamaica.

Tina had wanted to go this past winter. I hadn't wanted to dip into my savings.

Poor Tina. She'll think this is her fault.

I tried to roll over, to move from my side to my stomach and crawl. My vision narrowed. I stopped trying.

Blood pooled on the tile around me. It was on my clothes and covering my hands. It was on my lips and in my lungs.

I was dying, and I knew it.

Would Tina be the one to tell Thomas and Kai I died?

Blackness pushed in around me as the pain ebbed away.

How long until my brothers break their vow to never speak to each other again? How long until they sell the house?

At least I'll see my parents. I'll be with them again soon.

A figure loomed over me.

See there, that's my father now. Come to collect me. Come to take me to the other side.

My father said something and I tried to raise my hand. He touched my wrist and spoke again. I struggled to understand, to touch his face. Then everything went black.

At some point while she was talking, Dyson had sat on the edge of the claw-foot tub next to the sink.

Just for a second, she'd thought after exhausting herself looking through the bathroom cupboards and drawers. I just need to stop hurting for a second.

"As I died, I was hopeful," Dyson said. "As I died, I had faith. Faith that my parents would be there to greet me when I crossed over. Faith that we would all be together and happy. That we would wait for my brothers.

"That faith was in vain. I didn't know it at the time." She sighed. "I long for that kind of faith now."

Dyson hadn't felt like that in decades. Not really. Sure, there had been happy times, moments of light. But nothing sustained. It was hard to sustain faith and hope in times of war.

Even though that's when faith and hope were needed most.

"The next part was . . ." She remembered waking up in a small dark place, though those memories didn't come back to her right away. "It was all instinct at first. No thought. I felt, so I did. I wanted, so I took."

She looked over at the bathroom mirror. It reflected the doorway leading to the ruined bedroom.

"I was lucky it didn't last long. I was lucky someone was there for me," Dyson said, standing slowly and moving in front of the mirror. Without looking at herself, she reached for the bottom right corner of the ornate gold frame and pulled it open. Her eyes scanned the contents of the shelf she'd revealed. It was lined with small bottles, some dried flowers, and a small stack of one-inch-squared rough linen cloths.

Not here, she thought. It would be too easy if I found it here.

CHAPTER TWO

2014

You may want to slow down, said a voice inside my head, but I didn't want to hear it. I was too focused, too engrossed in what I was doing. Because a moment ago it was all black, then all dirt, then only thirst. I was thirsty a moment ago. Now I wasn't, and it was ambrosial. I wanted to keep drinking. I wanted to drink this—whatever it was—forever.

If your intention is to kill him, by all means continue, said the voice. But we don't want any of that, now do we?

Kill? No, I'm the one who's dying. Aren't I?

I paused, drew back.

There was a man in my arms. How had he gotten here? How had I gotten here?

It was no longer the hard ground of the subway platform beneath me. It was soft grass in a million shades of green.

And this man in my arms was older than those who'd hurt me, and I wasn't hurting anymore. Even the dry ache in my throat was gone.

The man's eyes rolled. They couldn't focus on anything. Not on the trees behind me, not on the stars above.

Trees? Stars? Kill? I don't want to kill anybody.

I looked around, and my eyes widened in shock. My crisp, clear vision of tombstones was surprising in the low light. To my right, I could see the bouquet of pale pink roses mixed with baby's breath in a vase on a wall covered in names. Across the lawn there was a wrought iron fence, and on the other side, an empty street. It was all so crisp, so clear, and so visible despite the darkness.

Then I looked up and swallowed a gasp. The city lights were too bright to see stars. But I could see them now. Not the bold brilliance of a cottage sky, but more. I saw more, and further than ever before.

There was a small exhalation of breath below me. I tore my eyes away from the galaxies above and dropped them to the man in my arms. I looked over the laugh lines in his pale face and the blood on his neck. His jacket and shirt were torn and blood trickled from the small and messy cuts scattered over his skin.

Did I do that? I closed my eyes and tried to remember.

An image of this man came back to me. He'd walked over from . . . somewhere. He'd seemed confused, worried, scared. He'd asked me if I was all right.

I'd tried to look at his face, I'd tried to take in my surroundings, but the trees behind him were a blur and all I saw was the pulse in his neck. Then, the sounds of the street faded to nothing and all I heard, as his eyes had glazed over, was the seducing beat of his heart.

I'd caught him as he fell. Then I—

Lick your finger, said the voice in my head. That voice that wasn't mine.

I obeyed. I couldn't help but obey. The words, so full of power, seeped into my mind and forced me to act.

My finger moved over tongue, then over the jagged cuts. They began to heal, though it would take several hours for the marks to disappear completely.

I can see his skin knit back together. How can I see his skin knit back together?

Good, said the voice.

I moved the man from my lap to the soft grass. Then, a loud crunch broke the still night air. It echoed in my ears, creating a map to its origin. It came from right behind me.

I whipped around, standing quickly. Knees bent, back hunched, and teeth bared, I growled. The growl was soft and low. I'd never made that sound before. I'd never stood like that either, but it made me feel ready, it made me feel strong.

"Oh, calm down." A man stepped out from behind a large cross-shaped tombstone. He had dark skin, darker eyes, and jet-black hair that fell in soft curls onto his forehead. He pushed the curls back with a hand and smirked. His mouth was a thin line turned up at the corner.

He threw a shovel down at his feet and I jumped at the sound it made as it hit the soft earth. Then, I heard a heartbeat. My heartbeat. Stronger and louder than I'd ever heard it before.

"What the—" I staggered backwards.

Had my heart not been beating before? Panic crept up my spine. My breaths came short and fast.

My heart should be racing. Why isn't my heart racing?

I looked down. I was wearing my favorite dress. The last time I'd worn it was my birthday party. Twenty-five years old, and neither of my brothers had come. Tina had been there, of course. She'd been determined to make sure I had a good time. We'd gotten trashed and I'd had to have the bright yellow dress dry cleaned. It had been a wine stain then. It was completely covered in dirt now.

"No," I whispered. "No, no, no."

I was waking up in a small dark box. It was filling with dirt. I was swimming up and out as earth poured into my mouth and down my throat.

"No, no, no, no." I turned away from the large stone marked with my name and the pile of upturned dirt in front of it.

This isn't real, this isn't real. I have a heartbeat; I just felt my heartbeat.

"No, no, no." My voice was a soft moan as I searched my neck with two fingers. Finding nothing, I wrapped my arms around myself as the volume of the world turned up.

The sound grew and grew until I could hear everything. Every single thing around me. Birds in the trees across the street, a skateboard on pavement, and heartbeats. So many heartbeats and none of them mine.

Then the panic was gone.

It washed away like a sand castle too close to the water's edge. As if a wave came up, and pulled it back, leaving only misshapen lumps of sand behind.

I opened my eyes and looked up at the stranger.

The feeling of calm gave my brain space to wonder aloud, "Who are you?"

He smiled. His teeth gleamed white in the darkness and against his smooth brown skin. They were whiter still against the red apple he brought to his lips.

I resumed my defensive posture.

Another loud crunch ripped through the night air as he bit the apple, spraying juice in a rainbow of color. My eyes followed the droplets, so small and so beautiful, as they sprang from the apple's flesh, falling in a myriad of color. I tracked the gentle progress of lights, from the man's lips to his well-shined shoes.

Biting into an apple shouldn't be that loud. Spray from an apple shouldn't be that bright.

"I don't know you." I stated, but really, it was a question. Do I know you? I wanted to ask.

He was a little shorter than me, though it was hard to tell, leaning against the tombstone as he was. I surveyed him, trying to keep every ounce of composure I could. Trying to forget the panic that had gripped my body a moment ago.

He was well put together—grey slacks, a navy button-up, an overcoat that had two odd bulges. One over his chest, the other like there was something round in his pocket. He was handsome, with a strong jaw line and sharp eyes.

I took a few steps back, away from him, and from the man lying on the ground where I'd left him. Then I stood to my full height.

"You seem a little . . ." The words died in my throat. I'd never met him before. I would've remembered those eyes that looked right through me. I would've remembered the aura of power.

He looked at me, eating his apple, giving me time to work it all out.

When he pushed off the tombstone. I took another step back. He tossed the apple core over his shoulder. It was an easy flick of the wrist, but the core soared through the air, over the tall wrought iron fence, and into the trees.

He scared me. I wanted to run.

"Oh, stop that," his voice was lazy and it held an accent I couldn't place. English and something else. "Besides, I could catch you, and what happens next is your choice."

"What part of this is my choice?" I held my hands out to my sides. "What part of any of this has been up to me?"

"Well, I assume if you've given it any thought, you've come to some kind of conclusion."

The answer sprung to my lips. I swallowed it down. It was impossible, and stupid, and I didn't want to say it. I wanted to get home. I needed to check on Tina. School started on Monday, and I had a life to get back to.

"I was attacked," I said.

I remembered the distant echo of Tina's heels on the tiled subway platform and rough hands shoving me. My head had cracked against the hard wall and I'd seen stars. I'd tried to fight back.

She got away, I'd told myself. She's getting help. She'll be back.

But she hadn't come back.

"I was killed," I amended, not wanting to believe it. But I remembered the flickering light. The ghost of my father coming to bring me to the other side. "Was I killed?"

The man nodded, and the last light of hope in my chest went out. He motioned for me to continue.

"When I was dying," I paused, grasping for the memory.

A fist to my gut. Another to my face.

I squeezed my eyes shut, but just for a moment.

"My father was there," I said. I examined this stranger's dark eyes. They were black, but for the flecks of brown running through them.

He smiled. It was a sad smile. Pitying. I hated it.

"Oh," I said. "It wasn't him." I felt the sting of tears, the swell in my chest, the emotion begging to rip from my throat in a scream. I was about to drown in the grief of losing my father all over again, but another wave of composure washed over me and I breathed through it.

"It was you," I stated.

"It was," the stranger said.

"Who are you?" I stepped forward.

"You haven't finished yet," he said. " 'Who' is not the first question."

His eyes were searching, intense. It was like he was looking at my soul.

"What." The word fell heavy off my tongue.

"Yes," he nodded. "What are you." He said it as a statement, not a question.

"No." I stepped back. "No way, no freakin' way."

I wouldn't say it. It couldn't be real. It was too bizarre. But I had known. A part of me had known. Even if I didn't want to admit it to myself.

The haze of panic lifted with another wave of composure, and I remembered knowing.

From the second my eyes had opened in that coffin. From the moment I'd realized I didn't need to breathe. When the dirt had spilled into my mouth and down my throat. When I'd heard worms moving through the earth, and hearts beating miles away. When the panic faded and I'd climbed up, and out of the ground.

When I read my own name etched in stone.

I'd known it then. I knew it now. I denied it. I couldn't believe it. I didn't want to believe it. Because I wanted my life. My life that I'd worked so hard for. My life that I was just getting back on track. I was finally feeling like my head was above water, and now this?

"I'm dreaming," I said.

"No," said the man.

"I'm insane," I tried. "Delusional."

"No," said the man.

"I died. I'm dead, and this is some kind of you-get-what-you-wish-for purgatory." I'd always wanted more time. More time with my family. More time to save money and go back to school, and learn and grow and see the world.

"No," he said. "Well, actually," he tilted his head. "That could be. I mean, not really but . . . but I think you know the right answer."

"It can't be," I whispered more to myself than the man.

"It can." He pulled a green apple from an inside pocket of his long coat.

"It's not possible." I shook my head.

"It is," he encouraged.

"I'm not a—" I started.

"You are," he assured.

"Vampire."

Sahrias's story continues in:

Blood, Kin, and Curses

Find out more at:

www.hspaisley.com

@hspaisley

www.ingramcontent.com/pod-product-compliance
Lightning Source LLC
Chambersburg PA
CBHW061113310726
48974CB00002B/517